Eleni Papanou

Jessie's Song

For Daphne

SET 1

"People are disturbed not by things, but by the view they take of them." Epictetus

Smoke and Stardust

Close your eyes,_____ and dream a dream._____ A hap-py lit -

Charcoal smoke surged over me in a thick stream obscuring the stars, along with the events that forced me down onto this cold, hard sidewalk. I stared into the flames streaking out of the second-story window until my senses were hypnotized, and the searing pain from the bullet that pierced my abdomen disappeared. "Stardust" began to play in my radio brain and transmitted the memory of my first meeting with Stella. I was at the Jazz Room with my band-mates, Donnie and Snaps. Most of our conversations were pointless, but I recalled them with startling clarity on this starless night.

The pain from my injury forced me back to reality, a reality I had no desire to return to. As blood surged out of my wound unrestrained, I thought this was it. I'd die alone and without my last dream realized. Just as I had given up hope, it came true.

"Daddy!" My daughter, Jessie, ran over to me wearing the pink pajamas I got her for her ninth birthday. She looked off to the side, hypnotized by the flames.

My sister, Leda, arrived next and knelt beside me. "Hang on little brother. An ambulance is on its way." She gently assisted Jessie down to her knees.

As I gazed at my daughter's face, an emotional storm struck me. *Is this real? Are you here?* I couldn't trust my own senses. I wanted this moment so badly. It sustained me all the way up to now.

"Why are you bleeding?" she asked.

"I'll be okay."

"That's a lot of blood."

"They'll fix me up at the hospital, and I'll be as good as new."

"Where's Mommy?"

Leda shook her head at me, and I took Jessie's hand. "She'll be here soon. How about you sing me a song while we wait for her?"

Jessie stared at the blaze, and the flames reflected off her light-brown skin. "I can't sing when I'm scared."

"As long as you sing, everything'll be all right…I promise."

Jessie cried, and I held her hand tight.

"What did Mowgli know about the red flower?" I asked. Jessie loved *The Jungle Book*. I read it to her every night when she came to visit.

Jessie looked down at me. "That's what the animals called fire, and it scared them but not Mowgli. He wasn't afraid."

"I want you to be brave, like Mowgli. Can you do that for me?"

Jessie nodded.

"Good. Now sing to me, brave one."

"What song should I sing?"

"How about your song?"

Leda put her arm around Jessie. "It would make me feel better as well."

Jessie nodded her head and began to sing softly at first and then with every ounce of her emotions.

Close your eyes and dream a dream.
A happy little summer in my jungle dream.
Where no one ever has to sleep.
Where wolves and tigers and panthers creep

I close my eyes, and they come to me.
I sing my song under a shady banyan tree.
A quiet place where I can stay.
Sit with my friends and play all day.

As Jessie sang, her voice calmed me. If I had to die, at least it would be to the sound of my daughter's beautiful voice inspired by my music. The way she shaped and improvised the notes made her sound way older than her nine years.

Jessie wrote the lyrics after she found out I was going to trash the song. It was a little too syrupy for my personal taste. She thought it was a waste to write something and throw it away, and she informed me she'd make me change my mind. Her comment amused me, and I didn't expect anything more to come from the discussion until she came to me the next day and sang my song with her words. I was deeply moved and named the piece, "Jessie's Song." I even had her sing it on one of my albums.

Jessie continued to sing to me. Her voice carried me further away from my pain, and the circumstances that led up to my injury.

Trust in me and follow along
Whenever you hear me sing my song.
Hear my call, you'll never go wrong
As long as you hear my song.

I go home when the moon is high.
I cannot stay because my mom and dad will cry.
Children have parents to go home to.
Out in the jungle that still is true.

I was ready to die. Accepting my demise came easy and was surprisingly atmospheric. The fire reflected off the cars and surrounding houses and made me wish I had Ezza around to write a song. I had the perfect title lined up, "Hymn of My Death." It's not hidden behind any fancy metaphor, but it accurately mirrored my mood. The music was beautiful, the stars were out, and the firefighters were coming to save the day. What more could any man ask for on the eve of his death? I turned my head away from the blaze to avoid answering that question. It took a bullet to my gut to make me realize I had a lot to be grateful for, but seeing the obvious was never easy for me. In a circumstance such as the one I found myself in, you can either ask God, "Why me?" or laugh and tell yourself, "What else did you expect to happen after all the bad choices you made?" I asked the latter because I was an atheist. I laughed. It seemed to make Jessie feel better, but on Leda it had the opposite result. Quite understandably she looked terrified.

Reflective thought is a typical reaction when you're about to die. You think about all the things you wanted to do but never bothered with because you believed you'd have plenty of time left. That's what I did as Jessie cycled through the melody again. I wished I spent more time with her, paid her more compliments, and told her I loved her more often. Not wanting my last moments to be about all the awful things I'd done—and I'd done far too many—I probed Jessie's face until I realized I got at least one thing right: I convinced Stella to have a child with me.

Jessie stopped singing when she noticed a few tears I couldn't hide from her. I asked her to continue to sing, and she refused. I reached into my pocket, removed a small box and handed it to her.

"What is it?" Jessie asked.

"Open it."

Jessie lifted the lid and removed a gold, heart-shaped locket with a ruby in the center. Leda helped her put it on.

"It's beautiful," Jessie said as she held the heart in her hand.

"Just like your voice," I said. "Can I hear some more of it?"

Sirens sounded in the distance as Jessie began to sing again. As she came out of the chorus, a mime mask blew past me in the wind, and I lost my sense of where I was. And here's where things started to get weird. My music teacher, Steve Pagels, showed up and stared down at me wearing his signature fedora and small, round spectacles.

"Steve? How did you get here?" I asked.

"The truth can't be undone, Markos. We all eventually must pay."

Leda started crying, and Steve hugged her. "He was a good man," he said.

Was? I'm still here! I could've sworn I spoke aloud, but my mouth didn't move. I felt disconnected from my body, not unlike the drug-induced haze I lived in during my teen years.

Steve tipped his hat forward. A small firefly flew out and fluttered around over me. *How cute, a firefly in the middle of winter,* I thought to myself. Only this cute little firefly started to whirl around, creating a wispy spiral that expanded until the circumference was larger than me. An arm of light reached down and wrapped around my whole body, and I surrendered with a smile on my face. *Death isn't so bad.*

Polarities

sum-mer in my jun-gle dream.＿＿ Where no one ev - er＿＿ has to sle

I opened my eyes to my ringtone song, "Crazy People," by the Boswell Sisters. I set it to remind myself to take my antidepressants. I was lucky it went off when it did, or the wind would've pushed me off the ledge of the roof on which I stood. As I examined the bustling street life below, I wondered how I got up here. My meds usually gave me clarity, but I had none tonight. I couldn't even trust my own senses. A trip to my bathroom mirror revealed I was as smashed up as my first Fender Strat. With my unshaven face and scattered hair, I could've passed for Medusa's brother. I was always vain but became even more so after the *incident*, which is what I called my failed suicide attempt. There seemed to be someone with a camera around every corner ready to steal a picture of me.

After I groomed myself, I took three doses of my meds to quell my anxiety. I hadn't played in six months, and my anticipated return to the spotlight that night came with many expectations. Everything I did was scrutinized. Privacy was a luxury. I longed for the days when the only people who knew my name were jazz enthusiasts.

I recently received an invitation to teach an improv class in Paris, and it started to look like a good idea. There was an added benefit: I'd been walking around in a haze since the incident, and I hoped that the city with catacombs and a celebrity graveyard would remind me that I was still alive.

On my way out, I picked up a letter that Stella slid under the door. This was the fourth one this month. I tore open the envelope and read through her most recent threat.

This is the last time you're going to pull something like this again. Jessie was really hurt when you didn't show up again. If you don't want to see your daughter, at least have the decency to refrain from making promises to her you have no intention on keeping.

Stella wouldn't answer her cell. I knew she screened her calls. She told me so herself. Stella was good at evading, but so was I. We were still a duo, even when we were apart.

Stella was in the middle of an early evening lecture. She stopped as I made my way to the back of the room. A few of the girls smiled as I walked past. I sat next to a guy who was in the middle of sketching a picture of a naked woman with snakes for breasts. He covered the sheet with his hand when I gave him the thumbs up.

Stella stepped away from the podium, and I waved at her. She glared at me and continued with her lecture.

"Some have envisioned our subconscious minds as plugged into a universal computer where the blueprints of our physical and mental data are stored. Our experiences are also kept on file in the computer, and they feed back into the appropriate species. You can think of us all as individual monitors that display a specific image that's unique to us both as a species and as individuals. What I find intriguing about this theory is it explains evolution from both a biological and sociological perspective. If all this is true, our minds aren't required to be in our bodies."

Some of the students laughed. I guess I heard my own voice in there as well. Stella had some wild theories about the afterlife. If you disagreed with her, you'd first have to present a cogent counterargument and then name your sources behind your claim. She would consider your position only if they were proven to be authentic.

Stella walked back to her podium and rifled through some papers. "Before you dismiss this possibility, ask yourself what would have to happen to shift humankind from a warring species to one that works interdependently?" She paused to survey everyone in the room. "What keeps us collectively repeating the same self-destructive patterns, even when they don't work to our advantage? What do we, as individuals, feed into the computer that prevents us from evolving intelligently and compassionately? Ponder these questions over the weekend, and we'll continue this discussion on Monday."

After the class let out, one of the adjuncts, Phil, stayed behind. He raced to get to Stella before me. "Are we on tonight?" he asked.

"Are we ever." Stella looked around the room, put her arms around Phil and kissed him.

I strolled over to them, whistling, "The Lady Is a Tramp." Stella placed her arms on her hips as though expecting me to say something to annoy her. She wasn't too far off.

"We need to talk," I said.

"About?"

I looked at Phil and back at Stella.

"I'll meet you back at the brownstone," she said to Phil, who nodded and walked away.

"Things look serious between you two. Is there a wedding in the near future?"

"What do you want, Markos? I don't have time to socialize right now."

"I want to apologize about my no-show the other day."

"It's not me you should be apologizing to."

"I'll make it up to Jessie this weekend." I rubbed my head. My meds didn't seem to be working.

"What's wrong?"

"I didn't get enough sleep last night. I was worried about Jessie."

"Why?"

"If I tell you, I know you're gonna take it the wrong way."

"I don't have all night. Either speak, or I'm leaving."

"I had a dream and—"

"Call the doctor I recommended. He'll do more than medicate you."

"It's not like that. Jessie was in it, and I had a feeling something bad happened to her. I wanted to make sure I was wrong."

"Get help before you can't tell the difference between what's real and what isn't."

"Could've used your diagnosis sooner. I thought *we* were real."

Stella walked over to the blackboard and erased a cool diagram of brains that were linked together by lightning bolts. They branched out to a giant cloud that surrounded them. I remembered the drawing because Leda, who was an accomplished artist, came up with a similar concept for one of her paintings.

"Either you get help now, or I'll call my lawyer," Stella said.

"There's nothing wrong with me."

She returned to the podium and put some stray papers into a folder. "Can you be certain?"

"The look on Jessie's face when she came to visit me in the hospital still haunts me. I won't ever hurt her again."

"I'm glad to hear that." Stella placed the folders into her briefcase. "Will we see you this Saturday?"

"I'll be there."

Stella picked up her briefcase. "Don't disappoint her. She really misses you."

As I watched Stella walk off, I recalled a poem I'd written about our first encounter. She wore a white orchid in her hair like Billie Holiday. Meeting her made me want to be part of a duo. I considered that only once before…with Ezza. Right now, my focus was on Stella. It was hard to think about anyone else. I hated her, and I loved her.

Slightly out of Tune

Where wolves and ti - gers and pan - thers creep._____ I close my

I arrived at the Jazz Room and admired the cute artwork on my promotional poster that hung outside. There was a goatee drawn on my face, along with a set of devil horns shooting from out of my head. Whoever did this knew me well. However, I didn't appreciate the word *sux* carelessly scribbled in after *The Markos Adams Trio*. You can make fun of me all you want, but never my band because it's not only about me.

My brother-in-law, Teddy, almost mowed me down when I entered. I didn't recognize him without a cigarette hanging out of his mouth. Leda had been trying to get him to quit since they started dating. His doctor told him if he didn't stop smoking, he wouldn't live past sixty, which was only three years away.

He pulled on my new black silk shirt. "Interesting style. It's like Robert Plant meets Jim Morrison."

"I was going more for a Chet Baker." I brushed my hair out of my face.

"How many times do I gotta tell you?...you don't look anything like Chet Baker." Teddy's eyes widened when he noticed my guitar case. "Holy anchovy! Ezza finally made it inside! Gotta mark this date down. Thought my funeral would come and go before this day arrived."

"I can help make that a reality if you don't drop your volume down to zero."

"Welcome back little brother." Teddy hugged me. "Thought you were gonna change your mind again and go home."

I stared at the stage, and my insides swished and whirled like the first time I played in front of a live audience. I got out my hand grip and squeezed it a few times.

"You're nervous," Teddy said.

I squeezed the grip again. "I'm okay."

He shook his head. "You saw the poster."

"What poster?"

"Markos Adams Trio followed by the *misspelled* word."

I pushed my hand towards Teddy. "Tshhh, I couldn't care less about that stuff."

Teddy believed me, but on that night if a baby gave me the raspberry, I would have picked up my guitar case and ran all the way home.

"I know. I just want this night to work out for you."

Leda walked over and gave me a quick hug. "Sorry I'm late. I was in the middle of a painting. I only have time to stay for one set." She squinted her eyes and examined my face. "You look a little pale. Are you sick?"

"Will you both stop treating me as though I'm ready to take another elevator ride up to the roof?" I should have thanked them. Their over-reactive concern made me forget about my stage fright.

I peered at my sister. "You don't have to worry about me anymore. I'll stick around until I die of natural causes."

I opened my guitar case, and my cellphone played my alarm tone. I got out my meds and took my dose.

Donnie and Snaps walked over. "All right, man. You're still here," Donnie said as he slapped my back.

Snaps shook my hand. "I told Teddy to chain you to the barstool if you tried to make a break for it."

"And I would've done it too," Teddy said.

I shook my head. "Can we please make this like any other night I played."

The bartender handed Leda a dish with a slice of baklava à la mode. A lit candle was planted in the middle. She held it in front of me as a small crowd gathered around. "It's not as good as yours, but it comes close."

"I told you not to make a fuss over this."

"Make a wish," she said.

"It's not my birthday."

"In a way it is. This is your first day back."

I shook my head.

"Just blow out the candle, and make your sister happy," Teddy said.

I forced out a smile, blew out the candle, and everyone clapped. I then sampled the baklava, which didn't come close to mine. The grin on Leda's face made me keep the remark to myself.

"Are you ready?" Snaps asked.

I picked up my guitar case and clutched the handle tightly. "Ready."

The three of us headed to the stage to set up. As I surveyed the crowd, I had trouble channeling Robert Johnson, and I had equal difficulty finding Wes Montgomery. They were like my mentors from the other side. I alternated between the two depending on whether I played the blues or jazz. I started doing this when I first learned guitar to ease my nerves, and it turned into a ritual.

Snaps tapped a four-count on the body of his standup, and the two of us played the first eight bars of "Reflections," rubato style. When Donnie came in with the brushes, I started to ease up. The first time through I played safe, sticking close to the melody. When I arrived at my solo, I closed my eyes and let my fingers explore as many potentials as the chords would allow. Wes showed up during the chorus, and I sailed through the rest of the song. All the stress from my encounter with Stella tuned out, and everything felt exactly as it had the last time I played here. The trouble is reality doesn't work that way. You can *feel* you've gone back somewhere, but you're only there in your head. A whole new reality manifests as you travel along, and no matter how hard you want to avoid it, change forces its way into your life.

After my first set, I spent most of the break hearing about how great it was for me to be back and how amazing I sounded. The platitudes continued as I signed a couple of CDs. A few of the local music majors flooded me with questions ranging from what kind of guitar strings I used to whom I named my guitar after. When I detected a clear path to the bar, where Snaps was talking with Leda and Teddy, I made my break.

"Thanks for leaving me behind," I said.

"Cut the modest act; you live to be worshiped," Snaps said.

"You know him well," Leda said.

"Is that true?" A woman in a skintight leather dress crammed herself between Teddy and me. She wasn't the usual type of woman you meet in a jazz club, but I dug her Sean Young-in-*Bladerunner*-style. I checked out her ruby red lips, moved down, and halted at her slim fingers holding a digital recorder. I wanted to leave, but my legs wouldn't listen.

"Mind if I ask you a few questions?" Ruby Red asked.

"Want me to get rid of her?" Teddy whispered.

"Markos prefers conducting his interviews back at his place," Snaps said with a grin.

Ruby Red leaned closer to me and spoke softly into my ear. "If I come over, will you answer them?"

"Depends," I said.

"On what?"

"The questions." Teddy leered at Ruby Red, and she put the recorder in her purse.

"What magazine are you with?" I asked.

"I run your fan club."

"Never knew I had one of those." I turned to Snaps. "Did you know?"

"Yeah, I told you about it."

I glimpsed back at Ruby Red. "Why am I worthy of a fan club?"

"Your cover album of classic alternative tunes is very popular. Even with people who don't like jazz. You're like the jazz version of Dead Can Dance."

I pointed my finger at Snaps. "And Donnie tried to talk me out of it."

Snaps flipped his hands up and shrugged his shoulders.

"Your version of 'Friday I'm in Love,' was the number one MP3 download for three weeks after your…absence from the music scene."

Ruby Red gave me a look I've become accustomed to. Everyone who directly or indirectly talked about the incident displayed an expression somewhere between pity and curiosity. It was further amplified when the topic was stumbled upon by accident. I called this expression the *Gray Pines*, named after the hospital I checked myself into. On Ruby Red, I found the look enticing. "If you think this is a way to score extra points with me…you're right."

"Will you play a song for me before I go?"

"Are you leaving?"

"I'll be at the Piano Bar." Ruby Red reached into her purse, pulled out a card, and handed it to me."

"Name it, and we'll play it." I inspected her card that read, *Samara Moon, vocalist.*

"'Personal Jesus.' You kinda remind me of Dave Gahan"—Samara smiled—"during his younger years, of course."

"That's a new one," Leda said.

Snaps slapped his hands together and laughed. "Donnie really hates that one."

I smiled at my treat for the night. "But I'll play the song for you, Samara Moon."

Samara Moon came into my life at the right time. Since I got out of the hospital, most of my nights were spent alone. On the occasions when I met a woman, I had to either be bored or angry at Stella. Tonight I was both, which resulted in some great solos. Snaps recorded all three sets, and our album was aptly titled, *Marcos Adams, Resurrected.*

I sneaked back to the bar after the second set to play darts with Teddy.

"Leda had to go." He threw a dart. "She told me her hand was missing the brush. The woman is obsessed."

"That's why she's a great artist."

"And so are you. Your solo over "How High the Moon" sounded incredible. It's like you never stopped playing." He handed me a bottle of beer.

"That's about the only thing that feels right." I sipped some beer. "I'm still feeling slightly out of tune. Think it'll take some time until I get back to my definition of normal."

"You? Normal?" Teddy snickered and handed me a dart.

"I said *my* definition."

I could feel Teddy's Gray Pines on me.

"Stop worrying. My nightmares have stopped"—I aimed the dart, picturing Phil as the target—"and I'm ready to bop." I took the shot, and it landed on the bullseye.

A bald guy with a toothy, over-enthusiastic smile raised a bottle of beer. "Markos Adamidis, still the champion."

"Thanks." I took another sip of beer.

The man's face seemed familiar. I knew he was someone from way back in my past. No one called me by my former surname in years. I had it legally changed to Adams to dissociate myself from a past I was trying hard to forget.

"You don't remember me?" he asked.

"Give him a hint," Teddy said.

The man laughed, and it sounded as though he was gasping for air. "Remember now?"

My memory returned. Only one person I knew laughed like that. "Gus Barras."

"Knew you'd figure it out. Is it still a G?"

He was referring to the squeaky overtone in his laugh. "It's now somewhere between F and G." I shook his hand. "When did you get back?"

"Been back for years."

That was a surprise to me. Leda was recently reacquainted with Gus's sister, who never mentioned anything about him returning home. He ran away when he was sixteen. That he was never mentioned told me he was a disappointment to his family.

"This is my brother-in-law, Teddy," I said.

Teddy raised his beer. "Cheers to you both. Wish I could stay and chat, but I gotta run. Gotta early day tomorrow."

"Come on, hang for one more pilsner," I said.

"Wish I could, but unlike you, some of us got real jobs."

Teddy walked off, and Gus probed my guitar on the stand.

"Is that Ezza?" he asked.

"Not the original, but she comes close in feel. Did you ever start playing again?"

"Music didn't have the answers I was seeking. I went looking for a new direction to get back on the right track."

"That's cool."

"Did a lot of traveling and soul searching, and I ended up back here. I work in a grocery store now. The hours are flexible.

I like it." Gus looked at the stage and then at me. "Glad to see music treated you well."

"Saved me back then and continues to do so now, but it hasn't always been the smoothest ride for me either."

"Know what you mean. That's why I work in produce. All I have to do is show up, do inventory, and help people find what they're looking for. Beyond that, there's not much to ponder in produce." He laughed, and I joined in, mostly to extract myself out of the strange vibe I was picking up from him.

Gus's eyes spooked me. There seemed a vacancy to them that didn't match up with his goofy smile.

"Have you seen Mr. Pagels?" he asked.

"We're working together."

"Really? I find that surprising."

I glanced at my watch hoping it was time to start the next set. I didn't want to continue this conversation. It was heading somewhere I didn't want to visit.

"Not a lot of people would've forgiven him," Gus said. "I wouldn't have."

"There wasn't anything to forgive."

"Guess what he said was true: God never gives us music that's too challenging to play. He told me that after my father had threatened to stop paying for my lessons. I believed it for a while until I found a song I couldn't master. And well, you know the rest."

Donnie and Snaps were getting ready to go back up.

"Got one more set," I said. "Why don't you hang out until the end? We can catch up then."

"I have an early day tomorrow, but who knows? Maybe your playing will inspire me to stay awake a little longer."

Apart from his irritating laugh, I didn't like being around Gus when we were kids, and this whole exchange didn't make me like being around him as an adult.

My unease went away on stage when we started off with "Round Midnight." After my solo, I searched the audience for Gus and was relieved when I spotted him walking out the door. He left, wanting me to know that my playing wasn't interesting enough to keep him up. If his motive was to bruise my ego, he failed. With Gus gone, my playing got more relaxed, and we ended the night with an encore.

Snaps and I helped Donnie break down his kit.

"I'm ready to start booking us again," Snaps said to me as he put the snare drum into its case. "You were burnin' up there."

"Japan, here we come." Donnie zipped up a cymbal bag. "I really need this one."

"Sounds like Nicole is the inspiration behind that statement," Snaps said.

"It's gonna take me the first half of the tour and several bottles of saki to de-stress myself."

"Don't tell her about the tour until the night before we leave," Snaps said. "The shock will leave her speechless."

"And then she'll kill me."

"You give her too much power over you." Snaps pointed a drum stick at me. "What do you think, Markos? Should he keep our tour to himself?"

"Haven't even said I'm ready to tour."

"After tonight, you're ready."

"So am I." Donnie stressed each word.

"You won't be on the plane with us if you don't do what I told you," Snaps said.

Donnie shook his head as he carefully lowered his bass drum into its case. "Why should I follow your advice? You got divorced four times."

"That translates into *four* times more experience than you."

I smiled reflectively at my friends. "I missed this."

"Missed what?" Donnie asked.

"All of it."

"Welcome back," Snaps said.

"Glad to be back."

The heebie-jeebies followed me home. Something about the way Gus looked at me reminded me of the evil eye. It's an old Greek superstition I never believed in. That was more my mother's territory. "You can see it in the way a person looks at you," she'd always say. "It's as though their eyes are staring into your soul, attempting to draw it out of you and into them."

I used to laugh at my mother when she said that, but it now gave me the creeps. Gus and I were always competing against each other. Our contest ended after I beat him out for an audition to get into the high school jazz band. He didn't take it well. He planned his whole future from the scholarship that was awarded to all the students who made it in.

An extra dose of my meds and an all night marathon of *Red Dwarf* videos failed to disconnect me from the Adamidis period of my life. When Cat couldn't make me laugh, I knew I was in bad shape. I shut off the television and glanced up at a picture of Stella and Jessie. It hung between two of my favorite guitars. On the left was my seven-string Palen Archtop acoustic and on the right, my Custom American Vintage '56 Fender Strat. On the opposite wall hung a charcoal sketch of Stella and me, perpetually reminding me how not to treat a woman if I ever fell in love again.

I popped a few more pills hoping to put a halt to the racing picture show inside my brain that kept playing the Stella channel. Something was trying to force itself out, and I didn't want to be alone when it did.

Sketching the Truth

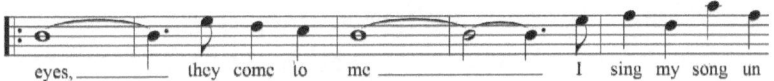

eyes,⸺ they come to me ⸺ I sing my song un

I went out for a walk in the Village. Disappearing in a crowd is an easy way to forget yourself. All you have to do is observe all the lost souls sleeping in alleys and doorways to appreciate what you have in your life.

I was friends with a few of the street people. The one I spent most of my time with was Crochet Man, named after the white-crocheted pants, shirt, and cap he always wore.

He technically wasn't a street person. Cro lived in one of those cheap motels where you need a gas mask to protect yourself from all the peeling lead paint.

I ran into Cro at a cafe on Charles Street. He was collecting money from a tourist whom he just finished sketching.

"Hey Markos, wait up." He ran to me. "Where you off to, bro?"

"The Piano Bar. Up for a beer?"

"You don't even have to ask." He put his arm around me. "You buying?"

"Don't I always?"

Cro was locally known for his unique charcoal art. He'd hit every cafe in the Village and when he found an interesting couple, he'd sketch them, usually without asking. He became famous when the *Village Voice* did a story on him. Couples who recognized him tried to make themselves appear interesting. He never painted them. "Art can't be contrived," he'd explain when asked why he wouldn't draw everyone who requested his services.

If Cro's circumstances were different, he probably would've had his own exhibit like Leda. This opinion came from her, after seeing his work. Cro had no interest in fame. His attitude reminded me of Music Man, one of my childhood mentors. He thought the aspect of fame detracted from art and as he implied when he told me, "Once you start creating art for public consumption, it isn't about the art anymore. You start thinking about what people will or won't like about your work."

I agreed with this sentiment, but once I started touring and recording, it was challenging to maintain that level of pureness. Once you're playing for the public, the need to impress the listener inevitably sneaks into your songwriting and performances. I held onto my artistic integrity by not allowing my reputation to overpower my creativity.

***

I watched Cro count a wad of bills. He slammed a few of them onto the bar.

"You make more than me," I said.

"Don't know how right you are, bro." He waved at the bartender.

"Why am I buying again?" I asked.

"Cuz I give you good advice and get people to show up at your gigs."

"Thanks for reminding me."

The bartender brought us our beers.

"Did you find your brother?" I asked.

"Got his last known address. He was stationed in Ramstein, Germany."

"What's he been up to?"

"He met a woman in Kaiserslautern and married her. I'm gonna try to call him tomorrow." Cro picked up his beer and took a sip. "How 'bout you? Seen Stella around?"

"Saw her today. She lectured, and I listened."

"When are you gonna tell her?"

"Tell her what?"

"You still got it bad for her. It's so obvious."

"It's not so obvious to me."

"Don't forget I caught you sneaking in here a few times to watch her play."

I leaned my elbow on the bar and rubbed my forehead. "If I thought she'd listen, I'd tell her."

"When I sketched you two, remember what I told you?"

I turned away to watch the pianist, who was in the middle of playing "It Might As Well Be Spring."

"You said we'd last forever. You were way off with that one."

"I'm never wrong."

"Hate to be the one to mess up your record."

"I said…I'm *never* wrong. I don't contrive what I sketch. Art captures life, and I'm only its projector." He placed both his hands in front of his face and wiggled his fingers. "I let its essence travel through me and draw whatever picture it wants."

"Are you sure you and Leda aren't the same person?"

"The truth recycles like clean, green energy."

"Does that mean we all tap into some all natural, GMO-free, cosmic brain?"

"Like that. Like it a lot. Mind if I use it?"

"So long as you put it in quotes with my name after it." I sipped my beer and listened attentively to the piano player.

"Seriously, bro, when I first sketched Stella and you, I sketched the truth, and that ain't no lie."

Cro said the same thing the first time I met him. Stella and I were dating a little over a month. We were in an outdoor cafe enjoying our espressos when Cro walked over and sat at a neighboring table. He pulled out his sketch pad and started drawing. He wouldn't listen when I told him we weren't interested in a portrait of us. We let him finish; not that we had a choice. After he showed us his drawing, Stella and I both agreed that he caught our essence. That's when he first told me he only sketched the truth. I didn't understand what he meant back then. Cro had a gift that transcended his painting. He captured what existed beyond the physical realm.

"Waiting long?" Samara asked from behind me.

I swung around to face her. "Long enough." I flashed her my best smile.

"Same here," Cro said. "Think I'll go and sketch me some more truth."

He took off, and Samara went to sit in his chair.

"Don't get too comfortable," I said.

She pointed to the door with her eyes. "Let's go. My apartment is three blocks away."

⚜

I spent the next few hours over at Samara's. I'll let you use your imagination to figure out what happened. The tabloids made my romantic life sound more interesting than it was in reality, so I'll pick things up from a little under an hour later.

Samara grabbed her digital recorder from the nightstand. "Ready for your interview?"

"Why do you wanna go and ruin the enchanting atmosphere we've created here?"

"You promised."

"And I already regret it."

"How was it for you tonight?" she asked.

"Think I'd rather keep this between us."

She threw a pillow at me. "I meant your first time playing in over a year."

"Started out great, got weird in the middle, and got better again in the last set."

Samara lay on her side and rested her head on her hand. "Why did you do it? Seems like you have lots of positive things happening in your life."

"Don't believe everything you read."

"Does that mean you still feel like you did on that night?"

"More or less."

"Would you try it again?"

"I wouldn't…for one reason only."

Samara positioned the recorder closer to my mouth.

"It hurt like hell when I woke up."

"Are you ever serious?"

"Not anymore."

Samara put her hand on my cheek. "What drove you to such a desperate act?"

"Desperation." I smirked.

"Why don't you like to talk about yourself?"

"I'm nobody's business but my own."

"You're in the public. Goes with the territory."

"If I didn't try to kill myself, you wouldn't have even asked me here."

"What makes you so sure?"

"A jazz musician doesn't typically have a fan club run by a beautiful female fan."

"Who also happens to be a singer," she said. "You inspired me to start my own band after I heard your joint project with

Steve Pagels. Some great stuff in there. The vocals are beautiful. I can see where you got your—"

"What type of music do you sing?"

"Trip hop. We reworked some jazz standards. Maybe I can sing for you one day."

How about right now?"

"Cool!" She sat up and crossed her legs. "Got a lot of extra energy tonight, and I always sing better when I feel that way."

"What song?"

"'Stardust'…in *A*-flat."

I got Ezza out from her case and played the song, not expecting to hear anything special. But when Samara started to sing, I got lost in her sensual voice as it smoothly glided through the melody. After I was finished, I was exhausted. The combination of sex and music had done that to me before, but never as intensely.

"What did you think?" Samara asked.

"Why haven't I heard of you before?" I placed Ezza back in her case.

"Getting a record deal is tough." She crossed her arms. "Now it's your turn to answer my question."

"About what?"

"Would you try to take your life again?"

"I won't answer that one."

"What can I ask you?"

"Anything about my music…" I felt lightheaded and leaned against the headboard. "…or my poetry."

"I read some of your poetry. Told me everything I wanted to know about you."

"Then why all the questions?"

"Not all the visitors that come to my website appreciate poetry."

"Besides the one question I won't answer, what else do they want to know?"

"What's the first thing that comes to your mind when you wake up in the morning?"

"Coffee. Black with four sugars."

Samara hit me with her pillow again.

"It's true."

She sat on my lap, straddled her legs around me, and put the recorder in front of my mouth.

"It's kinda hard to be profound with you sitting on me like that." I put my hands on her bare back and pulled her towards me. Samara tossed the recorder to the side and kissed me.

Two hours later she was asleep, and I gazed at her for a while. She was alluring, but she wasn't Stella.

Old Habits

der a sha - dy ban - yan tree. _____ A qui - et place where ___ I can sta

    I slowly cruised over the Williamsburg Bridge with my radio tuned to WBGO, of which I'd been a loyal supporter since I was sixteen. "Ornithology" was playing, and I whistled along to Charlie Parker's solo.

    Driving was my therapy. The traffic jams were a fair tradeoff for having the freedom to cruise beyond the island. Teddy thought I was nuts for keeping my car when I moved to the Village, even after the arrangement I made with one of the local parking garage owners. I could park for free as long as I played for all his social events and taught his son to play guitar like Les Paul. His son had other ideas. He wanted to be the next Elvis Presley and eventually started his own rockabilly band. Despite that, the space remained mine. There was always another birthday, wedding or funeral that was in need of a guitarist.

    I pulled in front of the brownstone feeling depleted of all my energy. Coleman Hawkins's version of "Body & Soul" was now on, and the light in Stella's bedroom was off. While we were together, we'd sometimes be up at this hour talking about world events or highlights from Stella's lectures on that given day. As I sat in my car, parked in front of the home we once shared, I remembered them all. After the song had ended, I tuned to *Behind the Curtain A.M.* It was a program that featured weird topics like U.F.O.s and Big Foot. Stella was interviewed on the show for a book she'd written about reincarnation. I got hooked on the format, even though I didn't believe in most of the topics they covered. Tonight they were discussing energy vampires.

The guest claimed energy vampires consumed light from their victims. It sounded eerily similar to my mother's description of the evil eye. I then had an unsettling thought. Stella was always telling me that I drained her of her energy. I always turned to her to feel better, and I was parked in front of the brownstone for the same reason. Knowing she was nearby alleviated my loneliness. She shone light into my darkness. *Or am I stealing it from her?* I switched on the interior light and stared at my eyes in the rearview mirror, hoping they didn't look anything like Gus's. They appeared more bloodshot than deranged.

When the guest on *"Behind the Curtain"* mentioned the name of her book, I jotted it down and thought about ordering it the next day. I never bought into anything metaphysical since I got a reading from a one-eyed Greek gypsy, but this night was weird enough to make me reconsider. I fell asleep in my car listening to Dinah Washington. The last song I recalled was "This Bitter Earth." I related to every word in the lyric. My life was like the dust that hid the glow of my daughter's smile. The night seemed darker and colder, and brought with it the most terrifying nightmare I'd ever had.

A small house burned in a fury of flames, and smoke came at me from every direction. I turned to face a human form that was engulfed in flames. It crept toward me and spoke with a voice I couldn't distinguish between male or female, "You're a coward, Markos Adamidis."

A pressure swelled inside me that made it feel as if my heart was about to burst out of my chest.

As the flame being was about to touch me, I ran off and felt a blast of heat on my back. I kept running until I ended up at the brownstone. The door was open, and Jessie stood in front wearing the heart-shaped locket I gave her. She held a red lotus in her hand and gave it to me. "Come home, Daddy… please," she said.

I took the lotus from her, and the fragrance brought on a violent fit of coughing.

"Why won't you come home? Please Daddy. Don't go away again. Don't leave me."

The coughing was choking me. I grabbed my throat.

"Please Daddy. Please."

Steve appeared and stood next to Jessie. "The truth can't be undone. We all eventually must pay," he said.

Jessie sang her song. When she got to the chorus, flames erupted around her and Steve.

I was pulled out of the dream when Leda tapped on the window of my car. I got out, and she handed me a cup of coffee.

"If you're gonna be a regular here, you can use the spare room. I'll even let you hang your guitars. But only two. Our house isn't a music store."

I grabbed the mug. "Am I that predictable?"

She nodded her head.

My attention shifted to Stella's unit of the brownstone where she was kissing Phil in front of the door. I clenched my teeth when Phil headed to his car.

I caught up with Stella as she opened the door. "Stella, I…"

"Please. Not now. I have to get ready for work."

She went inside, and Phil waited in his car until I left. I couldn't blame him; I would've done the same.

Combustion

Sit with my friends and____ play all day.__

    I sat on the couch with my hands in a prayer position in front of the fretboard of my guitar. Leda peeked her head over the canvas to inspect me. I started posing for her after her model had quit. The sessions were exhausting as I had to sit still, which wasn't easy for a Type A like me. For one sitting, Leda had me down on one knee while I held my guitar over my head. The basic sketch took her thirty minutes to complete, and another ten minutes when she took pictures of my pose from various angles. She then dismissed me and spent the next week turning my form into fine art. She painted in all these intricate vines and stems that grew out of the tuning pegs. They all extended outward and plugged into electrical sockets throughout my body. The painting outsold everything in her exhibit. Motivated by the sale, Leda created a music series with me as the model. I got some more offers to sit for other artists, and I politely turned them down, fearing I'd be better known for my physique than my music. It was bad enough the incident overshadowed my playing.

Leda stared at her canvas and then at me. "You didn't have your calves crossed five minutes ago." She pointed her pencil at me. "Uncross them."

I did as commanded, and Leda shook her head.

"That's not it either. Don't lean against the couch. It ruins your posture."

I sat up, and Leda shook her head again. "Why did you have to move?"

"I didn't move."

"My eyes can't be fooled. You moved."

"What is it this time?" I asked as my sister anxiously alternated her gaze between me and the canvas.

"If I lose one more night of sleep, I'm gonna throw him in the guest room." Leda removed the canvas, and leaned it against the wall. "I told him to lay off those beef jerkies. They keep him up all night. He used to get up to have a smoke; now he gets up to fart. I don't know which is worse."

"Both…at the same time."

"Ewww." She picked up a painting she had been working on and positioned it on the easel.

"Are we finished?" I asked.

"For now."

I rested Ezza at my side and slumped against the back cushion of the couch. My cellphone played my alarm tone, and I took my meds.

"Sorry I missed the last set. Teddy wouldn't stop talking about your solo over "How High the Moon.""

"A long stay in the psych ward can be inspiring. You should give it a try sometime."

After about sixty-seconds, I got bored with the silence and went to have a look at the painting. Shades of gray, black and white made up a typical looking New York City street. Quarter-note-rest cars were about to run over my guitar-shaped body. Flat-note symbols rained down on me in trails of red flames.

Positioned for battle, my fretboard arms were raised to the sky, and my tuning peg fingers stretched up and shot out sharp-sign projectiles of lightning.

"I like it…*a lot*, but I don't get it."

Leda put down her brush and studied me. "You need to lighten your load a bit." She picked up another brush and swirled it around a crimson shade on the palette. "Only then will you see you're taking on too much."

Leda dabbed some of the crimson around the body of the guitar for a bleeding effect. She put down her brush and inspected her work.

"Can I get a lithograph of this for my apartment when you're done?"

She slapped me on my forearm. "You're not really seeing. I want you to see."

"I'm seeing, I'm seeing." I examined the picture again. "After I was released, I did everything I was supposed to do, and everyone still treats me as though I'm about to take another jump off the roof."

"It's only because we care about you."

"I'll never hurt you or Teddy again."

"You didn't hurt us; you hurt yourself. And that's what makes me so sad." Leda got up and hugged me. "You're one of the most compassionate souls I know. Don't be afraid to show it."

"Think a change in my environment will help. I'm moving to Paris next month."

Leda took a step back. "When did you decide this?"

"Yesterday. Got an offer to teach an improv workshop. A new scene with new people will be the best medicine for me."

"Sounds more like you're running away from home."

"I prefer to think of it as running to a new life."

While I was indulging in my second cup of coffee, the doorbell rang. I didn't get up fast enough for Leda. She sighed, put down her brush and went to see who it was. When she opened the door, Stella rushed inside.

"Is Jessie here?"

"No," Leda said. "What's going—"

"She's missing! I can't find her anywhere!"

I got up from the couch and spilled a little of my coffee. I was shaken but not enough to think this was anything more serious than Jessie going off somewhere on her own. She'd done that before with me when she sneaked out in the early morning to visit the puppies in the neighborhood pet shop. I called everyone looking for her, and she casually walked in while Stella was yelling at me on the phone for being irresponsible.

"Take it easy, Stella. There's probably a logical explanation for this."

"When I went to her room, the window was left wide open." Stella cried. "She's gone."

"Did you call your sister?" None of this felt real. I heard the words, but I didn't want to believe them.

"She's not there."

My cellphone rang. The display read: *caller unknown*. Things were now starting to feel very real. No one called me this early in the morning. I answered with that feeling of dread you get in your stomach.

A synthesized male-voice spoke before I had a chance to get out my greeting. "Markos Adamidis, I have your daughter. If you want her to live, you must do exactly as I tell you."

"Who is this?" I asked.

"Don't attempt to put me on speaker. If anyone hears our conversation, your daughter will die."

I signaled for Leda and Stella to remain silent. "It's just between you and me."

"That is a rule you must follow to the very end. There are only two players allowed in our game."

"What are we playing?"

"Where is Jessie? Where is Jessie?" the kidnapper sang.

"I want to speak to her."

Stella put her hand over her mouth, and Leda placed her arm around her.

"You're not in the position to make demands," the kidnapper said. "I suggest you calm yourself before we continue our discussion. You wouldn't want to say something you might regret. That wouldn't be favorable to Jessie's well-being."

"Just tell me what you want." I clenched the cellphone so hard that I thought I'd break it.

"Identify who I am before it's time to pay up, and you'll win Jessie back. If you fail, you—"

"I'm not playing until I talk to Jessie."

Stella clutched my forearm, and I could feel her trembling.

"Is he putting her on?" Stella whispered.

"Hi Daddy," Jessie said cheerfully.

"Thank God," Stella mouthed as I positioned the receiver near her ear.

"Are you okay, baby?" I asked.

"Did he tell you about the game?"

"Yes. And I'm gonna make sure you win this one."

"I can't wait to play. It sounds like fun." She giggled. "Catch us if you can!"

There was a few seconds of silence, and the kidnapper's synthesized voice returned. "Those are the last words you'll hear from your daughter until our game is over."

Stella was about to speak. I pressed my pointer finger against my lips to silence her.

"Tell no one what I'm about to tell you. If you don't comply, Jessie dies. If you don't follow my instructions, Jessie dies. Do you understand?"

"Clearly."

"You have twenty-four hours to figure out who I am. If you win, Jessie goes home with you. If you fail to identify me, you must end your own life at a location which I'll reveal to you as the deadline nears. Those are my terms. They are nonnegotiable."

I glanced at my watch. It was 7:30 a.m.

"I'll call you back with further instructions when you're alone." The kidnapper hung up.

"Is she all right?" Stella asked.

I clutched Stella's arms. "I need you to stay here with my sister."

Stella pushed me. "Where is she? Where's my baby girl!"

"I don't know…but I'll find her."

"How?"

"I don't have time to discuss this. I have to go now."

"If you expect me to sit here and wait for your call while our daughter is missing, you're more out of your mind than I thought you were!"

"The kidnapper says I have to do this alone."

"I want my daughter back now. What are you going to do to ensure that happens?"

"Whatever it takes, Stella. Whatever it takes." And I meant it.

Teddy entered the room eating a beef jerky. He stopped chewing when he noticed us.

"Looks like I picked the wrong week to quit smoking. What happened?"

Stella ran over to Teddy. "Jessie's been kidnapped."

Teddy switched on his cop persona and spoke calmly. "Did you get the call?"

"Just now," I said.

"Can you tell me anything about it. Like was there any background noise, or anything else that sounded peculiar?"

"I only heard the kidnapper. He spoke using a synthesized male voice."

"Where's the drop?"

"All I got is the time. Twenty-four hours from now."

Teddy eyed his watch.

"He's calling back later with the rest of the details. Think he knew I wasn't alone."

"What was Jessie last wearing?" Teddy asked Stella.

"Her pink pajamas."

Teddy pulled out his cellphone.

"Who are you calling?" I asked.

"The station." He turned to Stella. "When did you last see her?"

"No police," I said. "The kidnapper will kill Jessie if he finds out."

"We need to get a team in here before he calls back."

"I gotta do this alone."

Teddy put the phone to his ear, and I gripped his arm.

"You need to pull yourself together, Markos! Time's in short supply here, and we're wasting it."

"Make the call, and I'll hold you personally responsible if Jessie dies."

"You won't do Jessie any good if you lose control," Leda said to me.

I tried to grab Teddy's cellphone, and he pulled it away from me.

"Stop playing cop. I need you to be my brother now. The kidnapper will kill her if I don't do what he says."

"They all say that."

"I can't lose her, Teddy. I won't be able to survive that. There's been too much loss in our lives already."

Stella walked over to Teddy. "If the kidnapper is threatening to kill Jessie, we have to keep this between us."

"I can't do that, Stella. I'm a police officer. It's my duty to serve and protect."

"I don't want to give that bastard an excuse to harm my baby." Stella placed her hand on Teddy's forearm. "I trust you. I know you can help Markos bring Jessie back home safely."

Bruised ego aside, it seemed Stella was close to persuading Teddy to stay quiet. To help move things along, I flashed him a picture of Jessie on my cellphone screen. "You know what it's like to lose a child."

"Keep his son out of this!" Leda yelled. "I know you're upset, but opening up old wounds won't help us find Jessie."

"I'm sorry. But I don't know how else to show him how serious this is. I believe that whoever has Jessie wouldn't hesitate to kill her."

"Whoever has her is motivated by the ransom," Teddy said. "They won't risk it by harming Jessie."

"All I'm asking for is twenty-four hours. You can do whatever you want after that." I showed Teddy the picture of Jessie again. "Give me the chance to save my daughter. If I don't find her by tomorrow, you can go ahead and report it."

"How much is he asking for?" Teddy asked.

"Too much, but I'll manage."

"I got some money. If you need it, it's yours."

"I said I'll manage."

Teddy shook his head. "Something about this doesn't fit. Kidnappers usually target wealthy people."

"Why don't you tell him he's not playing by the rules. Maybe he'll feel guilty and bring Jessie back." I glanced at the picture of Jessie. "This is personal."

"What makes you say that?" Teddy asked.

"He told me so."

I took a little too long to answer, which made Stella panic.

"Call the police now!" she yelled.

Everything around me was spinning. How the hell was I going to explain that the ransom was my suicide? Whoever was desperate enough to want me dead hated me, and I knew the power of hatred all too well and what it could do if left unchecked. It's what led to the incident, and I had no doubt it was powerful enough to make the kidnapper kill my daughter. I wasn't going to let anyone turn that possibility into a reality.

Teddy tried to make the call again. I snatched his cellphone and smashed it against the wall.

Teddy clutched my arms. "You gotta stop this now! You're not helping Jessie!"

I pushed Teddy away. "I gotta do this alone! There's no other way!" I turned to Stella and grabbed her hands. "I know I haven't been reliable lately, but you know I love Jess and would never put her in danger."

Stella pulled away from me, got out her cellphone, and handed it to Teddy.

"Make that call, and I'll disappear until this is all over," I said.

Teddy narrowed his eyes. "If you know something more, now's the time for full disclosure."

"Please." I closed my eyes for a moment and tried to calm myself so that I wouldn't lose it in front of my family. Teddy wouldn't have taken me seriously if he thought I regressed back to the days before the incident. "You have to let me handle this. It's the only way."

Leda, who'd been silent up to now, had been watching me closely enough to pick up what I was going through. She was the only one who knew what desperation looked like on me.

"Give him the twenty-four hours, Teddy," she said quietly.

Teddy peered at my sister. Her insight had proven to be valuable through the years, and he'd come to rely on it almost as much as I had.

"Give him what he wants!" Leda yelled.

Stella cried. "You can't do that! You can't leave this all up to Markos!"

Teddy nodded his head at Leda and pointed his finger at me. "Twenty-four hours. That's all I'm giving you."

Leda hugged me tight. "Whatever is going on, please be careful."

"You've all gone as crazy as Markos!" Stella swiped the cellphone from Teddy and went to make a call.

I seized her forearm. "You gotta trust me."

Stella tried to pull her arm away.

"I need you to trust me with this. I never lied to you before. That should be worth something."

"If anything happens to her, you'll be responsible."

"I know, which is why I have to leave now. Jessie's life depends on me following the kidnapper's instructions, and I'm not gonna risk pissing him off when he has her with him."

Leda put her arm around Stella. "I know my brother well. We have to trust him with this."

"Just find her." Stella broke down and hugged Leda.

"Do you have any idea who's behind this?" Teddy asked me.

"I'm tossing around some names, but none of them stand out yet."

"Keep me posted," he said. "I want to know everything you find out."

"I'll keep you in the circle, but if you're thinking about calling your friends after I leave, I'm asking, I'm begging you not to."

Teddy creased his forehead.

"I'll make sure he doesn't," Leda said.

I left, doubting whether Teddy or Stella would keep this to themselves. They treated me as if I had one foot back in Gray Pines. In all honesty, if I were Teddy, I would have reported the kidnapping. Bringing up his son was cruel. Johnny died while on vacation. He and his fiancée were at a beach in Greece swimming. They both got caught in an undertow and drowned. After this was all over, I vowed to make it up to Teddy…if I lived past the deadline.

I made a list of people who I thought would be mad enough at me to want me dead. The kidnapper addressed me by my previous surname, and I recalled my meeting with Gus who'd done the same. I hadn't seen him in years, and he showed up at my gig, goading me as he had when we were kids. *Could he hate me enough to want me dead?* I laughed at the thought. Sure, we had a troubled past but nothing severe enough to warrant a kidnapping or my suicide. Nevertheless, I still couldn't get my mind off the way he looked at me, and I put him on my list of suspects. I also had to consider all the other rivalries I dealt with in my life. There were many, and remembering them all would be impossible. For Jessie's sake, I hoped it was one of the names I jotted down on my note pad.

SET 2

"There are no facts, only interpretations." Friedrich Nietzsche

Sunburst

Trust in me and fol-low a - long, when ev - er you hear m

While I sat in traffic, I thought about the terms of the ransom and who would want me dead. Gus's name came to me again. He showed up at the Jazz Room unexpectedly and then disappeared without so much as a goodbye. A few other people also came to mind, but Gus emerged as the strongest suspect. He acted weird during our whole meeting. However, being weird was normal for Gus. I went over my conversation with him, searching for a clue that would explain why he showed up after a nineteen-year absence.

Gus and I had spent much of our childhood together and not because we both liked to play with Matchbox cars or toss a football in the park. We were friends by default; our mothers were friends. While they discussed the current plot of their favorite soap opera, Gus and I either fought or tried to outdo each other. When it came to sports, I ruled the field. Gus was the music guy. The only time I liked him was when he shut his mouth and played guitar. His technical ability impressed me enough to want to learn to play. I asked him on various occasions if I could check out his guitar, but he refused to let me even touch it. I didn't understand his neuroticism until I got Ezza. I've been near the threshold of rage when someone so much as stood next to my guitar stand.

Things got worse between Gus and me on the Sunday before our first day of the ninth grade. While I was hanging altar robes in the closet, he came barreling in, excited about starting high school.

"I just met the new music teacher at student orientation. His name is Mr. Pagels." Gus took off his robe. "After I played for him, he said I'd have no trouble getting into whatever music school I want." He hung up his robe. "Got it all planned out. I'm going to go to Berklee where I'll study with the best music teachers in the country. By the time I graduate, I'll be able to play better than Yngwie Malmsteen. Everyone's going to want to jam with me."

I hung up a robe, trying not to listen. Hearing Gus go on about how fabulous his life was made me realize I still didn't know what to do with my own.

Gus pulled his coat off the hanger. "I'll then front my own band and tour the world. We'll go everywhere, even to places we're not allowed to visit because it's too dangerous for Americans."

"Like where?"

"Egypt, China and Saudi Arabia. I want to visit all those places." He snapped his fingers. "I'll perform a concert in front of the Giza Pyramid. That would be so cool."

"They'll never let you put on a concert in any of those places."

"They will for me. My playing will transcend all borders."

I put on my coat. "You got that from the Rolling Stones."

"Did not."

"I think it was Keith Richards who said that."

"No way! He'd never say anything that deep."

"Whoever it was, it wasn't you." I laughed. "If you can't be original when you speak, how do you expect to be original with your music?"

Gus sneered at me. "Where do you want to go after you graduate?"

"The Playboy Mansion."

"You have to have a lot of money to get in there."

"You don't need too much."

"How much?"

"I'll get it."

"You can always make money working over at the Fun Palace. You play video games every day. Might as well get a job working with them before they kill whatever brain cells are left in your head."

Gus laughed, and I shoved him into the closet.

"I was only joking," he said.

When Gus stepped out of the closet, I punched the side of his face. I would've struck him again if Father Nicholas hadn't entered the room.

"Markos Adamidis!" he yelled. "Your father will be very disappointed when he hears about this." He turned to Gus. "Are you all right?"

Gus ran out of the room with his hand over his nose. I think it was bleeding.

"Please don't tell my father," I said.

"I will not lie to your father."

"I'm not asking you to lie. Just don't tell him."

"You're too young to understand now, but we learn from our mistakes, not by covering them up."

I picked up some robes that had fallen on the floor.

"Has something been bothering you lately?"

"I'm okay." I placed the robes on a table.

"You can tell me anything, and it will be between us."

I hung up one of the robes. "I heard a priest can't talk about a private conversation he has with someone. Is that true?"

"That's right."

"What if I have something to say about my father? Would you still want to listen?"

"Of course, I would. I'm here for all my parishioners."

"And you won't tell him what I tell you?" I placed another robe on a hanger.

"I won't say a word."

I hung up the robe as the inside of my stomach writhed and twisted. "My father hits me whenever he gets mad."

"Did you do something to deserve it?"

"I guess."

"Does he ever hit you for no reason?"

"No, I...he...sometimes he gets mad for stuff most people don't get mad over."

"Such as?"

I wanted to tell him something, but I got scared. Father Nicholas liked my father. I didn't think he'd believe me. And if he told my father that I talked about him, things at home would get worse for me. My father detested family matters being discussed in public. To all the members of the parish, we were the perfect family. My father was a masterful conman.

"I understand how you might think your father is being too hard on you. I've known him for over thirty-five years. He's strict with you because he wants what's best for you."

I hung up the last robe.

"Don't take things so seriously, and enjoy these years. They only come around once. When you grow up, you'll remember them with a smile on your face." Father Nicholas picked up an open box of used candles and set them on the table. "Anything else?"

I shook my head.

"I'll see you next Sunday."

After Father Nicholas left the room, all I could think about was my father and what he was going to do to me when we got home from church. I flew into a rage and pulled all the robes off their hangers, knocked over the box filled with candles, and overturned a table that housed a coffee machine and ceramic cups. As my senses returned to me, I realized I made it worse for myself, and I ran out of the church ahead of my parents.

I stopped in front of a small music shop where a few guitars were displayed outside on stands. My eyes went straight to an electric with a sunburst body that was one of those cheap made-in-Japan models. When I held it, I knew I was meant to play guitar. I glanced inside the store. No one was around.

Gus told me two hippies owned the shop, and they spent most of their time in the back room getting high. After his guitar lessons, Gus came around here to hang out and supposedly even got high with them a few times. I never took him seriously as I'd seen Gus at parties, and he wouldn't even have so much as a sip of beer. He claimed he didn't like the taste, but when offered something else, he'd turn it down as well. Gus could never pull off high school cool.

After one more peek inside the empty store, I ran off…with the M.I.J. in my hands. Someone screamed, "Stop that kid!"

A stocky man, who just exited one of the stores on my escape route, grabbed me by the sleeve of my shirt. He dragged me all the way back to the shop where he introduced me to the owners as *the punk who stole the guitar*.

Music Man sat behind the counter reading with his wiry mane hanging over his face. Flipper wore his hair in a tight braid that dropped down past his waist, and he wore a Deep Purple concert tee-shirt that looked as though it was ironed.

He wiped down the counter with a dust cloth. "Didn't your old man teach you about the little pieces of green and white paper you can use to exchange for goods and services?"

"I don't have any *pieces of green and white paper*. That's why I stole it."

Flipper laughed. "I dig your honesty." He removed a pack of cigarettes from his pocket.

"Are you gonna call the cops?" I asked.

"And bring them here? No way." He took out a cigarette. "Unlike me, smoking isn't Music Man's only vice…if you know what I mean."

"Can I have one?" I asked.

Flipper laughed again. "Want me to smoke it for you too?" He handed me a cigarette.

"Got a light?"

Flipper shook his head, took out a lighter from his pocket and lit my cigarette along with his. "Why did you swipe the guitar?" He took a drag from his cigarette.

"I wanna play." I puffed out a few smoke rings. "It's all I ever think about."

Flipper glanced at Music Man and laughed. "The kid's got it bad." He peered back at me. "You're in love." He leaned his cigarette in the ashtray and wiped off some ashes that fell on the counter from Music Man's joint. He then picked up the guitar I tried to steal and played "Hotel California." I hated the song with a passion. It seemed as though everyone selected it on the jukebox at Jake's Diner.

"Why don't you ask your parents to get this for your birthday? It's more honorable than stealing."

"It'll never happen. My father thinks music is a waste of time."

Flipper stopped playing and gawked at Music Man who appeared angered by my comment.

"Did you catch that?" Flipper said to Music Man. "The kid's father told him music is a waste of time. Sounds a lot like your old man."

Music Man shook his head. "That's wrong on infinite dimensional levels."

"Couldn't have said it better myself." Flipper looked at me. "What's your name?"

"Markos."

He let me hold the guitar again.

"This isn't too expensive. It'll be going on sale early spring."

"How much?" I asked.

"Ninety-nine, ninety-nine. If you can get the cash, I'll hold her for you."

"Her?"

"Guitars are like women. You'll get what I mean once you start to play."

A police car pulled up in front of the store. Music Man grabbed the ashtray and hurried to the back room. Flipper got a can of air freshener from behind the counter and gave a few quick pumps. The room now smelled like pot and garden fresh springtime. I could tell the two officers who came inside smelled it, but they didn't bring it up. They were more focused on the punk who tried to steal a guitar...and some other merchandise.

Before I ran away with the M.I.J., I stole a few cassettes from a record shop. The clerk chased me down two blocks, and I lost him. I would've gotten away with it had it not been for one of the customers who recognized me when Stocky Man apprehended me. He called the police, and I was brought down to the station until they could get a hold of my parents.

As I waited for my father's arrival, a police officer sat at the desk in front of me filling out a crossword puzzle. He stopped to light a cigarette. "Your father will be here soon."

"Can I stay here for the rest of the night?"

"Why would you want to stay here?"

"I wanna see what it's like." What I really wanted to say was my father was probably going to pound me to a pulp when I got home, and a night in jail seemed like the more peaceful alternative.

"How's everything at home?"

I hesitated to answer as I always did when the question was asked. "Okay."

The police officer leaned back in his chair, and it creaked. "If there's anything you'd like to say to me? I'm here to listen. It's my job."

"I don't know why I stole the cassettes. It sort of just happened."

"Better figure it out soon. The only reason you're not in a lot of trouble is because this is your first offense. The next time, the state won't be as forgiving." He glanced towards the door as Leda entered. I recognized the expression on his face. Lots of guys looked at my sister the same way when they saw her for the first time.

"Dad's filling out the release forms," she said to me.

"Is he pissed?" I asked.

"What do you think?" Leda looked at the police officer and gave him one of her flirty smiles. "Hi."

I rolled my eyes. "This is my sister, Leda."

"I'm Teddy."

Teddy and Leda spent the next few minutes getting acquainted. She told him about her art, and he told her he wanted to see it. She visited the station on her own the next day with her portfolio, and he asked her out for dinner. Their union was the one good thing that came out of my arrest, but for my father, it became another item on a list of things I did wrong.

He dragged me out of the station and said in a quiet voice, "You're in big trouble. The biggest you've ever been in your life." The low volume didn't hide his anger, and several times on our drive home, I was tempted to push the steering wheel into oncoming traffic. I might have done it had Leda not been in the car.

Mask

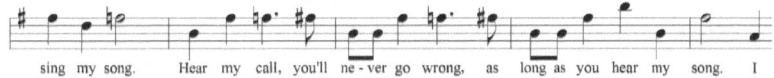

sing my song. Hear my call, you'll ne - ver go wrong, as long as you hear my song. I

The blast of horns, police sirens, and people yelling out their windows never appeared more distant. No one was moving, and I considered ditching the car, but I didn't want to add to the problem. I drummed my hands on the steering wheel to Joe Williams singing, "Teach Me Tonight." His mellifluous vocals helped bring down my heart rate that shot right up again when the kidnapper called.

"Are you alone?" he asked, still using the synthesized voice.

I turned down my radio. "Yeah…Gus."

A fleet of pedestrians crossed the road in front of me.

"I know it's you. So now that I guessed correctly, I want Jessie back."

"I never said you were correct."

"It can only be you."

"Is that your answer?"

"Can't think of anyone else who'd want me dead." I put the cellphone on speaker mode and placed it on the cradle. I looked ahead into the crowded intersection. A cab driver pulled a U-turn and almost plowed over a row of tourists crossing the street. I longed for yesterday when this scene would've been the worst part of my day.

"What's troubling you?" the kidnapper asked. "I'm only helping you finish what you failed to accomplish yourself."

The light turned green, and the traffic started moving again, albeit slowly.

"I read about how your wife left you after the wedding fiasco. That must've been difficult for you."

"Not as difficult as what I'm going through now."

"Your problems won't disappear by jumping off a building this time." The kidnapper paused for a moment when a faint crackling started. "You have to stick around until the very end to get the answer to the one question you're afraid to ask me: will I keep up my end of the bargain? You have no guarantees of anything in life, so you shouldn't expect one from our arrangement. The only thing you can do is have faith that I'll honor my word. Do you have faith, Markos?"

The crackling stopped, and I had that feeling you get when you wake up from a daydream. "If you want me to answer that, you have to let me talk to my daughter."

"If I like your answer, I may."

"I take action. Faith is for the weak and desperate." I jammed on the brakes when I almost went through a red light.

"What do you call sleeping in your car, parked in front of your ex-wife's home?"

I looked at my rearview mirror. A bus had just stopped to let off passengers. "How long have you been watching me?"

"Long enough to know that action, in your case, is equal to being weak and desperate."

"Put my daughter on. I answered your question."

"Or maybe you do have the faith that your ex-wife will one day come back to you? Maybe faith does equal desperation after all." The kidnapper laughed.

"I want to talk to my daughter now!"

"I think you're forgetting who's in charge here. So I'll have to remind you by denying your request."

I pounded on the door until my hand went numb. "Why don't you show your face, you coward! You fucking coward! You don't have the guts to deal with me, so you go after a child!"

"Here I am. Over to your left."

I faced the sidewalk and fixed my gaze on a man wearing a mime mask. He was performing an air-guitar routine near a subway station while a few people watched. He ended his show, and when the crowd cleared away, I spotted Jessie standing beside him. He took her hand and pointed in my direction. Jessie looked at me and smiled.

The kidnapper got out a cellphone from his pocket and placed the receiver against his ear. "Did you like my act? Was it realistic?" he asked, still using a synthesized voice.

I opened the door, ready to jump out.

"Stay where you are. The last thing you want is the N.Y.P.D to tow your car away."

"My car can be replaced."

"But your daughter can't." The kidnapper reached into his pocket and stealthily revealed the handle of a revolver.

I slammed the door shut.

"I've gotten to like her, and I don't want to have to cancel our game when we're having so much fun playing." The kidnapper looked down at Jessie. "Are you having fun?"

Jessie nodded her head and smiled.

"Do you want your father to end this game?" He placed the cellphone next to Jessie's ear.

"Keep playing, Daddy. If I win, the mayor of New York will let me speak on TV about freeing the animals in the zoo."

Seeing Jessie smile gave me the strength I so desperately needed in that moment. "You're gonna win, Jess. I promise you."

"Thanks!" Jessie's smile got bigger. "We followed you all morning. Now it's your turn. Catch us if you can!" She ran down the stairs of the subway station with the kidnapper.

Drivers behind me beeped their horns as the light had turned green. I floored the gas pedal, and the tires screeched.

"I'm trying to find a redeeming trait about you," the kidnapper said. "So far I found none."

"Your opinion means nothing. What do you want from me?"

"Your silence. If you tell your old cop brother-in-law about our plans, your family will be attending two funerals, maybe even three if you get out of hand again."

I squeezed the steering wheel with both my hands until my arms shook. "My mistake. Everything's cool. Don't take this out on Jessie."

"Since I'm a good sport, I'll forgive your transgression... once. I won't be as forgiving if there's a next time. Failure to play by my rules can easily make Jessie the loser in this game."

Two police cars raced ahead of me with their sirens glaring. The loudness of it made my head ache.

"Try to be extra careful. I wouldn't want you to die before our deadline."

I rubbed my forehead with my fingers. "What's the difference? The end result will be the same."

"Your self-centered explanation doesn't take into account my personal stake. I didn't go through all this trouble for you to take the easy way out. We must finish this together if you want the outcome to be advantageous for your daughter. Will that be problematic for you?"

"I'm playing to the end."

"Glad to hear you're motivated. Meet me at Jake's Diner in twenty minutes. If you find me, Jessie will go free...and so will you."

I looked at the clock on the dash that read 8:30 a.m. "It's always packed at this time."

"If I'm who you think I am, this should end quickly."

A bus parked in front of me, and I pulled to the other side of the street, almost hitting a car.

"I know you don't like to work too hard, Markos, but anything worthwhile takes effort. A musician of your great talent should understand that basic truth. I'm sure you'll agree Jessie is worth a little extra effort on your part. And you better start applying some of that right now. I won't be here forever. See you soon…if you're smart enough to find me."

I turned on the radio, but whatever came on was long forgotten. The only thing that stood out was a large billboard with a picture of newlyweds standing on the steps outside a church. It made me think of Stella and our wedding song, "Our Love Is Here To Stay." The song played in my mind as I blew the horn and shouted a few expletives out the window. Neither action made my car move any faster, but my heart had no trouble shifting into high gear. Jake's was four blocks away, but the traffic was so dense that I knew I had a better chance of making the deadline on foot. I turned into the next side road and couldn't find a legal space to park. I pulled in front of a fire hydrant. What did I care? My car getting towed was the least of my worries. I got out and ran all the way to the diner.

Jake's was packed, and I inspected all the booths searching for anyone on my list. None was present. I carefully surveyed all the patrons. The kidnapper could've been any of them. I was more focused on the mask and Jessie and paid no attention to what the kidnapper wore. Another thing troubled me. Since the kidnapper was here, that meant there had to be someone working with him, keeping an eye on Jessie.

Dottie came over and handed me a container of coffee.

"Not now," I grabbed a napkin off the counter and patted it against my face to blot the sweat.

"Would you like an egg cream instead?" she asked. "You look like you just ran a marathon." She smiled as sirens shrieked in the near distance.

"Not now, Dot."

The diners rushed to the window as a line of police cars, followed by two fire trucks, turned down a side street a block away. Terror swallowed me whole. Steve lived on that street, and I hoped all of this was nothing more than a coincidence.

I bolted out of the diner, followed the crowd and froze when I caught sight of the kidnapper wearing the mime mask. He stood at the intersection, and when he noticed I spotted him, he lost himself in the swarm of people. I ran after him and turned down the side street where firefighters had their hoses aimed at a blaze raging furiously inside Steve's duplex.

I pushed myself through the crowd looking for the kidnapper, but he vanished inside the pandemonium of fire engines, police cars, and people running in every imaginable direction.

I approached one of the police officers directing people behind barricades. "What happened?"

"Step away, sir."

"I know who lives there. Are they okay?" I asked as medics rolled out two stretchers, each with a filled body bag.

"Who are they?" I asked the medics and went to follow them when I got no response.

The police officer I spoke with pulled me back by my shoulder. "Stay back."

"I have to know who they are!" I said, although I knew the answer. I couldn't think of Steve and his wife in the past tense. I'd seen Steve several days before at our weekly acoustic gig at the Village Gate. "How did it happen?"

"I can't give you that information." He walked away to talk to another officer.

I took some of my meds to calm my nerves. My heart hadn't slowed down since my conversation with the kidnapper. The last thing I needed was to die of some heart event before I had the chance to pay the ransom.

I hung around longer and learned that a gasoline can was found outside, and arson was suspected. The synchrony of events confirmed in my mind that Gus started the fire. His showing up at my gig the previous night and his mentioning of Steve and my past seemed beyond coincidence. The deluge of flames that continued to burn as the ambulance took off for the morgue did more than take away my dear friends; they ignited my rage toward Gus, and they also terrified me. *If Gus was behind this and was crazy enough to kill Steve and his wife over not getting into a high school jazz band, what's to hold him back from doing the same thing to Jessie?* I popped two more pills after answering the question. *Nothing.*

Parole Hearing

home   when the moon is   high.   I can-not stay be - cause my mom

Steve showed up with his fiancée on the day of my father's last parole hearing. I hadn't seen Steve in eighteen years. Without his fedora and spectacles, I wouldn't have recognized him. Scar tissue covered his face, and it was hard to look at him. His appearance brought back memories of the night my father caused his injuries.

My father avoided eye contact with Steve and me. Unlike his friends, we knew his true identity, underneath his fancy suit. I was surprised he still managed to spend money he didn't have on clothes that made him look as if he had a full wallet.

He turned and smiled at a young, excessively made-up jailbird groupie who sat behind him. My Uncle George said he met her through some internet-dating service. Things got serious, and if he got paroled, he was going to marry the woman who was seven years younger than me.

The parole hearing official appeared to sympathize with Steve as he read his statement. I didn't think my father would be released.

"Simon Adamidis, I've been asked to speak regarding your possible parole. I don't think you deserve to be released after what you've done. While you've been serving your sentence, I've lived through my own. You've caused me a great deal of pain, which I still feel both physically and mentally. Not a day goes by when I don't think back to the night when my injuries were caused and the destruction you left behind for everyone involved."

Steve glanced over at me, and I turned away.

"I spent the next year all alone in a hospital. Unlike you, I had no family to visit me. Seeing the reflection staring back at me was hard. It was a constant reminder of what you did. My right hand was severely burned, and three of my fingers were fused. It took several operations before I could play guitar again. I spent hours re-teaching myself to play with my left hand. I'm almost blind in my right eye, and I still have nightmares that force me to relive what happened."

Steve's fiancée held his hand.

"I've lived the past eighteen years in my personal hell. I only left my apartment to teach and buy groceries. The rest of the time I stayed home alone. I was appalled by my appearance and didn't think anyone would want to be with me ever again. I spent many nights thinking about taking my life. After a failed suicide attempt, I joined a support group and met the most wonderful woman. I thought no one would ever love me again." Steve wiped his eyes with a handkerchief.

"Would you like to continue later?" The parole hearing official asked.

"I'm okay." Steve gazed at his fiancée. "She made me care again. Made me want to look forward to the future. We're going to get married and begin a new life together."

He handed the paper he was reading from to the parole hearing official and then looked at my father. "This will be my last appearance at your parole hearing. The only reason I'm here today is to tell you my will to forgive and get on with my life is stronger than your will to destroy. I forgive you, Simon. Mostly for my own sake. I can't move forward if I have to relive what happened every year. My testimony won't change. I've instructed my attorney to record my statement here today on video and have it played back during subsequent hearings. It's time I put this behind me."

Everyone in the room talked at once. Steve got up with his fiancée, and they headed for the door. He paused to look at me, and I turned my head away. Steve's speech moved me, and I didn't want to be moved. As far as I was concerned, he got what he deserved.

After everyone had settled down, a prison warden made a statement about how my father was a changed man. He led a weekly prayer group and helped counsel some of the youth who ended up in jail. As usual, my father managed to charm all those around him.

My father then read from his prepared statement. "I'm not even going to attempt to apologize for my actions. I did what I did because back then I was selfish and couldn't see beyond my own problems. I was not only a terrible husband, but I also failed my children. I realize I can't make it up to them. I wouldn't even attempt to if I could because the truth can't be undone. We all eventually must pay."

I bit my tongue to remain silent.

"All I can do now is leave my fate in the palm of God's hands. If I didn't find Him, I would be lost today. If by the grace of God I'm released, I'll begin my new life as a servant of the Lord and devote the rest of my life to His word."

The parole officer's expression softened, and my father's lawyer finished up by saying he was an exemplary prisoner and had no priors. Too bad he wasn't an exemplary father.

I sat on the couch, infuriated by Leda's flippant attitude about the parole hearing. As usual, all she cared about was her painting. Everything else seemed insignificant to her, or so I thought back then.

"If Dad gets out, it'll be his fault," I said. "You should've heard him. He made his testimony about himself."

"You've got him all wrong."

"As far as I'm concerned, he's as much to blame as our father."

"You don't know enough about what happened to make that judgment. You were only sixteen."

"I know enough."

Leda put down her brush and slid her chair over to her desk. She opened one of the drawers and removed a CD. "You can't avoid this any longer." She tried to hand it to me.

"I prefer vinyl. Digital kills all the warmth."

"You have to listen to it."

"I don't need to listen to anything. Pagels is a manipulator, and I want to keep the past where it belongs…in the past."

"Don't blame this all on Steve. All the silence led to what happened. There's so much I never knew about Mom and Dad."

"How can you be so easy on him?"

"I heard the truth." She tried to hand me the CD again.

"None of that is gonna make a difference because it can't change anything."

"No, but it will at least explain it."

"I don't want an explanation. I want justice."

"Sounds more like revenge."

"You were always too forgiving."

"And you were always too stubborn. Talk to Steve. Get his side of the story." Leda put the CD back in the drawer and returned to her painting. "I was as angry as you when this all happened."

"What changed your mind?"

"I met Steve. He could've done the selfish thing and continued on with his life. Even with all those burns throughout his body, he was more concerned about your feelings."

"Guilt will do that to you."

"Probably…but he also believed in you. Steve didn't want you to give up on your dreams. After he got out of the hospital and found you still holding a grudge, he quit his job so that you wouldn't quit the band. He showed a lot of loyalty…and courage."

I shook my head, not wanting to listen. "The truth can't be undone. We all eventually must pay. Dad actually said that."

Leda walked behind her easel, picked up a palette and removed a brush from a jar.

"I can't get that phrase out of my mind," I said.

"You have to get over this."

"I can't. The night keeps playing back in my mind."

Leda painted as I rambled on. It was like that with us. She understood when to sit back and let me talk myself out of whatever mood I was in. I examined Leda's painting towards the end of our discussion and refused to look at it again as it reminded me of the day justice died. My father was freed from prison.

What a Little Bullet Can Do

dad will cry.____ chil - dren have par-ents to go home to.____ Out in

I returned to my car, shocked it hadn't been towed. When I opened the door, someone grabbed me from behind. I swung around and stopped my fist short of hitting Stella's face.

"Why are you here? I told you I'd call," I said.

Stella slammed my car door shut and blocked me from getting inside. I sensed a lecture coming.

"Take off your cape. You're no superhero."

Stella's speech sounded a little slurred, but who was I to judge after all the pills I just took?

"You can't do this one alone," she said.

"Every minute we spend arguing is a minute I lose searching for Je—"

A bullet pierced the window inches away from Stella. I pulled her down to the ground and lay on top of her.

"What the hell is going on, Markos?" Stella yelled.

"I have an ex-wife who doesn't know how to follow instructions." I got up on my knees and opened the door.

"Get in."

Stella crawled inside the car while I surveyed the street. I got in after her and started the car.

"Someone just shot at us. Don't you think we should call the police?" Stella asked.

"And spend hours at the station answering questions? No time for that." I pulled into the street.

"What are you involved in?"

"Nothing."

"Come on, Markos. Stop the lies and tell me what kind of trouble you're in."

"I never lied to you. Why would I start now?"

"Who would want you dead?"

"The shooter was aiming for you."

"Don't even try to lay this one on me!"

"I'm still piecing this together, and you interrupting me isn't helping."

"Whoever is doing this is serious. Maybe you should get Teddy to help you."

I punched the side window. "When did you figure that one out? When Jessie got kidnapped, or when you almost got shot!"

Stella started to cry. I hated that I had to yell at her, but the prospect of dying in less than twenty-four hours didn't come with a manual on how to be pleasant to my ex-wife while searching for my daughter's kidnapper.

"If you listened and stayed with Leda, I'd be searching for Jessie rather than wasting the little time I have taking you home."

"Not knowing what's happening to her is unbearable. I want to be with you when you find her."

"Even if I could take you with me, I still wouldn't. It's too dangerous…for Jess and for you."

"Why was she taken? Why our daughter?" Stella pounded her fists on top of the dashboard. "Why our daughter!"

Anything can happen in a godless world, I answered to myself to justify my own firmly held belief at the time. *It doesn't play by the ten commandments or any other religious edict. We're on our own.* I had no other response that Stella would've appreciated, so I said nothing.

"I know how horrible I must sound," she said. "No child deserves to be kidnapped, but I miss my sweet little girl. Ever since Jessie was born, she's been the light that shined brightness into my life. If anything happens to her, the darkness will be unbearable. These last few years have been difficult, but I managed to hold on because of her, along with my faith that something greater than us exists. That such an awful thing was allowed to happen to Jessie tells me I probably spent a lifetime believing in lies." She wept and covered her face. "I'm trying to be strong, but my faith is slipping away. I don't know if I can ever get it back."

To hear Stella paraphrase my own thoughts disturbed me. I could offer her no words of comfort; I had no faith in anything. She cried all the way to the brownstone, and I tried my hardest not to join her.

The decor of the living room had been changed since I moved out. Gone were my guitars that hung in perfect symmetry along the wall. They used to drive Stella crazy. "Guitars aren't art…they produce art," she'd always argue.

My once-assigned wall now flaunted Stella's and Jessie's travels. Stella thought it was more important for Jessie to see the world than just read about it. Each picture featured them posing in front of a famous landmark. My favorite was of Stella and Jessie on a camel in front of the Giza Pyramid. My face never made an appearance on Stella's wall of travels, which was limited to one side of the room when I lived here. I spent the last few years of our marriage traveling with my trio and never gave my absence much thought, but the omission now bothered me. As I stared at each picture, I finally admitted to myself that Stella and I were worlds apart, even when I lived here.

My attention returned to Stella when she tripped as she entered the living room. When I tried to help her up, she pushed me away.

"I can do this myself."

Stella wasn't handling this well. Does anyone handle a kidnapping of their child well? I didn't think so, but the way Stella grabbed hold of the coffee table to prop herself up made it seem as if she was drunk.

"Are you sure you're okay?" I asked.

"Our daughter just got kidnapped. Are *you* okay?" She sat on the armchair across from me. "Give me a minute to rest and then I'm coming with you."

"You nearly got shot! Doesn't anything scare you?"

"Yes." Stella gazed at the wall of travels. "Not seeing Jessie again."

"If I bring you along, you won't."

"You're still not telling me why—"

A vision cut off Stella's comment. I lay in front of the home that was on fire. Jessie was kneeling beside me, wearing the heart-shaped locket. In her hands was a red lotus. She sang her song to me, and I felt my consciousness drifting away as I mentally sung along. *Trust in me and follow along, whenever you hear me sing my song.*

Steve loomed over me. "The truth can't be undone. We all eventually must pay."

"Markos!" Stella snapped her finger in front of my face.

I massaged my temples. "Got any aspirin? My head is killing me."

I followed Stella to the bathroom. She opened the medicine cabinet, which was filled with prescription bottles.

"What are all those for?"

Stella swiftly shut the cabinet and handed me the bottle of aspirin. "You know how I never throw anything away."

I took two aspirin and handed the bottle back to Stella. "After Jessie returns, I'm gonna see your doctor friend." I turned on the faucet and splashed some cold water all over my face.

"For real?" Stella handed me a towel.

"And as a bonus, I'll leave you alone when this is all over." I wiped my face. "No more late-night phone calls, no more parking in front of the brownstone, and no more discussions about my visions and nightmares."

Stella's eyes filled with tears. "I don't want you to think I don't care about what you're going through, but I'm having a hard time with this…a really hard time."

"I'm gonna bring Jessie home." I took Stella's hand. "Believe that with all your heart. I'm gonna bring her home to you."

"I know you will." Stella hugged me.

I longed for her to do that since the night she threw me out. Today, it was the last thing I wanted, not only because of the circumstances behind the gesture but also because it reminded me of everything I lost and could never get back.

The Culture Trap

jun - gle   that   still   is   true.

A blow from my father's hand had knocked me to the floor. "Why did you have to go and do something so stupid and shortsighted? Everyone in the diner is gonna know I got a criminal son!"

My mother entered the living room. "Why don't you take the time to listen to his side of the story before passing judgment?"

"This is gonna be the talk of the church next Sunday at coffee hour."

My mother helped me up to the couch and sat next to me.

"Father Nicholas called before and said he attacked Gus and trashed the rectory."

My father pulled me back down to the ground where I remained to avoid another beating.

"You progressed from vandalism to grand larceny all in one day. Congratulations…you're the biggest loser of the family."

My mother headed towards me, and my father pushed her away.

"Stay out of this, Maria! I'm handling him from now on! You're the one who turned him into a loser by always babying him and not letting him suffer the consequences of his actions. The boy needs to learn how the real world operates."

"And you think what you're doing is teaching him?"

"What do you want me to do? Hug him and tell him it's okay to break the law?"

My mother kneeled down and held my hand. "Why did you do this? You know the commandments. God doesn't like stealing, and I didn't raise you to be a thief."

"Dad's right. I'm a loser."

My mother cried and hugged me. "Why would you say such a thing?"

"Cuz it's true."

"I don't agree." She peered into my eyes. "You're a smart boy, and you got lots of friends."

"It's not enough. Something's missing."

"So you think stealing will help you find what you're looking for?" My father asked.

"I wanna play the guitar. It's all I ever think about. Even Flipper gets it."

"I don't care what that hippie loser told you."

"At least he understands."

My father pushed my mother away from me and pulled me up by my shirt. I thrust my face close to his, grunted, and stomped my foot on the ground. He backed off a couple of steps. That was the first time my father ever retreated from a confrontation.

"Of course he gets it. It takes a loser to know a loser." He sat on the couch.

I helped my mother up. "I still want a guitar," I said.

"Life isn't about what you want," my father said. "When you leave here, you're gonna have to make a living, and music won't pay the bills. I'm talking from experience. I gave music up because I couldn't support your mother and Leda with the money I was making. You need to concentrate on your studies so that you can get a scholarship and go to college."

"What if I don't wanna go to college?"

"The moment you graduate you're either in college, or you'll have to find another place to live."

"Don't listen to him," my mother said. "You're always welcome here."

"This is exactly what I'm talking about. You always give him the easy way out, and he takes it." My father faced me. "I talked to Jake. Starting this Saturday, you're gonna start bussing tables at the diner. You need to learn the value of money."

My father believed he was condemning me, but I thought it was a great idea. I could use my earnings to buy the M.I.J. for only ninety-nine, ninety-nine.

I stared at a poster of Jimmy Page on my wall and wondered if he had a father who gave him so much trouble over music. You'd think my father, who was once a musician himself, would have understood my need to play guitar. His whole speech about not earning enough money was probably a lie he told to convince himself his decision to leave music was a good idea. Back when he still played, he was offered a gig with a touring big band. Supposedly they were a famous act. He refused to mention their name whenever I asked. I believed he regretted turning down the offer. He traded in his sax case for a cash register at Jake's because his idea of family overshadowed his own desires, which he viewed as selfish. He once told me life on the road wasn't for him. He wanted to be around for his family. While his story sounded honorable on the surface, his actions didn't match up. He was a martyr who lived his life to appease an idyllic version of himself, instilled by culture and religion. One thing I've learned from my father is that I would never compromise. I had to find what I wanted and live it out to the best of my ability. Sometimes it's knowing what you don't want for yourself that makes you fight harder.

Written in the Grounds

Close your eyes, _____ and dream a dream. _____ A hap - py lit -

Mrs. Barras laid down a tray of sugar cookies and two cups of Greek coffee. Everything looked exactly as it had when I last visited, from the family pictures on the wall to the plastic slipcovers that protected the gaudy red-velvet couch. I used to hate it when my mother dragged me here, but I now found the memories amusing. I could still hear my mother and Mrs. Barras laugh as they told each other's fortunes by reading the coffee-ground shapes formed at the bottom of their demitasses.

"I'm surprised to see you," Mrs. Barras said. "You haven't been around in years."

"My mistake. I missed these." I took a bite of the cookie.

"I still can't believe my eyes. Markos Adamidis, all grown up and famous. Your mother was right about you."

"Hopefully about the good stuff."

"Of course." Mrs. Barras poured some sugar into her coffee. "Can't say I'm surprised about her accuracy. You were always so self-disciplined."

"Not until I got my guitar." I glanced at a picture of Gus's sister with her three small children. "Lina, Athena, and George Jr. are getting big. You must be a proud *yiayia*."

"I am."

"How about Gus? How's he doing?"

"He hasn't been around in five years."

Mrs. Barras mixed the sugar in her coffee. The tapping of the spoon against the ceramic rang in my ears somewhere between C and D, not quite deciding what it wanted to be.

"Know where he is? I need to find him." I picked up a cookie and jammed the whole thing in my mouth. I wanted to get as many of these in before I left. They were the next best thing to cigarettes, of which I probably would've gone through two packs by now had I still smoked.

"Why now?" She picked up her demitasse and took a sip.

"It's been a long time. I wanna see how he's doing." I checked out another picture hanging on the wall. Gus and I stood on either side of Steve in a typical rock-star guitar pose. We were both about fifteen.

"Gus admired you," Mrs. Barras rested her demitasse on the saucer. "Everything you did made him try harder."

"It was the other way around when it came to music."

"Maybe...but you had many friends, and Gus felt self-conscious around the other children. He wanted to fit in." Mrs. Barras picked up a cookie and broke it in half. "I held on to his guitar after you returned it to me. He refused to even open the case." She ate one of the cookie halves.

"When did you see him last?"

"He returned home five years after he ran away." Mrs. Barras stirred her coffee with the other cookie-half. "He told me he found God. I was relieved until I learned he was in one of those cults where people live all together in one house. They worshipped a scientist in L.A. who said he came to Earth to end all wars by transmitting a peace signal from his spaceship. Gus told me there were other scientists who were working with him to develop the signal." Mrs. Barras shook her head. "Have you ever heard of such a crazy thing?" She finally removed the soggy cookie and ate it.

"I've heard crazier." I took another sip of my coffee.

"George made a mockery of the whole thing and told Gus he was where he belonged. That only an alien would like him because everyone on Earth knew he was a failure. He kept putting Gus down until he finally had enough and left."

"Have you seen him since then?" I bit into another cookie.

"Not for another seven years. He left his group when they wouldn't let him marry one of the members he fell in love with. He wanted to quit the cult so that they could get married, but the woman refused to leave. He came home brokenhearted. George had died the previous year, so Gus stayed here for a while. He got himself a job, and he seemed all right for a time…until the ghost came."

"Ghost?"

"Gus said everywhere he went, the ghost followed him, and he needed to find a place to hide." Mrs. Barras picked up the demitasse, gently rocked it in a circular motion and rested it upside down over the saucer. "I think he was talking about his father."

I glanced at a picture of Gus and I dressed in our altar-boy robes.

"That was the last time I saw him." Mrs. Barras brushed some crumbs off the table with her hand, emptying them onto a napkin. "I don't know what went wrong. We tried to do the best for him. Every day I ask God what went wrong with my Gus? He was a sweet boy. Always loyal and willing to help out. Then one day he woke up a stranger. The change happened so fast…but you didn't have it easy either."

"I still don't."

"How have you been since I've last seen you?"

"It's been tough for a while, but I'm okay."

"Another cookie?" Mrs. Barras pushed the tray towards me, and I snatched two more.

She lifted the demitasse and examined the grounds. "Why are you looking for Gus?"

"He came by the Jazz Room the other night and left before I could get his number."

"He came to see you? Really?"

"He told me he worked in a grocery store."

Mrs. Barras smiled. "I know where he lives. Sorry I didn't tell you sooner. I'm very protective of him. He's been through a lot."

She walked over to a stationary desk, got out a sheet of paper and jotted something down.

"I understand." I turned over my demitasse, waited a couple of seconds, and flipped it upright to see the shape formed inside. It looked like a blob of nothing to me.

"Watch out for him...please." Mrs. Barras handed me the address.

"I will." I showed her my coffee-ground pattern. "What does this look like to you?"

Mrs. Barras stepped back and made the sign of the cross. Never in all my years had I seen her or my mother take coffee-ground reading seriously. It was only a game.

"Go," she said. "Go find him now."

"What do you see?"

"Ghosts. Gus was right. They're real. Keep him safe and don't condemn him. He's been through enough."

A Foggy Brain

summer in my jungle dream._____ Where no one ev-er____ has to sleep

The smell of urine and Chinese cooking from the restaurant below followed me down an empty hall with paint peeling off the walls. I stopped when I got to 31C and rang the bell. After a few minutes of waiting and pondering over Mrs. Barras's bizarre reaction to the coffee grounds, I turned the knob. The door was locked. I removed a credit card and after several attempts, I managed to get it open. My father was wrong again; my delinquent days paid off.

I walked over a mountain of newspapers and magazines, making my way to what appeared to be a desk. It was hard to tell at first glance. Torn pages covered the entire surface. I rummaged through them and noticed they all had a common theme, me and the incident. I picked up one of the newspaper clippings. The headline read: *Local Jazz Musician, Markos Adams, Takes Leap Off the WXQX Building While on a Cigarette Break*. I tossed the article onto the desk, and my cellphone vibrated, startling me. All the talk about ghosts got me a little jittery, and this whole apartment complex seemed like the perfect setting for them to take up residence. My cellphone rang, and I answered.

"Tick tock, tick tock, by this time tomorrow you'll have already paid up," the kidnapper said.

"I know it's you, Gus. Why don't you tell me why you're doing this?"

A car door slammed, and I ran to the window to have a look outside. A passenger had just gotten out of a cab.

"You sound certain."

"You're the only one who makes sense."

"So…is Gus your final answer?"

I had a feeling he expected me to say yes, and I wasn't going to give him what he wanted. "I prefer to keep my options open until the deadline."

"A wise decision. Be in your car for my next call, which will come in two minutes. If you miss the call, I'll assume you've quit our game."

The kidnapper hung up, and I ran down to my car. My cellphone rang as I opened the door.

"Thought you wouldn't make it," the kidnapper said after I answered. "I never saw you move so fast."

I inspected the area. "If you're following me, who's keeping an eye on Jessie?"

"I assure you, she's being well taken care of."

"Is there someone else involved in this with you?"

"That's for you to figure out."

I slid into my seat and started the engine. "Where to now?"

"Nowhere in particular. I enjoy making you jump to my every command." The kidnapper laughed. "You're easy to train."

I tightened my grip on the steering wheel. "Since you're in such a festive mood, why don't you put my daughter on so I can speak to her?"

"If you stick to the rules I gave you, I'll let you talk to her before you have to pay up. I have to leave you now and get back to my new hobby. I'll call you after I'm finished." The kidnapper hung up.

I headed to the police station to ask Teddy if he could run a background check on Gus. I passed the lot after I spotted Stella talking to Teddy. They never had any intention of letting me handle this alone, and that meant trouble for Jessie if I didn't get Teddy off my trail. I parked a block away, searched my car and found a tracking device under the hood. Teddy involving himself shouldn't have surprised me. I hadn't given him or Stella a reason to trust me. I left the tracker in my car and decided to play the manic-depressive, suicidal-type of guy Teddy and Stella believed me to be. If they wanted crazy I'd give them my best performance, which wasn't really a far stretch. A quick glimpse in the rearview mirror told me I was perfect for the role. I made the graffiti art from my poster look like an improvement.

I sat on a stool and played "Moody's Mood" on a Les Paul jazz acoustic while a salesperson was helping a father select an electric bass for his son.

Teddy entered the music store and hurried over to me. "Care to explain why we're meeting here?"

"This is the last place your friends would be hanging around."

"How did Jessie look?"

"She thinks this is all a game."

"At least she's not scared."

I stopped playing and ran my hand through my hair, which was saturated with sweat.

"You're a mess. Looks like you were shot at." Teddy pulled out a beef jerky from his jacket pocket and tore open the wrapper. He took a bite and stared at me while he slowly chewed.

I put the guitar back on the stand. "Stella was never in any harm. The kidnapper only wanted to scare us."

"Did it work?" Teddy asked in the same condescending tone he used when I was a teenager, whenever he wanted to hear me admit I screwed up.

I always dealt with Teddy's grilling by hiding behind my guitar, and today was no exception. I walked over to a row of electric guitars on display. "I haven't been here since Music Man sold this place." I picked up an M.I.J., similar to the one I tried to steal and played "Over the Hills and Far Away." My regression was now in full swing. I expected the proverbial knock on my door, followed by Teddy entering my room to state how I couldn't hide behind a guitar for the rest of my life. No, I couldn't, but music certainly helped block out most of my problems. Nevertheless, I now had a problem I could no longer block out, and I didn't know how to function without a guitar in my hand.

"Heard the incident happened near Steve Pagels's building that burned down this morning," Teddy said. "Is there a connection here I should know about?" He took another bite of his jerky.

I stopped playing and reached into my pocket. "That's why I called." I handed Teddy a sheet of paper with some details I'd written about Gus.

"What's this?" He examined my notes.

"Think there's more than one person involved, but Gus Barras is my main suspect. He more than likely started the fire at Steve's and shot at Stella. I checked out his apartment—"

"Are you trying to blow this whole thing?" Teddy yelled quietly. "The only reason I'm covering for you is because of Leda, and I'm close to changing my mind. You can't break into people's homes without a warrant. No evidence you find will be useable in a court of law."

"I don't give a damn about the evidence! I want my daughter back!"

The father, son, and the salesperson stared at me.

I put the M.I.J back on the stand and a siren sounded, making my head ache. "Gus has been keeping track of me. His desk was filled with articles about the incident."

A fire truck raced by, and another vision of Jessie singing and holding a red lotus came to me.

"Markos!" Teddy hissed.

I rubbed my forehead, hoping I could fool Teddy as I did Stella.

"Holy anchovy, what planet did your head just come back from?" He took a bite of his jerky and talked with his mouth full. "Stella told me your nightmares started up again."

"It was only one. I'm cool now."

"If that's supposed to make me feel better..." Teddy cut himself off when the bell from the front door rang and a customer entered.

The bell was the same one from when Flipper and Music Man owned the shop. The ringing amplified the most painful memories from my childhood and intensified my anxiety. I reached into my pocket for my pills and stopped myself. I needed to remain lucid. "Your *feelings* aren't top priority," I said. "Jessie's missing, and that's the only thing I'm gonna focus on until I find her."

"You told me they were gone for good."

"I don't have time for a psych evaluation, but if that's what it'll take to get you off my back, fire away." I crossed my arms. "It's not as if I have a pressing engagement to attend to."

Teddy pointed the jerky at me. "If you want my silence, you gotta count me in from now on." He paused when the customer walked by us. "Call me every two hours with updates. If I don't hear from you, I'll assume you're in over your head." He glanced at his watch. "It's now 12:30. I'll be expecting a call from you at 2:30. Got it?"

I threw my hands in the air. "You win."

"I always do." Teddy took a proud bite of his jerky, and I grabbed it from him.

"Stop with the hotdogging. I'm starting to get comfortable in your world."

Teddy stole the jerky back and pointed it at me. "Stick to bebop. The disheveled-cop-who-hasn't-slept-all-night-look doesn't work on you."

"I could never fool you. How do you stay so calm in situations like this?"

"After all the years I spent on the beat, it's like second nature to me. But I'm nearing my breaking point today. Teddy waved his beef jerky and took a bite. "Doesn't work nearly as well as cigarettes. Since my shift started, I came close to buying a pack three times."

"Sorry I brought up Johnny," I said.

"The only reason you're still standing is that I know what you're going through. I would've clobbered anyone else for using my son to get to me."

We walked to the door. "I want you to make sure Stella is taken care of in case anything happens to me."

Teddy narrowed his eyes. "Why would anything happen to you? Jessie is the only one in trouble here."

"You know me. I never could rely on faith alone. I wanna make sure everything and everyone is covered."

Teddy nodded. "In the meantime, I'm gonna run a check on this Barras character."

"Thanks. I appreciate it."

"You understand the risk I'm taking keeping quiet with this?"

"I know, and after this is over, I'm gonna owe you big time. If it wasn't for you and Leda, I don't know where I'd be today."

"You don't owe me a thing." He slapped his hand against the side of my arm. "We're family."

"Thanks, Teddy."

"Now go get your daughter."

The kidnapper called me at exactly 1:00 p.m. "Just finished with my new hobby. Would you like to know what it is?"

"Not really."

"Painting is therapeutic and a great way to reduce stress. It's been a while since I've held a brush in my hand, so I thought I'd give it a try. I think what I've done here is exhibit material, but I can't take all the credit. I had a beautiful model. Would you like to know who she is?"

I gripped the steering wheel as I braced for the answer.

"I admire her work, especially the ones with you as the subject. They're very revealing."

"If you hurt her, I'll kill you!" I made a hard left turn to take the next side street and almost plowed into some oncoming cars.

"Do you understand what it means to be hurt, Markos?"

"All too well."

"I'm hurting too. Maybe that's why I do what I do. I could never seem to make people happy, so I gave up trying. I am what I am. A pain-making man living in a pain-driven scam called life."

I let him continue with his psycho-rap, hoping to pick up anything revealing about his speech pattern. The synthesized voice protected any accent present in the human voice, so I listened to the word selection and phrasing, trying to see if it connected to Gus in any way.

"A part of me wants to get caught. I'm tired of living and hoping the next day will get better. It never does."

"If you truly mean what you're saying, doing the right thing will clear your conscience. Tell me where I can find Jessie."

"I would, but you deserve to suffer for everything you've done to me."

"Is it because I got the scholarship and you didn't?"

"Oh. We're back to that again. You're too easy an opponent. Be more challenging when I call back, or I'll move the deadline ahead out of boredom." The kidnapper hung up as I pulled in front of the brownstone.

Won't You Teach Me Some Night

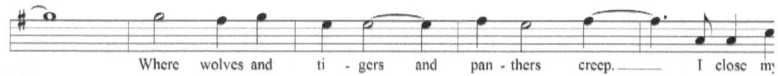

Where wolves and ti - gers and pan - thers creep._____ I close my

Jake owned the diner my father had managed. They spent their boyhood summers on the island of Paros in Greece, so they were tight. My father always used to tell me he wanted to open up his own restaurant, but he didn't have a business mind. I think it had more to do with laziness. He didn't like working. He always sat at the corner booth next to the register, chatting with some of the local boys. When he worked the late shift, he'd also throw in a few games of backgammon along with a bottle of three-star Metaxa. If you never heard of the latter, you're not missing much. While my parents were both out working at one of the annual festivals at the church, I tried a shot and ran to the bathroom to spit it out. Nevertheless, if I had to choose between ouzo and Metaxa, I'd choose Metaxa. For decorum's sake, I won't mention what I did after I took my first shot of ouzo.

A few cute girls motivated me to get up each Saturday morning, but only Ezza managed to hold my attention for longer than a week. I dug her from the moment she bent forward in front of me to refill a ketchup bottle. She was older than me. Think she just turned thirty. Her euphonious voice never failed to pull me into whatever topic she discussed. She sounded like one of those old pull-string dolls Leda used to play with before her right-hand found the paint brush. Ezza was shorter than me and had unusually large blue-gray eyes that shot out behind her thick, black-rimmed librarian glasses. I never considered glasses sexy until I saw them on her.

Ezza kept to herself. On her breaks, she always hid behind some book in the back-corner booth. When things got hectic, she'd sneak outside to smoke. Dottie would follow her out to catch up on current affairs.

"They don't tell you anything about what's going on in the world anymore, but if you bring Ezza out to the back for a smoke, you get a whole week's worth of world events," Dottie told me as I bussed one of her tables.

When Ezza walked by us and smiled, I nervously smiled back and turned away.

"You got a crush." Dottie smiled and wagged her finger at me.

"I don't get crushes." I grabbed a cup and saucer from the table and threw it into the bus bin.

Dottie picked up a broken piece of ceramic and waved it at me. "You're right; you cause them."

I shifted my attention to Ezza, who was wiping down the counter.

"Don't worry, your secret is safe with me," Dottie said.

I yanked away her towel. "Say anything, and I'll tell her you made the whole thing up because you hear voices in your head."

Dottie pulled back the towel and whipped the side of my thigh with it. "Markos Adamidis, you better watch your mouth, or I'll tell your father you're the one who's been stealing his cigarettes from behind the counter."

"If you do that, I'll tell him you were the one who put salt in his coffee."

The exchange was all in good fun. Dottie and I were close, even before I started working at Jake's. She was the hip grandmother I never had. Both my grandmothers' houses smelled like mothballs, and they always wore black because they were widows. The only time they left their apartments was to attend a holiday function or to go to church.

On days when my father was tough on me, Dottie wouldn't stop talking to me until she was satisfied I was sufficiently cheered up and ready to do battle with my father again.

"How's school going with you?" Dottie asked.

"Flunking out in math." I wiped down the table. "I gotta go to summer school."

"Thought you were good in math?"

"I am. I get confused during tests. The way the questions are worded makes it seem there's more than one answer."

Dottie pointed at Ezza. "You should get her to help. She's one of those egghead-types. She has two degrees and is working for another one over at N.Y.U."

"Wonder why she's wasting her time here then."

Dottie hit me with her towel again. "Watch your attitude before you turn into a snob like your father."

I stared at Ezza as she poured some coffee into a patron's cup. When she caught me watching her, I quickly redirected my attention to the table I was bussing. Approaching girls wasn't difficult for me. At fourteen, I'd already broken a few hearts. Ezza was a whole new challenge for me. She was the older woman, meaning she had more experience. It made me feel inferior.

"I'm going out for a smoke," Dottie said.

I didn't respond. I was busy watching Ezza giggle as she talked to one of the customers seated by the counter.

Dottie snapped her fingers in front of my face. "Meet me out back in five minutes."

"Why?"

"Meet me, and you'll see."

Ezza and Dottie were in the middle of a conversation. I stayed close to the door, thinking of ways to introduce myself without coming across like a lovesick teenager.

"I never thought about what happened before the big bang," Dottie said, "I always thought it was the start of everything."

"That's only a theory," Ezza said. "Absolute knowledge about our place in the cosmos is impossible. All that we observe in space is based from our vantage point; therefore, our interpretation is subjective. And it's no better here. The belief that we're in control of our own environment is equally illusory. An asteroid or comet can come at us from the deepest reaches of space and bring us to the brink of extinction. We're all too scared to admit to that because we'd then have to accept we exist in the midst of chaos."

"Exactly," Dottie said, appearing confused.

I strode over and asked, "What's up?" with all the cool attitude I could muster. I might've exaggerated more than usual to account for the stained apron I was wearing. It knocked my level of cool down a few notches. I pulled out a cigarette from my front pocket. "Got a light, Dot?"

She smirked at me and handed me her lighter. "Markos needs help in math. Can you tutor him, Ezz?"

Ezza peered at me. "I'll consider it if you tell me what you think happened before the big bang."

"Never bought into it." I cocked my head to the side, lit my cigarette, and gave the lighter back to Dot, who shook her head at my performance. Can't fault her for it as I do the same thing whenever I recall that memory.

"How do you think everything began?" Ezza asked.

I couldn't answer. I was fastened into one of those intense stares where you're not aware you're staring.

Dottie pushed the side of my arm. "Answer her question."

I took a drag from my cigarette while formulating an answer, which wasn't difficult. I watched countless documentaries about space. "Everything was already here, and all the galaxies are held together by ether." I took a drag from my cigarette. "It's like we're living in a giant bowl of fruit Jell-O. The ether is the Jell-O, and the galaxies are the little pieces of fruit."

Ezza squinted her eyes as though probing me. "I'm surprised I didn't pick up on this sooner." She turned to Dottie. "You know who he reminds me of?"

"I told you. James Dean."

"I think he looks more like John Stamos."

Dottie shook her head. "Nah, I don't see the similarity other than them both being Greek."

"How old are you?" Ezza asked me.

"Fourteen."

"Gemini?"

"How did you know?"

"Sorry, I don't have time."

"Cuz I'm a Gemini?"

"I have three orders to get out."

"What are your degrees in?"

"Philosophy and world history."

"And you believe in astrology?" My passion for debating pseudoscientific piffle overpowered my shyness. "That all started because people from a long time ago didn't understand anything about science."

"No need to argue. I don't believe in it either."

"Then why did you ask?"

"Cultural conditioning." She pointed her cigarette at me. "You claim you don't buy into astrology, yet you have all the characteristics of your sign because horoscopes saturate our societal landscape. You can't escape from culture unless you move into the woods and live the life of a hermit."

"What did I tell you?" Dottie said. "You don't even need the *Tonight Show* with Ezza around."

"It was a lucky guess," I said.

"Wish it was." Ezza started to pace. "If we're so easily suggestible, everything passed down to us from a historical perspective must be doubted until it can be proved with certainty."

The pickup bell in the kitchen rang.

"Shit." Ezza put out her cigarette and hurried off.

"Strange girl," Dottie said as we followed her into the kitchen. "She can't have a normal conversation."

"That's why I like her." I smiled and watched Ezza as she picked up a plate of fries.

"So do I. But I can't help but worry about what's going on with her. She seems to forget things a lot lately. For someone as smart as her, that doesn't seem right."

Dottie handed me an egg cream and fifteen dollars in tips that brought me closer to my M.I.J. I went over to where Ezza ate her dinner and sat in the booth across from her. When I took a sip from my drink, Ezza slapped the table and startled me.

"What's wrong?" I asked.

Ezza put her burger down and cried. "Nothing." She picked up a napkin and wiped her eyes. "I'll tutor you if you leave me alone." She got up and left. When she returned a few minutes later, she seemed more relaxed.

"All better?" I asked.

"Than what?" Ezza smiled as she picked up her burger.

"You seemed upset."

"I'm okay now. I meditated. It helps to calm me." She took a bite of her burger.

"When can we start?"

Ezza creased her forehead as she finished chewing her food. "Refresh my memory."

"You said you'd tutor me in math."

"When did I say that?"

"Before you left to meditate. You told me if I left, you'd help."

"Then why are you still here?"

"I wanted to make sure you were okay."

"That's so sweet." She tore off a small scrap from a place mat and wrote down her number. "Call me."

Ezza handed me the paper, and I got locked into her gaze again. She slammed her hand on the table, and I jumped out of my seat thinking she got angry at me.

"See you Friday, and don't be late." She grinned and returned her attention to her burger.

Meditation

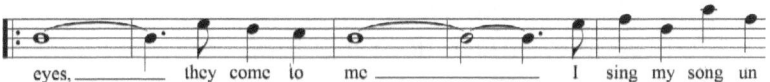

eyes,_____ they come to me _____ I sing my song un

I found Leda gagged and tied to a chair. "Was it Gus?" I asked as I freed her.

"Not sure. He wore a mime mask, and he didn't say a word to me."

"Teddy was right. I should've let him report this." I got out my cellphone.

Leda grabbed my hand. "Not until after we find Jessie." She pointed at my cellphone. "Put that away...*now*."

I obliged, and she rushed over to the easel to appraise the kidnapper's artwork.

"You may want to look at this. He painted me as you found me, except that my hands are untied, and I'm holding a red lotus."

I went to inspect the painting.

"Any idea what it means?" she asked.

I reflected over my vision of Jessie holding a red lotus. *How could the kidnapper know about my visions? Maybe the bug in my car didn't come from Teddy, and the kidnapper is spying on me and listening to my private conversations. Whenever he called, he knew exactly where I was.*

Leda replaced the painting with a piece she had been working on and then picked up a brush.

If someone threw a guitar pick at me, I would've fallen over. "How can you paint after what just happened?"

Leda dabbed the brush onto the palette. "There's no better time to create than when I'm freaked out. And believe me, I'm freaked out. The best art comes from the most extreme emotions. I'd rather spend them on something productive." She peered at me. "You, of all people, should understand what I'm saying."

"Not me. Can't play a single note when I'm freaked."

"You spend too much time analyzing things before you set foot on stage. But once you start playing, that all goes away. You gotta learn to trust what you're receiving completely and without judgment…*before* you start playing."

"Easier said than done. Without Wes or Robert J. hanging around, I'm useless."

Leda's hand moved faster as she painted. "I refuse to let this experience kill my inspiration. If I do, that monster behind the mask wins, and you know how I hate to lose."

"Think you're onto something. I was spooked before we went on last night. After Wes showed up and I let go, my playing seemed more detached than usual. I felt like I was in the audience watching myself."

"What spooked you?"

"It all started with a dream I had before my gig. It seemed so real. I was lying on the sidewalk bleeding, and you brought Jessie to me. There was a fire, and she was scared. Jessie loves *The Jungle Book*. I told her to be brave like Mowgli, who wasn't afraid of fire like the rest of the animals."

"They called it the red flower." Leda looked at the painting and then at me. "Do you think your dream is somehow connected to the kidnapping?"

"Can't be. You're the first person I told about the red lotus."

"Did you see anything else?"

"Jessie started to sing her song to me."

"'Jessie's Song,'" Leda smiled.

"Her voice calmed me…until Steve showed up."

"Pagels?"

"Yeah. And after he removed his fedora, a firefly flew out of it and morphed into this large vortex that swallowed me whole. Next thing I know, I'm awake, standing on the ledge of my roof, staring down at the street. Since then, I've been having visions of Jessie singing and holding a red lotus."

"Doesn't sound like any of your previous dreams."

"Try telling that to Stella and Teddy. They've been following me. They think I had a relapse. Teddy probably has all his friends involved by now."

"He's doing it on his own."

"You knew? Why didn't you tell me?"

"If I did, and he found out, he would've ended up reporting the kidnapping. I didn't want to risk it. Let him think he's in control of the situation, and he'll keep quiet."

My sister had a gift of making everyone feel as though they're on the winning side. She probably told Teddy something similar about me.

"Do you think my dream has something to do with Jessie's kidnapping?"

"You think you had a premonition?"

"You know I don't buy into that metaphysical jive, but I can't find any other rational explanation." I looked at the picture of Leda holding the lotus.

"There have been many instances of people who've dreamed about events before they occur. And after the fire at

Steve's building…" Leda cried and wiped her eyes with her forearm. "Maybe you are seeing into the future, and since Jessie is with you in it, that means she's gonna be okay."

"I wish I could see more. The same vision keeps playing back in my mind like a needle on a record that skips back to the same place only I can't pick up the arm to move it ahead." I got out my cellphone and glanced at the picture of Jessie and me on the screen. "I'm probably gonna have to pay the ransom."

"Money can easily be replaced."

"All I want is to see her again so that I can tell her I love her."

"And you will. All you gotta do is open your heart, and you'll get through this."

I sneaked back inside Leda and Teddy's unit and peeked into the studio. Leda was still painting. An earthquake, tidal wave, and tornado could hit at the same time, and she probably wouldn't notice. Snaps insisted I was the same way when I played. I never believed it until he decided to prove it to me. During one of our gigs, he stuck a sign on the back of my shirt that read: *Wave to me whenever you read this.* Whenever I soloed, I moved around a lot on stage. After we finished the set, he pulled the sign off my shirt and showed it to me. When I insisted no one raised their hands, Teddy played me back the video Snaps instructed him to record. All the members of the audience raised their hands when I turned my back to them. Teddy compared my hyper-focusing to Leda's; however, she lived in the zone while I only visited during recording sessions and gig nights.

I crept into the bedroom, opened the closet, and removed a shoebox from the overhead shelf. Inside was Teddy's old gun, along with a supply of bullets. I took both and made it out on time to check in with Teddy.

"Any news on Gus?" I asked.

"Just got off the phone with the LAPD. Turns out Gus got in serious trouble with the law there."

"What did he do?"

"He was stalking some girl. Claimed she was his fiancée."

"His mother told me about her. They were members of the same cult."

"Here's where things get interesting. The girl disappeared shortly after Gus left the cult. He was ruled out as a suspect because he had an alibi…his mother. That would've been the end of my suspicion if I didn't remember all the stories about how overprotective Mrs. Barras was of her kids. She wouldn't let Sophia talk to Leda after she moved in with me. She thought Leda was a bad influence. Couldn't believe Sophia, who was eighteen, still listened to her mother. The more I think about it, the more I agree with you about this guy. I'm keeping a watch on him. I'm parked in front of his apartment right now."

"Is he there?"

"No. But I'll be here when he shows up."

"I appreciate your help, Teddy."

"If you find him, call me. Don't go anywhere alone with him."

I laughed. "I'm not afraid of Gus."

"I'm serious. If he's grown up to be a murderer, let's not help him make a career out of it."

I was relieved Teddy was helping me. Now that Gus was a suspect, he'd be focused on him for a while. This gave me more freedom to move around. I had to keep it that way to ensure that if there had to be a funeral after this was all over, it would only be mine.

Too Darn Hot

der a sha-dy ban-yan tree._____ A qui-et place where___ I can sta

I stood in the church hall and watched my father marry his young bride. By the time they had exchanged their vows, I'd finished off a pint of whisky. When Father Nicholas asked if anyone objected to their union, I smashed the bottle on the floor. "Opa!"

The old groom, his trophy bride, and all the guests turned to face me.

I staggered down the aisle. "My father has no right to be here!" I approached the altar and pointed at him. "You should be burning in the hell you believe in, but because it doesn't exist, just as your god doesn't exist, justice won't be served. You'll probably die of old age, honored and respected by everyone in this damned church!"

The guests talked all at once, and two of the ushers seized me by my arms.

"You have them all fooled!" I said as I tried to break free.

My father walked over to me. "How dare you come in the house of God speaking the words of the devil."

"The devil is already present here, and I'm looking right at him."

"You have no right to judge me. Only God can do that, and I've put myself at His mercy for the rest of my life."

"Bravo," I pulled myself free and clapped my hands. "That was quite a performance. What will you do for an encore? Perform an exorcism on me?"

Father Nicholas stepped between my father and I. "Who are you to come in here and spoil this wedding? The bride did nothing to deserve your disrespect."

"I'm trying to save her."

"You should go home and sober up," Father Nicholas said. "Try to remember the good things your father did for you. He never gave up on you, even after all the trouble you caused. If you can be forgiven, so can he."

Father Nicholas nodded to the ushers. They grabbed my arms and dragged me to the door.

When I returned home, I passed out on the couch and had the worst nightmare I'd yet to experience. I was a shadow, surrounded by flames. Firefighters arrived and turned their hoses on me that shot out bullets instead of water.

I woke up to a cold splash of water on my face. Stella stood over me holding an empty glass. I sat up and braced myself for the scolding I thought was to follow.

"I can't do this anymore. I want you out of here today."

"I had a difficult night. My father got married."

"I know." She shook her head. "Father Nicholas called me and told me everything."

"He never could mind his business."

"He wanted to make sure you were okay, which was very kind of him considering you preached your atheistic views to his congregation. That was so cruel, even for you." Stella sat down beside me. "I don't recognize who you are anymore."

"I didn't mean for any of that to happen."

"Why did you go last night?"

"I was angry. Couldn't hold it in anymore. They shouldn't have let him out."

"But they did. And you have to accept that."

"He fooled them all, but not me. He hasn't changed."

"You have to let go of this and get on with your life."

"I can't."

"Talk to me. It's the only way I'll understand why you've been acting like this." Stella got impatient when I didn't answer fast enough. "I'm going to be late." She stood and fell back onto the sofa.

I placed my arm around her to see if she was okay, and she pulled away.

"I'm sorry I can't be forgiving and *perfect* like you," I said.

Stella shook her head. "I'm tired of your sarcasm."

"And I'm tired of all your preaching!" I got up and overturned the coffee table. "Lay off me!"

"As you wish." Stella said without a hint of emotion. She got up while holding the armrest. "Be out of here before I come home." She walked to the door, picked up her briefcase and left

After I had moved out, I started hanging with Snaps as in the old days, but I wasn't enjoying it as much. Snaps insisted I needed something new in my life to fill in the void left after Stella dumped me. He convinced one of his friends over at WXQX to let me host a Saturday-evening jazz program. The slot was open after the regular host quit to take a better-paying job in L.A. Snaps always went on about how I had the perfect late-night radio voice, so I gave it a shot and enjoyed the experience. Spending the night talking about my favorite music was something I used to do for free and now I was getting paid. That was definitely my kind of gig. The program director liked my *jazz pizazz*—his words. I'd never say anything so trite. He gave me a regular slot and moved me to Sunday nights. Something about sitting alone, talking to faces I couldn't see sparked my imagination. In my second week, I began to throw in anecdotes about the songs I played and where I was at the time of my life when I heard them. I talked about my unrequited love for Billie Holiday and how I would ask her for a date if I ever met her on the other side. One of my female fans called in pretending she was Billie Holiday.

"I dig your style," she said to me. "I saw your pic on the WXQX website. You look real slick."

"How slick?"

"Very slick."

"Like Chet Baker slick?"

"Nah. You don't look a thing like him. I was thinking of Tyrone Power."

"That's a new one."

"Just do me a favor and live longer. He died way too young."

"Does that mean I'm your type?"

"Oh no, silly boy. Things could never work between us. You should go with a woman closer to your reality."

"How about we meet up after I die?"

"That'll take way too long, baby, and I'm feeling bored. There aren't many jazz clubs up here."

"When I join you, I'll open one, and you'll be the only singer."

"Is that a promise, or are you just saying it to make me wait?"

"Both."

The program director liked the exchange so much that he made my position permanent and named the program, *Markos Adams, From the Other Side*. Each week, I'd select a dearly departed jazz or blues artist and run a mock interview. It was never staged. The screener would pick a caller he thought would sound good, and we'd just roll with it. It was the perfect escapist vehicle for me, and it helped to get me through some rough nights.

I took Jessie to the Bronx Zoo once a month. The tigers were her favorite. On our last trip out, she stood in front of their cage and pensively stared at them as they slept.

"Do you think Shere Khan would like being locked up?"

"Probably not."

"Why do they put animals in cages?"

"People like to appreciate them, but they can't do it in the wild."

"Why?"

"Shere Khan would eat them." I tickled her.

Jessie looked at the tiger. "It's sad. No animal should be in a cage. Even Shere Khan." She crossed her arms. "I'm never going to the pet store again or any other place where an animal isn't free."

That was my Jessie. She was almost eight, but she already showed a great deal of compassion. She decided she'd no longer support a business that kept animals locked up, and that was our last trip to the Bronx Zoo. I was disappointed as I enjoyed going there with her, but I was glad she took a stand for something she believed in.

A few months later, we were watching a documentary on television about American cuisine. Jessie got excited when the narrator started talking about chicken nuggets. It was her favorite meal until she learned how the chickens were killed. Jessie watched the whole program that covered hamburgers, hotdogs, meatloaf and sloppy joes. At the show's end, Jessie announced she would no longer eat animals. Stella thought it was a phase but after three months, she had to accept her daughter was a vegetarian. The two of us had a talk with Jessie to try to get her to eat meat again. She ended up converting us to her side when she asked us if we'd kill an animal for food. I'll never forget the look Stella and I gave each other. We both became vegetarians that night.

I became an expert with spices. I had to. It was the only way to make vegetables appetizing to my palette. Indian food became my favorite cuisine, and I could cook all the popular dishes served in the restaurants. Before I became an absent father, I prepared home-cooked meals for Jessie on all her weekend visits, always ending them with my famous baklava. That was typically her favorite part of the meal, which was understandable. No bakery, restaurant or market had baklava that compared to mine. My secret blend of spices were guessed at numerous times, but no one ever came close to reverse engineering my recipe. I promised Jessie I'd give it to her after she was all grown up.

She appreciated my first attempt at Aloo Palak. I'd been avoiding the recipe as it seemed like a lot of work, which turned out to be true. I spooned my first batch into Jessie's bowl. "Don't worry, I went light on the spices."

"I don't mind. Your cooking is *way* better than Mom's, even when you mess up. She always ends up putting in too much cumin." She winced. "It's gross."

"Never admit that to your mother. I don't want a food war to break out."

"What's a food war?"

"Your mother is very competitive. She won't accept that my Aloo Palak is better than her Aloo Palak."

"She never made Aloo Palak." Jessie laughed. "I don't think she ever will. She's too busy with Phil, and you said it takes too long to make."

"He's around a lot?"

Jessie nodded.

"Do you like him?"

She swirled her spoon around in the bowl.

"It's okay if you like him."

"He's really nice. He got me a doll from China. It's made of porcelain. I keep it on my dresser."

"It seems things are getting serious between the two of them."

"I think he's going to ask her to marry him."

I poured a little extra cayenne pepper into my food. I wanted to feel the burn.

Every Time We Say Goodbye

Sit   with   my   friends   and‗‗‗   play   all   day. ‗

Paying the ransom seemed more likely than finding Gus before the deadline. After I checked in with Teddy, I went to Stella's to say goodbye. As my eyes explored all the pictures on the wall, my mind drifted to the happy times I spent with her and Jessie. I wished I brought Ezza so that I could hear Stella sing "Angel Eyes" for one last time. I loved how she sung it.

Stella entered with a tray of tea and set it on the table. My cellphone played my alarm tone, and I took my meds. There was no reason for me to remain lucid anymore. I raised my tea cup, and Stella poured me some tea. The aroma of cardamon awakened more old memories.

"I missed your Bengali spice tea," I said.

"Those pills work well." She sat beside me.

"How so?"

"You're calm."

I shook the bottle. "There aren't enough of these in here to keep me calm." I sipped my tea, and it soothed my throat that felt raw after all the yelling I did today. "I know you don't trust me to find Jessie."

"If I didn't, I would've already reported the kidnapping."

I glanced towards the window and then back at Stella. "Can we please start being honest with each other tonight?"

"How will I tell the difference? You haven't been honest with me throughout most of our marriage."

"Let's not discuss our past," I said.

"Tonight isn't about us."

"Why did you bring it up?"

"Only as it relates to tonight," Stella said. "It's obvious you're keeping something from me, and I want to know what it is."

"So are you. Why did you tell Teddy my nightmares started up again?" I got up and went to the window to see if anyone was parked outside. "I'd sink my life's savings and bet Teddy's friends are hiding somewhere around the block, keeping an eye on me." I shut the shade. "Please tell me I'd go broke."

"It astounds me how you've managed to turn the focus away from Jessie and onto yourself." Stella picked up her cup of tea and lost her grip. The cup fell onto the table.

I watched with concern as she blotted the spill with a napkin. "Are you okay, Stella?"

"No I'm not!" She got up. "I can't sit here anymore. My mind keeps coming up with horrific scenarios of what's happening to Jessie."

Stella went to her piano and started playing "How High the Moon," up-tempo and cheerful. She used music to calm herself. It was another thing we had in common.

I walked over and leaned against the body of the piano. "I miss playing with you."

Stella glared at me. "The song was enjoyable on first hearing. Please spare me the refrain. It's old, tired and predictable." Stella fumbled over a few keys and stopped playing. "Sorry." She pushed back the bench and got up. "I'm the one who feels old, tired...and scared." She went to the couch and sat. "I don't know how to deal with all three at once."

"No apologies necessary. I deserve your wrath." I sat next to her. "Fire away. I can take it."

"Not tonight. But I might take a few shots after Jessie comes home."

My eyes wandered around the wall of travels. "I took you both for granted. Realized it only last night. I was always slow at picking things up."

"Except when it comes to music."

I faced Stella. "I appreciate that you stayed with me for as long as you had. You tried to make things work while I tried to escape reality by touring. I wanted to be as far away from my past as I could get."

"You can't escape your past, Markos. It's always there, no matter what you do."

"But a new environment doesn't have any memories attached to it. Whenever I'm on the road, nothing bothers me. Every street I walk on, club I play at and restaurant I eat at is a new experience. Even the way people speak to me sounds different. That's why I decided to accept a teaching gig in Paris. I'm tired of looking back."

Stella widened her eyes. "When were you going to tell me...and Jessie?"

"I just got the offer recently." I glanced at my watch. It was nearing three.

"Please stay," Stella said. "Until you have to drop off the ransom."

"Why now? My presence wasn't needed before."

"Every action we take is a consequence in Jessie's life. It's going to take extra effort on both our parts to help her get over this. You have to stop running away and take the time to get to know her again."

"And what action will you take?"

"Work at trusting you. Deep down I know you're a good father. It's my fear for Jessie's safety that makes it hard for me to trust you. I don't want to do that anymore." Stella wiped her eyes. "It's probably what pushed you away from her."

"No, Stella." I held her hand. "My absence had nothing to do with you…or Jess." I was about to cry as it had just struck me that I wouldn't be around to see Jessie again. My eyes re-scanned every picture on the wall so that I could take them with me and hold on to them during my last moments. "I wish I could tell you what you wanna hear, but I'd be lying. You were right not to trust me, and it's better that I stay away." I got up. "My presence would only hold Jessie back from all the great things she still has left to do." I hurried to the door before I lost it in front of Stella.

She ran ahead and blocked my path. "No matter what you think now, Jessie will always need her father."

"She's done all right without me, and she'll continue to do so when she comes home."

"I don't think Jessie would agree with your assessment."

"She will when she realizes I did what I had to do to save her."

Stella slowly stepped back. "What are you trying to say?"

"After tonight, you'll never doubt my loyalty."

"You're scaring me, Markos."

"Don't be. Jessie will be home by tomorrow morning."

"What are you keeping from me? Tell me."

I gazed at Stella for what I thought would be the last time. With nothing left to lose, I grabbed her and kissed her. She pushed me away as I expected.

"You'll never change," she said.

"You're probably right." I turned the knob. "But I got you to move out of my way."

"Don't go." Stella clutched my forearm.

"Tonight may not be about us, but we'll always be a duo whether we're apart or together." I left as tears spilled out of my eyes, and I despised each one of them. If I had to die, I didn't want to die feeling defeated. I wanted to make every last moment count.

After You've Gone

Trust in me and fol-low a-long, when ev-er you hear m

After I had stolen the guitar, my father sent me to Dr. Frank to uncover what mental condition I had. I sat in the office and listened as both my parents recounted every private detail of my life.

"Why are you so angry?" Dr. Frank asked.

I glanced at my father.

"Go ahead and tell him. That's why we're here."

I faced Dr. Frank. "I wanna play guitar, and my father thinks it's a waste of time."

"I told him if he takes his studies seriously, I'd get him a guitar," my father said. "He obviously didn't have the patience to wait. I don't know what else to do. I'm hoping you can help him see he's hurting his own future with his reckless behavior."

I started to believe something might be wrong with me. My father knew how to make me look bad, even to myself.

"What are your thoughts about everything that's been said here today?" Dr. Frank asked me.

"I got no thoughts."

"Surely, you must have some."

I glanced at my mother. "This is a waste of time."

"See what I mean, Doctor Frank?" my father said. "He's got a bad attitude."

"I got it from you."

"You son of a…" My father cut himself off, but it was too late. The way Dr. Frank probed him made it seem as though he saw through my father's facade of being a caring and supportive parent.

"Let's all stop and take a breath for a minute, okay?" Dr. Frank gave me one of those pillows with a handle and pointed to an empty wall. "We don't need to restrain our emotions here. Feel free to hit the wall as hard as you want."

"Why?"

"If you release your anger, it won't have any power over you."

I glared at my father and then at Dr. Frank.

"Try it," my mother said.

"This is retarded." I tossed the pillow on the floor. "I'm out of here." I walked out of the office with my father trailing behind me.

"You get back in there, right now!"

"Hitting a wall is not gonna fix anything."

"You can't know that unless you try."

"I already did. I punched a lot of holes in my bedroom wall. All that did was make my knuckles bleed."

"A guitar won't fix what's wrong either. Dr. Frank said you have to get to the root of what's bothering you, and he can help you find it."

"I'm leaving."

"Find another place to live then. I'm not paying for your freeloading ass to sit in the house anymore."

I had too much to lose by running away, mainly the M.I.J. I was working for and Ezza whom I didn't want to lose either, so I returned to the session. The cushion proved to be useful. I dug my nails into it each time my father said something that got me angry.

Dr. Frank diagnosed me as having ADD and manic depression. He wrote me out a prescription for antidepressants, but all they managed to do was make me sleepy. On most days, I'd go to sleep after school and not wake until the next morning. I wanted to stay in bed forever. One day drained into the next, and I longed for something to shake things up so that I could feel alive again. I started snorting coke around this time. It gave me more energy, but I still didn't want to wake up most mornings.

A month after my session, I had stopped taking my medication. Fooling my mother was easy. I'd slip the pill under my tongue and spit it out in the bathroom. I'd then go to my room, snort a few lines and top it off with a joint. This became an after school ritual until the day I found my father on the recliner, reading the paper. He was supposed to be at work by now for his twelve-hour shift, which ran until 3:00 a.m. I wished he worked the same shift on Saturdays. Having him around made it harder to sneak out back for a smoke, and my nicotine fits made me very irritable. It took a great deal of effort to keep from mouthing off to him whenever he reprimanded me in front of the waitstaff.

I slinked upstairs to my room to hide a residual high left over from a joint I smoked behind the bleachers at school. My mother came up later, knocked on the door and entered. She took a few sniffs around the room and then sat next to me.

"I smell smoke."

"I didn't smoke."

"What's that smell then?"

"Your imagination. I told you I'd never smoke in here again."

"What do you mean? You smoke somewhere else?"

"No. What's with you today?"

"I care about you." She pinched my cheek. "And to prove to you how much I do, there's a tray of baklava that just came out of the oven."

"A guitar would be an even better way." I gave her a toothy smile.

"You have a one-track mind." She got up. "Come on down in about ten minutes. I'll have a plate ready for you with a dollop of vanilla ice cream."

"Make it two scoops."

"You got it. Just stay out of your father's way. He's in a bad mood."

"When isn't he?"

My mother opened her mouth to respond and then shook her head and left. She probably didn't have anything to say to counter my remark. My father was always angry about something.

The smell of my mother's fresh baked baklava soon entered my nostrils. I waited for my high to ease up and went downstairs to satisfy my munchies. I crept past my father, who still had his head behind a newspaper, and entered the kitchen where my favorite dessert was waiting to be eaten. In the middle of my third piece, Leda barreled into the kitchen crying. My father and mother rushed in behind her.

"You have no right to tell me what to do anymore!" Leda yelled.

"You're not to see that old man again," my father said. His face was as red as a Roma tomato.

"I love him."

"Grow up. Love is for the movies. I promised you to Mihali's oldest son who has a chain of pharmacies in Thessaloniki. You'll be set for life."

"I'm not marrying someone I never met."

My father rubbed his forehead. Anyone who wasn't Greek wasn't good enough for his daughter. Had Teddy's skin been a few shades darker, I believe my father would've shipped Leda off to a convent in Greece to become a nun.

Leda hugged our mother and cried. "I don't want to get married."

My mother didn't say anything, letting my father take the lead, as usual.

"I should decide who I'm gonna marry," Leda said.

"We have traditions that we follow in this family."

"They're your traditions. Not mine."

My father thrust his finger at Leda's face. "You are not to see that man ever again! He has no respect for our values and customs!"

"You have no right to say that. You never even talked to him."

"He never came inside to introduce himself, and he sneaks around and drops you off a block away, thinking I won't notice."

"Because you came outside yelling at him and wouldn't let him explain."

"There's nothing to explain. I saw it all. He had his hands all over you in front of our home. He has no respect for you."

"I love him. I'm gonna see him again, and you can't stop me."

My father slapped Leda across the face.

"That won't stop me either!"

He struck her again.

Leda cried and ran out.

"If you see him again, you're no longer my daughter!"

Leda was throwing clothes into her suitcase when I entered her room. Still feeling a little wired, I sat on her bed and fell onto my back. "That was fast."

"When you love someone, you can tell right away."

"He's gonna blame me."

"No, he won't."

"I technically introduced you guys." I laughed.

"Why do you find that funny?"

"If you two get married and have kids, they'll have a cool story to tell their friends. 'Daddy and Mommy met each other when Uncle Markos got arrested.'"

Leda walked over and stared down at me. "You're high again." She threw a shirt over my face.

"It's only pot." I threw the shirt back at her.

"It can lead to other things, Markos." She sat next to me. "I'm not gonna be around to watch after you."

"I got Mom."

"She's a robot who follows Dad's orders. She just spent the past hour trying to talk me into giving what's-his-name's son a chance. 'Maybe you'll fall in love with him,' she told me. That's why I'll never get married. I don't want to end up like her, a slave to a man who doesn't appreciate me. I want to do my own thing. Live my own life."

"Where will you go?"

"Teddy's"

"Doesn't sound like that's living your own life."

"Only until I find a place of my own."

"Dad's gonna flip out."

"Think we passed that stage today."

"I can hear the main topic of discussion at coffee hour: Leda, the *boutana,* is living in sin with her non-Greek, old pervert boyfriend."

"I hope I embarrass Dad so much that he can't show his face at church again. It'll be my payback for all the years of hell he put me through."

"Why do you think it matters to him—what people at the diner and church think of us?"

"It's how he was raised. Mom too. They want to make our life appear perfect to everyone so we can be envied and admired."

"With you gone, Dad's gonna be even more on my case."

"That's why you have to stop getting high and find some direction in your life."

"I don't have a talent like you."

"You're not trying hard enough. Stop hanging out at the arcade so much and maybe you'll figure things out."

"I did. But dad won't get me a guitar."

"Then earn enough money to buy one yourself."

Leda left that night. With her gone, I had no ally to stick up for me. My mother would always remain on my father's side, and all I could do was prepare myself for the coming war.

This Old Room

sing my song.   Hear my call, you'll ne - ver go wrong,   as   long as you hear my   song.   I

The door flung open, and the smell of my mother's home cooking zoomed into my nostrils. "When's dinner?" I asked.

My mother inspected me from top to bottom. "Wash up first. You're a mess."

I went up to the bathroom and had a good scare when I caught a glimpse of myself in the mirror. After splashing some water on my face, I splattered some more on my hair and slicked it back.

"There's a pack of razors in the medicine cabinet," my mother yelled from downstairs.

I checked the time on my cellphone display. It was 3:30 p.m.

"Shave before you come downstairs," she said.

I opened the medicine cabinet. *Might as well look good for my last supper.* After I made myself presentable, I took a peek at my old room. It was a shrine of my former self. An old faded poster of Jimmy Page still hung on the wall, and a small picture of Robert Johnson posing with his guitar rested on my nightstand. All the holes in the wall that I punched were carelessly spackled over and painted.

My mother entered and knocked on the opened door. "Your food is gonna get cold."

"Why didn't you change this into a guest room?"

"I'm not ready to let go of the memories."

"This would make a perfect sewing room."

"I like things as they are. The familiarity is comforting."

"Not for me. Every time I enter this room, I feel like I'm suffocating. It's as if time stands still in here." I picked up a model B52 plane that sat on the dresser. I built it with my father when I was around ten. "Why did he stop doing things like this with me?"

"You became more independent. It scared him."

"Why?" I repositioned the plane on the dresser.

"You're a lot like him, and he wanted better things for you."

"I did all right, didn't I?" I turned around, and my mother was standing in front of me.

"Yes, you did." She leaned up and kissed my cheek. "Now come downstairs and eat."

"In a few minutes."

"Don't lock yourself in the past, Markos. You survived, and that's reason to celebrate."

"With a piece of your spanakopita."

"You never have only one." She smiled and left the room.

Food tempered all the storms in the Adamidis household. Most of our problems were discussed over dinner and resolved over coffee. The ones that weren't were carried over into the next meal. My father was less agitated with a full plate of food in front of him, which is why I usually waited until dinner was served before I asked him for something.

My mother placed a plate of spanakopita in front of me. I wasted no time getting it all down. I wanted to be filled with my mother's cooking before the end came.

"I was going to make a tray of pastitso, but then I remembered you don't eat lamb."

"You never said that to me before."

"Said what?"

"That you made a vegetarian meal just for me."

"You changed. Why can't I?" She pulled out a chair and sat. I raised a brow and had another bite.

"How is it?" she asked in her sweetest-sounding voice.

"Delicious." I served myself a second piece of spanakopita.

"Too much feta cheese?"

"There can *never* be too much feta cheese."

"If you treated your wife better, you wouldn't always be so hungry."

I put down my fork. "I did most of the cooking when we were together."

"Why are you here?"

"To visit my mother."

She crossed her arms and leaned back into the chair. "You looked more beat up than the walls in your bedroom. What's going on?"

"Nothing. Why does everything have to be a Homer-style epic with this family?"

"I know you well, Markos. You never leave the house looking like you just crawled out of a puddle of mud."

"Got a lot on my mind." I rubbed my head.

"Why did you come here?"

"I need you to keep an eye on Stella and Jessie."

"Where are you going?"

"Away for a while."

"To where?"

"Paris. Got a teaching gig there."

My mother got up, walked over to the phone and picked it up.

"Who are you calling?"

"Stella. Maybe she'll tell me why you're acting strange."

"Jessie's been kidnapped."

My mother dropped the phone. "*Ah, Xristouli mou.*" She made the sign of the cross. "When were you going to tell me?"

I picked up the phone and hung it up. "Please don't go hysterical on me, Mom. I'm having a hard enough time dealing with this."

"Answer me!" She cried.

"I wasn't going to tell you."

"Why not?"

"I wanted to avoid a scene like this."

"How the hell can you come here, acting like this is another ordinary day when you don't know who has your daughter? He could be a pervert who stalks little girls. Ah, *Xristouli mou.*" She made the sign of the cross again. "What if that's why he took her?"

I clutched my mother's arms. "It's not like that. The kidnapper contacted me this morning. He's gonna release her after I pay the ransom."

"Did he let you speak to her?"

"I saw her. She looked okay."

"You saw her? Where?"

"In front of a subway station on Broadway. She thinks all of this is a game."

"I don't understand any of this. Why would anyone take Jessie? You're not rich."

"This isn't about money. Whoever took her wants to hurt me." I heard Jessie singing in my head and rubbed my forehead with both my hands, covering the entirety of my face in an attempt to hide my delirium. "And I'm hurting bad." I peered at my mother. "I need you with me, Mom. If you fall apart, I won't be far behind you, and Jess needs me to stay strong until I find her."

"I'm with you, Markos. You know that."

"Thanks."

She held my hands. "Stay strong and know God will help you and Jessie. He doesn't abandon the faithful."

"If I sit around and wait for God to fix this, Jessie will be killed. Faith and God are for people who can't deal with reality."

"Watch your mouth!" She pulled her hands away. "We don't speak of God like that here."

I tried to stop myself, but the words came out anyway. "I don't believe in God. And if I did, I'd accuse him of sentencing me to hell and doing the same to Jessie by allowing her to be taken by a psychopath. How does your faith resolve that?"

My mother cried, made the sign of the cross, and ran out of the room.

I hung up my cellphone after checking in with Teddy. He was fuming because I was a little late in calling. I had good reason; my mother locked herself in her room, probably praying for my soul in front of her perpetually burning tealight candle that sat under an antique icon of Jesus.

I knocked on her door. "I'm sorry. I'm finding it hard to censor myself today."

"How long have you been an atheist?" she asked.

"Not now, Mom…please. We don't have time for a religious debate. I was upset, and I couldn't shut myself up."

"You've been like that ever since I can remember." My mother opened the door. "But I never doubted the kindness of your heart." Her eyes were swollen from all the crying. "What's really going on here, Markos?"

"Soon as I pay the ransom, the kidnapper will let Jessie go. Then everything will be right with the universe again."

My mother showed me her checkbook. "I wanna help. How much money is the kidnapper asking for?"

"I have enough."

"How much?"

"All I'm worth."

"I could always tell when you're holding something back."

"I'm not holding anything back."

My mother leered at me, slammed the door and locked it.

"Why do you do that?" I yelled. "Why do you turn everything off around you when you're mad? You've been doing that ever since I can remember. You'd either lock yourself in your room to sew, or run to Mrs. Barras's house to avoid what was going on here."

My mother cried louder.

"You wouldn't be a martyr anymore if you said what's on your mind."

"You've grown up to be a cruel man. That's what's on my mind!"

"I thought you never doubted the kindness of my heart?"

"That was before it stopped beating."

"It stopped in this house on the day I stole the guitar… when you watched Dad hit me and did nothing!"

My mother opened the door. "Your father had a point. You took things to the extreme to get what you wanted."

"Stella and Teddy would agree. They're treating me like I'm still a patient at Gray Pines. And I think they believe I took Jessie."

"You scared us all. It's hard to forget what you did."

I slapped the palm of my hand against the wall. "I had nothing to do with what happened to Jessie!"

My mother held my arms firmly. "You don't have to fight me, Markos. I believe you."

"Then why are you all treating me as if you're ready to convict me?"

"I see such pain in your eyes, the same pain you had when you were a boy, only I didn't realize then how deeply you felt it."

I shook my head. "Jess is kidnapped, and you and Teddy seem to be more concerned over my mental health."

"We don't want to lose you either."

"You should've shown your concern when I needed it, but back then you only saw what you wanted to see, and we all suffered because you married a devil who pretended to be a saint. And when you finally recognized it for yourself, you still stayed with him."

"What's with the biblical reference? I thought you were an atheist."

"I am." I turned to leave.

"Where are you going?"

"As far away from here as possible!"

"Why are you angry with me?"

I turned to face my mother. "All you cared about was yourself. You should've been watching out for us, but it was easier to let him destroy everything while you ran around town like a whore."

My mother slapped me.

"Strike at the problem and pray it'll go away?" I laughed. "Why not? It's always been the Adamidis way."

"You only know his side. It's my turn to explain."

"I don't care about your side." I walked downstairs and headed to the front door.

My mother followed me. "Wait. You're right."

I stopped when I heard her crying.

"I felt trapped," she said. "There were so many times I wanted to pack up and leave with you and Leda, but I was afraid. How would I support you? I had no job skills. I dropped out of college, and the only place I worked at was Jake's to help out your father whenever one of the waitresses called in sick. I know that's no excuse. I was a terrible mother. I failed you both."

I would've agreed with her before tonight, but we were now on the same team rooting for Jessie. That put things in a whole new perspective for me. I hugged my mother. "Forgive me. I didn't want to lay this all on you tonight, but as usual I can't keep my mouth shut. Sometimes I think it has a mind of its own." I took a step back. "I want you to stop blaming yourself for what Dad did."

My mother rubbed her eyes. "Not as long as the pain continues to exist in you. I know you're suffering from my bad choices, and I know you hate me because of them."

"I could never hate you, and I don't wanna leave you with all this baggage. Dad should be carrying the whole load, but he's being rewarded for what he did."

"Did you let go of yours?"

"I'm trying."

My mother stopped crying and peered into my eyes. "You need to...for Jessie and yourself. When she returns home, let her grow up living her own childhood, not yours." She put her hand on my cheek. "We're okay. Take that with you tonight and always, and bring Jessie home safely."

The traffic started to lighten up, and I turned on my radio in time to hear Wes Montgomery's solo over "'Round Midnight." The appropriate music that fit my mood always seemed to come on at the right moment. In the middle of his solo, the kidnapper called.

"Tick-tock, tick-tock. My watch tells me it's 6:00. I left a going-away present at your place. I hope you like it."

"As long as I've got breath in me, I'll search every sewer in this city until I find the one you're hiding in."

"Why did you try to kill yourself?"

"If you wanna hear my life story, it's gonna cost you."

"How much?"

"Put Jessie on the phone."

"I can't do that. I play by the rules once I set them."

"Rules can be broken."

"Not mine."

"Why?"

"Without rules, there's no organization; with no organization, there's no compliance. The world would be lost in chaos."

"Doesn't sound so bad. I never liked structure."

"Maybe you should reconsider your position. You're about to die."

"I won't know the difference, so why worry?"

"If you're correct, and there's no god, your awareness will end as well."

"I came to terms with dying a long time ago."

"So you looked death in the eye and think you conquered it?" The kidnapper laughed. "Your shortsightedness explains why I'm winning."

"I'm not sure," I said.

"Not sure about what?"

"Why I jumped."

"This is a waste of time. If you can't be honest with me, I don't think I want to continue this game with you."

"I don't feel a damn thing." I was on Broadway, and the sidewalks were filled with pedestrians, but I never felt more isolated. Although I'd driven here many times before, it seemed my car warped into another dimension, and that I was the only human in existence driving along some road on an alien world.

"Maybe you wanted to die to feel something," the kidnapper said.

"You might be right. My heart rate sped up on my way down. Why do you do what you do?"

"I've been angry at you for many years. I've tried to let it go, but then I kept thinking you had no right to get away with what you did to me."

"I never did anything to you, Gus."

"Is that your answer?"

I wanted to say yes, but I still couldn't commit to a response.

"I'll leave you to ponder for a while, but don't take too long. The last verse will be played soon."

Repeat Performance

home   when the moon is   high. _____   I can-not stay be - cause my mom

A box with red wrapping paper and a pink ribbon sat on the dining table. I untied the ribbon and delicately tore off the paper. I did this because Jessie liked to use the paper for her art projects. Along with music, she picked up the Adamidis gene for art.

I examined the box and wondered if I should call a bomb squad in before opening it. You'd be astounded over what frightening outcomes your mind can conjure up in situations like this.

I lifted the lid and removed a red lotus. As the scent entered my nostrils, I had a vision of Jessie singing to me.

The kidnapper stared down at me wearing the mime mask, and he spoke with the synthesized voice. "The truth can't be undone. We all eventually must pay."

I stroked the petals between my fingers, and the lotus burst into flames. Upon second glance the fire vanished, and the lotus was unharmed. To ease my nerves, I got out Ezza and played "Sometimes I'm Happy." I made it through three more songs before my cellphone rang in the middle of my first pass of "Well You Needn't."

"Did you like my gift?" the kidnapper asked.

"What does it mean?"

"That's for you to figure out."

"How is a flower supposed to help me figure out who you are?"

"If I say any more, you'll know. Where would be the challenge?"

"I need something more."

"I have a few more clues to give you, but I don't think they'll make much difference. You're proving to be an easy opponent."

"Arrogance leads to sloppiness." I put Ezza in her case.

"And lack of faith leads to defeat."

"I haven't given up yet."

"Why are you an atheist?"

"What makes you think I am?"

"I read about it in one of your interviews."

"A little girl getting taken by a psychopath contradicts everything I learned in Sunday school."

"I also struggled with the contradiction. How could God make a man like me? A man who inflicts pain and suffering on others and gets off on it. I'm an abomination."

"You know yourself well."

"Do you have faith in anything?"

"I'd rather swim to shore than wait to be rescued."

"What if you can't swim?"

"I'm a fast learner."

"We'll see about that soon. Do you know where the WXQX Network Building is?"

I twirled the lotus stem between my fingers.

"Oh, that's right. Of course you do," the kidnapper said. "That's where you tried to take your life a year ago, tomorrow."

"Was it tomorrow? I don't remember." I tossed the lotus on the table.

"I enjoyed your last program when you interviewed Chet Baker. I bet you can relate to him."

"So is that it? You want me to jump again?"

"It's about time you scored a point. To continue your trend be on the ledge at exactly 7:30 a.m., or your daughter will die."

I glimpsed at my watch. It was 6:30 p.m. "You owe me another clue."

"We'll talk again after I have everything set up for you." The kidnapper hung up.

I opened a drawer in my desk and removed a box. Inside was the same heart-shaped locket from my visions. I was going to give it to Stella on our anniversary. She left me one month before our eighth year together, and I never returned it. I planned on giving it to her after we reunited. I couldn't figure out if I was an optimist or pathetic. Perhaps that implied I was an amalgamation of both.

I picked up the locket, recalling how Stella admired it in the display case at Fortunoff's. She loved the rubies that outlined the heart. Stella's ideal proposal called for a ruby engagement ring camouflaged in a glass of Pinot Noir. I took the mention as a hint, so I brought her to our favorite restaurant in Little Italy. When she wasn't looking, I slipped a ruby engagement ring into her glass. She said, "Yes," after she screamed so loud that everyone in the restaurant applauded. I thought to myself, *what did you just get yourself into?* The apprehension was short-lived. When I slipped the band around Stella's finger, it looked as though it belonged there.

I returned the locket to the box and put it in my pocket. My ringtone alarm played, and I skipped this dose. I wanted to face whatever was coming sober and sure of myself. And if I had to die, I wanted to go out doing what I did best. I called

Snaps, grabbed Ezza, and left for what I thought was going to be my final gig.

Singing Cats

dad will cry. ___ chil - dren have par - ents to go home to. ___ Out in

I tapped my pencil on the desk to the rhythm of "Another One Bites the Dust." It had looped in my brain until Ezza slapped her hand on the table.

"Have you even been paying attention?"

"I was."

"Then what did I just say?"

Before I even had a chance to answer, she smacked her hand on the table again. "I thought you wanted to get better in math."

"I do."

"Then why are you spacing out?" She went to pick up a glass pipe that was leaning against the ashtray and then quickly retracted her hand. "Nothing I hate more than time wasted."

I tossed my pencil on the table and got up.

"What's wrong with you today?" Ezza asked.

"My sister's gone, and my father's on me all the time. He's making me go to a shrink."

"Did he give you a diagnosis?"

"ADD and manic depression."

"And I thought I was a wreck."

"I'm worse now than before I went to him. He gave me these pills, and all they do is make me wanna sleep, so I stopped taking them."

"Give them to me. I haven't slept in weeks."

I sat back down. "If I could, I would."

"Your father isn't the easiest guy to get along with at the diner. Can't imagine what he's like at home."

The phone rang, and Ezza picked it up. "I have to take this in the other room. Get started with the next problem." She went into her bedroom and shut the door behind her.

Curiosity made me pick up Ezza's pipe and take a hit. It was like magic. The smoke flowed into my mouth and slithered down my throat in a warm, caressing stream. After a few more hits, I repositioned the pipe against the ashtray. Seconds later, the secrets of the universe revealed themselves to me, and I went to work on my next math problem. I couldn't sense the pencil between my fingers, or the motion of my hand as I wrote down the numbers. It was as though I was no longer linked to my body. The experience seemed weird and breathtaking all at once. I stopped writing and fixed my eyes on the eraser tip as a whirlwind of thoughts surged into my mind from every conceivable direction. They came in random order, but they somehow made sense to me.

Ezza sat down. "Where were we again?"

"In your apartment." I laughed, still staring at the eraser.

Ezza gawked at me and picked up her pipe. "You didn't take a hit, did you?"

"Just one." I raised my pointer finger in the air. "Or two." I lifted another finger.

Ezza slapped her hand down on the table. "Why the hell did you do that? You're only thirteen!"

"Fourteen, and if you didn't want me to take a hit, you shouldn't have left your pipe here."

The reason Ezza was so upset was that what was packed inside the bowl was more than a little sprinkle of pot. My sweet Ezza was a heroin addict.

She grabbed her forehead with both her hands. "Get out."

"I'm sorry. I didn't mean to…"

"I said get out!"

I slapped my notebook shut.

"Let me ask you a question," Ezza said. "What do you want to do with your life?"

"I don't know."

"Don't do this again. Ever"

"Why not? You do it."

"When I was your age I still played with Barbies."

"You played with dolls at fourteen?" I laughed. "That's so funny."

"Shut up!" She bashed her fist down on the table.

"All right. Just stop doing that."

"The point is I grew up functional…for the most part. I wasn't a kid pretending to be an adult."

"You seem okay to me now."

"I'm a mess, not a role-model."

"A beautiful mess."

Ezza picked up her pipe. "I can't think here." She grabbed my hand and pulled me off the chair. "Let's move this conversation upstairs."

Ezza and I lay on a blanket on the roof. The full moon, and a sky full of stars shone down on us.

"I come up here whenever things get too confining," Ezza said.

"Do things get better?" I asked.

"Than what?"

"When you get out of school and have your freedom, does it get easier?"

"Sorry to be the one to tell you this; it gets harder."

I peered at Ezza's milky skin under the moonlight. She turned to me and smiled, but her eyes betrayed her sadness.

"Why do you keep getting college degrees?" I asked.

"I still don't know what I want to be when I grow up."

"Then why should I rush?"

Ezza sat up and took a hit from her pipe. "Now that you know, there's no use hiding it. Just keep this to yourself. I need my job."

"Your secret is safe." I craved another hit, but I didn't want to risk her throwing me out.

"To answer your question, I don't like uncertainty. It's unsettling. It's like I'm adrift in the middle of the ocean on a small raft. No matter what direction my internal compass points to, I can't find land." She took another hit. "I want to know what it's like to drop anchor somewhere…anywhere."

"Sounds boring. I wanna visit every country before I die and never live anywhere longer than six months."

"How are you going to pay for all those plane tickets?"

I gazed up at the stars until I couldn't tell myself apart from them. It was as if I became the sky, looking down on myself. "Haven't thought that far ahead yet." I turned to face Ezza. "Why didn't you ever get married and have kids like most other women your age do?"

"I had a relationship with my philosophy professor. We had a similar worldview. It really connected us." Ezza lay on her back. "On our first date, we went to the planetarium and fantasized that enlightened aliens came down to Earth and invited us to their home world. We both left the planetarium depressed. The chance of meeting an enlightened alien was next to zero, and neither of us wanted to live on Earth."

"Did you change your mind since then?"

"I want to leave now more than ever. Most people don't care about what happens beyond their own self-dictated reality. When I first got that, I realized I was powerless. I can't do anything to turn things around. The inertia of destruction is too powerful to counter. I want to scream at all the leaders of the world and the people who give them the power to destroy, 'Wake up! You're killing yourselves and taking the rest of us with you!' But hardly anyone cares. The whole world will continue to smell like crap as long as people can buy their cheap stuff from cheap stores that get their merchandise from cheap labor. We've all become nothing more than commodities to be exploited." She turned to me. "Stay young for as long as you can. Only in ignorance can you find happiness."

"I'm happy being here with you."

Ezza returned her attention to the heavens. "Conventional wisdom says you suffer if you're born in the wrong part of the world. But it's worse if you're born on the wrong planet. You're stuck here unless someone invents a propulsion system that can take you somewhere else. There are no more Plymouth Rocks to sail away to. We now all live in a prison."

"That's what it feels like at home to me." I gazed at the stars, which now seemed to be moving towards me. And then an answer to a question I never even asked came to me as clear as the windows in our house after my mother cleaned them. "Art, music, and poetry."

Ezza looked at me. "What about them?"

"I always wanted to get a guitar, but I never knew why until just now. I hear music in my head all the time. It's like I'm a radio receiver, and the music is being transmitted to me."

"What's stopping you?"

"I don't have a guitar."

"I can see how that might hold you back."

A few cats fought down below. Their screeches echoed all around and sounded beautiful to my ears. My inspiration was more than likely brought on by the heroin, but one of my first pieces came from that night. I called the song, "Moonlight Cat Serenade." It was on my first album.

"We were soul mates, and we planned on getting married," Ezza said.

"Who?" The singing cats made me forget our discussion.

"Me and my boyfriend, the philosophy professor."

"What happened?"

"He killed himself."

"Woh!" I sat up, overwhelmed by everything. Singing cats, guitars, dead fiancés, and space flight all vied for their time in my brain.

"There's no escape for those of us who want to leave." Ezza wiped her eyes.

I wanted to kiss her, but my body wouldn't respond to my brain's request. I lay beside Ezza and put my hand on her arm to comfort her. I wish I understood the full extent of what she told me, but I was a kid in love. When she hugged me, I thought the night couldn't have been more perfect. Reflecting over the memory, I only feel sadness. Sadness that I couldn't recognize Ezza's pain.

Last Gig

dad will   cry.   chil - dren have par-ents to go home to.   Out   in

Snaps got us a late-night gig over at the Music Box. The club was virtually unknown, and most people who played there were just starting out in the scene. During the week, the place was half-empty, and I wondered how the owner turned a profit. Snaps asked why I needed to play tonight, and when I told him my reasons were personal, he left me alone as any respectable bandmate would do. I asked him to bring along his recording gear to capture my performance that I hoped would define my music career. Tonight, I'd play without calling on Wes and Robert J. Tonight, I'd play like Markos Adams.

During my walk to the club, I mused over being channeled by the successor of my radio show.

"Markos Adams is on the line from the other side. Welcome back to your show, Markos."

"It's your show, now."

"Very true, but you started it all," my successor said. "Why did you do it? Why did you jump again?"

"To save my daughter's life."

"Yeah. Heard all about that. Your ex has been on every talk show telling everyone how you insisted on playing the superhero, but you weren't very good at it because you couldn't save yourself."

"She may be smarter than me, but I'm the better musician."

"That you are, which is why you're here."

"It doesn't make me feel any better."

"What would?"

"Seeing my daughter again."

I shut off my thoughts and roamed around the Village, capturing the ambience until a calmness filtered into me. *Had I just stepped into the acceptance stage of grief?*

I caught up with Cro at a cafe. He sat alone at a corner table, sketching. Floating out of the overhead speakers in a mellow, rhythmic stream was John Coltraine soloing over "Stardust."

"Looking smooth and calm tonight, bro," Cro said as I pulled out a chair to sit. "You must've taken my advice." He continued to sketch.

"You are the sketcher of truth."

"Was there ever any doubt?"

"I'll never doubt you again. Any news about your brother?"

"Still waiting. Did I ever tell you he almost beat me in an art contest?"

"You never even told me he was an artist."

"The day before the admission deadline, he decided to enter the contest with me. Took him only two hours to finish his painting."

"I've seen you work that fast."

"Not back then. If my brother put in a little more effort, he would've beaten me. Drugs destroyed him, destroyed his talent and destroyed his passion. He never got what it meant to sketch the truth." Cro showed me the drawing. "This is from the day before he OD'ed. He just finished telling me how art didn't matter to him anymore. All he saw was the ugliness in the world, and he didn't want to paint ugliness." Cro returned to his sketching. "He joined the Air Force after he got out of the hospital, and I left home shortly after he did. I tried to make a name for myself as an artist, and you know the rest."

"Do you believe in life after death, the kind where you live for an eternity with your family and friends?"

Cro stopped sketching and put his pad on the table. "I do."

"Wish I did."

"All you need is faith, and the rest falls into place on its own."

"Whenever I hear people talk about faith, it seems as though they expect things to happen because they pray for it. In all the years I spent going to church with my parents, I've never seen anything miraculous. Just a lot of promises that were never paid out."

"The faithful don't expect payment."

"Another reason why I'm not religious. I'd go broke if I played for free." I glanced at my watch. "Which reminds me, I have to be at the Music Box."

"The Music Box? Why the hell are you going there?"

"I'm in the mood to play some truth."

"Say no more, bro. I'll be there to hear it."

I sat at the bar and rolled a shot glass between my hands. I limited myself to six shots of Jack Daniels, which the bartender lined up in front of me. By the time I emptied my last one, I'd have a light buzz to ease my nerves and still be focused enough to play.

"Didn't get enough last night?" Snaps held out his shot glass, and we toasted.

"Something like that." I gazed at Snaps and marveled over how far we'd come. "Thanks."

"For what?"

"For everything."

We both drank our shots.

"Did you get a hold of Donnie?" I asked.

"Nicole was all riled up as usual, but he'll be here."

I stretched my left wrist as far back as it could bend and then did the same with all my fingers.

"You played right in the pocket last night," Snaps said. "It's like you never took a day off."

"Had my Archtop with me while I was in the hospital. I played for the patients in the dayroom."

"How many nurses' phone numbers did you get?"

"Three."

"Only?"

"I wanted to take baby steps. It's been a while."

"From what I heard, you took *giant steps*. And you burned on that tune as well. Coltraine was probably cheering you on from up above."

"When it comes to music, I recover fast." I stretched my thumb back to touch my wrist.

"Good to know. We pulled in a big crowd last night. Harry asked if we wanted to add in an extra day. What do you think?"

"Sounds tempting, but I need some time to think about it."

"You got it, but don't take too long…" Snaps snapped his fingers. "Oh yeah. Almost forgot to tell you. That baldheaded guy came back and asked about you after you left."

I shifted my arm to the side and knocked over a shot glass. "What did he tell you?"

Snaps creased his forehead. "If I knew he was that important to you, I would've called him to come and hear us play." He reached into his wallet and removed a slip of paper. "Got his number right here if you want—"

I snatched the paper, got out my cellphone and called the number.

The bartender wiped the counter and left me with a replacement shot while I left a message on Gus's answering machine. After I hung up, I guzzled down two shots.

During the whole time, Snaps had been staring at me while cupping his chin between his thumb and pointer finger. "Can I be honest with you?"

"Keep me in suspense." I drank a shot. "It's easier to handle."

"Sorry, can't do that. You're acting freakier than the summer you spent going to the Limelight looking like the Crow. What's up?"

"I was in love." I slugged another shot. "I always act freaky when I'm in love."

"That's true." Snaps laughed. "Man, was I glad when you moved past your girls-who-look-like-Elvira phase. I thought you were gonna give up jazz to play guitar for Marilyn Manson."

Donnie slapped my back and sat next to me. "Would've fit him perfectly. Leda told me all the girls back then said he looked like Robert Smith."

"No they didn't," Snaps said. "They said he looked like Henry Rollins."

Donnie raised his brows and grabbed a few peanuts from a bowl.

The bartender handed Snaps and Donnie their shots. I raised mine and smiled. "To the best musicians I've ever played with."

We clanked our glasses together, drank our shots and slammed the glasses on the bar.

I went on stage and played the gig as a last gig should be played. I poured all my emotions into my solos and engaged in more pointless banter with Donnie, Snaps, and Cro, who showed up in the middle of our second set. For two hours, I forgot about everything, including myself. The reality of what lay ahead returned after I left the Music Box and headed to Jake's, where Gus told me he'd meet me.

Beginning to See the Light

Close your eyes, _____ and dream a dream. _____ A hap-py lit-

Gus and I sat in a corner booth at Jake's. The fluorescent lights made the floaters in my eyes more prominent than usual, and I put on my shades to calm them down. "Interesting you'd pick this place."

"It was an instinctive choice for me. This used to be the most popular late-night hangout on the eastern side of the Williamsburg Bridge until Jake retired to Limnos and left it to Jake Jr." Gus seemed disturbed as he examined the taped-over repairs on the seat cushions and stained ceiling panels. "He ran this place to the ground. Wonder what his father thinks of him."

"Unlike our fathers, Jake Sr. was cool."

Gus smiled, but it looked forced. "Yeah, I remember. All the kids loved hanging over at his place because he let them smoke. If he did that in this day and age, he would've gotten sued." Gus laughed. "Those were some great—"

"Why did you show up at my gig?"

"I wanted to see what you've been up to after all these years."

"I was surprised you called me back tonight."

"At this time of night, the roaches rule my apartment. I'd rather be out enjoying a fresh cup of coffee." Gus raised his cup and took a sip.

"When I lived on this side of the bridge, I always ended a gig night with a cup of Jake's best." I sipped some coffee.

"Haven't set foot in here since I ran away. It reminds me of my family. I try not to think about them."

"Then why did you pick this place?"

"I know how much you like it here."

Dottie came by and topped off our coffee.

"Since when do you work the graveyard shift, Dot?" I asked.

"Two waitresses called in sick, and Jake Jr. needed yours truly to come to the rescue." She shook her head. "I should ask him to set up a cot in the storage room. Sometimes I feel like I live here." She glanced at Gus. "Who's your friend?"

"You don't remember me?" Gus asked.

"Should I?" She examined him.

"Gus Barras," he said.

"Mildred's son?" Dottie asked.

"That's me."

"Heard you were in L.A."

"I was."

"Welcome back to the East Coast." The kitchen bell rang. "That's probably your food. Be back in a jiffy." Dottie scurried away.

Gus emptied a creamer into his coffee. "Can't believe Dottie is still here. She was old back in the day, and she looks almost the same."

"Dot's the best," I said agreeing with him. It was as though Dot was perpetually stuck in the early nineties.

"How long did you work here again?"

"One too many Saturdays."

Gus poured some sugar into his cup. "What was the name of the other girl? The one who used to tutor you?"

"Ezza."

"That's right. How could I have forgotten? She inspired the name of your guitar."

"Why did you come to my gig last night?"

"I already answered that—"

"The real reason."

"I like hearing you play. Mr. Pagels was right. He knew you had it in you to be a world-class musician." Gus laughed. "Remember how he used to introduce himself? 'It's like bagels except with a P.' He was such a funny guy."

Dottie served us our fries and handed me an egg cream. I tapped a straw on the table and peeled off the wrapper.

"You deserved the scholarship," Gus said.

"Didn't end up using much of it." I placed the straw in the glass.

Gus picked up the ketchup bottle and grunted as he opened the lid. "I heard." He violently thrust the bottle, releasing a surge of ketchup over his fries. He capped the bottle and wiped it. "I could never satisfy Pagels, no matter how many fancy chops I played him." He picked up a fry and swirled it around in the ketchup. "What do you think makes you so different?"

"I put my cross down a long time ago."

"Was that before or after you tried to kill yourself?"

I swept everything off the table and stood. "What do you want from me?" I yelled.

Everyone in the diner stared at me.

"What are you all looking at? Get back to your own business, and leave mine alone!"

Dottie rushed over. "What's going on here, Markos?"

Gus brushed some french fries off his pants. "It wasn't my intention to offend you, Markos. After I read about your suicide attempt, it hit me pretty hard. I always thought you were the one who had it all together, and that I was the one who was all screwed—"

"Shut your fuckin' mouth before I shut it for you!" I turned to face Dottie. "Tell Jake Jr. I'll pay for the damage." I reached into my wallet and pulled out a twenty. "For you and the busboy's trouble." I faced Gus. "Come with me."

"I'm not going anywhere with you."

I pulled out Teddy's gun and aimed it at him. "I wasn't asking."

Dottie's eyes widened. "Markos, what are you—"

"Stay out of this Dot. This is between me, and the man who kidnapped my daughter." I pulled back the hammer of the gun. "Get up...*now*."

Gus did as I said, and I shoved the barrel against his back. "Move."

I picked up my guitar case and followed him to the door. Some customers clung to each other as we passed them, waking me up to the reality that I'd become what my father predicted...a criminal.

I walked fast to ease my temper and keep myself from shooting Gus.

"Where are we going?" he asked.

I quickened my pace. "It's a surprise."

My cellphone rang. Teddy's number came up on the I.D., and I answered.

"You're overdue for your call."

"Arrest me," I said loudly. "Any news?"

"I'm still looking. Did you see Gus again?"

"Haven't seen him."

"Good. Be sure to call me if he shows—"

I hung up, and I picked up my pace when I heard police sirens.

"Any news?" Gus asked.

"About what?"

"Your daughter."

"That's what you're going to tell me."

"I already told you I had nothing to do with it."

"You seem to think you were the only one back then who had it hard. I faced my share of demons as well."

"Heard all about it. Your father told my father you were possessed by the devil."

"My old man confused me for himself."

We turned the corner and saw what used to be Steve's duplex. All that remained was part of the frame.

I pushed Gus ahead of me. "Tell me what you see."

"A burned-down building."

"It belonged to Steve and his fiancée." I put my guitar case on the ground. "It was arson."

"Who would do such a terrible thing?" Gus asked.

"Someone who's mad at him for something he thinks he did wrong."

"Hope he got all his guitars out in time."

"If he made it out, I think his Les Pauls would've been the last things on his mind."

"He died?"

"Along with his fiancée." I aimed the gun at Gus. "Did you do this?"

"Is that what you think?" He shook his head. "I admit I was disappointed for not getting into the band, but I wouldn't set a man's home on fire over it."

"I saw your mother. I know the trouble you've been in."

"That explains your confusion. She always used you to gauge my progress. I could be as good as the great Markos

Adamidis if I wasn't such a klutz. She wanted a flashy son to show off to her friends. It didn't matter I was the best guitar player in the school."

"I don't have time for a recap of our competitive years. I know you've been keeping track of me, and I wanna know why."

"I showed up to one of your gigs. That hardly counts for stalking."

"Where's my daughter?"

"I never thought of you as the paranoid type."

"Where's my daughter!"

"It's late. I would imagine she's sleeping."

I grabbed Gus by his collar and pressed the barrel of the gun against the side of his head. "I know you have something to do with this."

"I swear I don't know anything about this!" He cried. "Please don't kill me."

"It's you. I know it's you."

"Why? I haven't seen you in years, I…"

"You're the only one it can be." I forced him to the ground.

"How about your father?" Gus got onto his knees. "He blames you for ruining his life. He said that to my Uncle Manny, who told my mother. I'll bet she didn't mention any of that to you."

I stared up at the charred remains of Steve's home that reflected my current state of mind that was about to get worse. My cellphone rang and *unidentified caller* flashed across the screen. I answered and slowly lifted the receiver to my ear.

"Still think I'm Gus?" The kidnapper laughed.

"Who are you?" I yelled.

"If you listened to me, you might've figured it out by now."

"Who are you!"

The kidnapper hung up, and I helped Gus to his feet. Something seemed amiss. All the clues still pointed to Gus: the newspaper articles, him following me around bringing up our competitive years. None of this made any sense.

"Looks like your cross just got heavier than mine," Gus said.

"You're right. I'm throwing mine down now."

I picked up my guitar case and left.

A Mentor to Watch Over Me

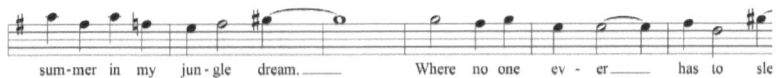

sum-mer in my jun-gle dream.____ Where no one ev - er____ has to sle

Ezza had managed to hold my attention better than any of my teachers at school. Dottie was right. I didn't need newspapers or television when I had the Ezza channel to turn to. It seemed no matter what question I asked, she had the answer, and she gave it to me straight. She viewed the world with her own unique ideological lens, which more than likely contributed to her sadness. Ezza's mood progressively darkened after a philosophy magazine turned down an article she recently submitted. During most of our tutoring session she brooded over her rejection letter, which she let me read.

"They told me they liked my angle of creating a society that would protect us from the dark side of human nature. That understanding our weaknesses and being proactive against them would guarantee us to progress further than we ever have."

"Our founding fathers already tried that, and it started to fail them after they signed on the dotted line."

"Which is why I proposed we should go back to a nomadic type of existence. Ever since we settled in the fertile crescent we started fighting with each other. The Earth doesn't belong to us, yet we carve it up as though we own it. If we back off and realize that ownership leads to greed, which leads to fighting, I think people would naturally gravitate to a nomadic lifestyle. What do you think?"

"Sounds good…in theory. But we can't move backwards." I handed Ezza back the letter. "The past already happened, and the future is ready for us to screw up. I say copy the Vulcans. They got it all figured out." I positioned my hand like Spock. "Live long, and don't be stupid."

"The asshole who wrote the letter said something similar."

"He's a Trekkie too?"

"Who the hell knows! He went on to say how we can't move backwards, but that wasn't what I meant." Ezza poured some powder into the bowl of her pipe. "Never expect anything in your life, Markos, and you'll be better off." She heated the bottom of the bowl over a lit candle.

"How come?"

"When something doesn't go your way, you feel like shit. You then end up doing anything to kill that feeling." Ezza took a hit from her pipe. "And what you sometimes do to kill the feeling ends up killing you."

I reached into my pocket and removed a pipe I recently bought.

"Don't even think of smoking in here."

I pointed to her pipe. "Why not? You are."

She banged her hand on the table. "I'm old enough to know what I'm doing."

"What are you doing?"

"Killing a feeling." She took another hit.

"Do you want me to go out and find a condemned building to light up in? That's dangerous for a kid my age."

Ezza squinted her eyes at me. "So is doing drugs, you wise ass."

"What's the word? The one that stands for a person who tells someone what not to do, even though they do the same thing themselves?" I took out a baggie, and Ezza seized it.

She dipped her finger in the bag and tasted the contents. "There's heroin mixed in here. Where did you get this?" She shook the bag.

"From my dealer." I snatched it back.

Ezza shook her head. "You're a smart kid, but you won't be for long if you keep that up."

"You're still smart." I sprinkled some powder into my pipe and got out my lighter.

"Only because I just started. My ex got me hooked on the junk by telling me I wouldn't worry about the future of humankind. When I'm high, I laugh about it...most of the time."

"I wouldn't waste one brain cell worrying about humankind. You were right. Most people don't give a shit about anything but the reality they invent for themselves and force their kids to live in with them." I took a hit from my pipe.

"That's why I took my first hit." Ezza leaned back against the chair. "I can't shut off my feelings, and they're sometimes too much for me to handle, even when I'm high."

She took off her glasses. Without them, she couldn't see anything close-up. Maybe that was her way of shutting everything out for a while.

We sat on the couch and listened to an Alice Cooper album. "Hard Hearted Alice" was on. The only reason I remember is because the song that followed led me to the blues.

"Do you honestly want to learn how to play the guitar?" Ezza asked.

"It's all I think about." I took a hit from my pipe.

"You're going to have a hard time learning if you're high all the time."

"I don't have a guitar, remember?"

"Who's your favorite guitarist?"

"It's a toss between Page and Hendrix."

"They're both amazing, but do you want to hear the master?"

"As far as I'm concerned, the two Js rule."

"In rock they do, but I'm talking about the J who was the master of the blues. My ex turned me on to him." She went to her vast record collection displayed across two long wall shelves. It was impressive as Ezza categorized them by genre, artist, and release date. She removed a Robert Johnson album, put on "Terraplane Blues," and I was hooked.

"You can borrow it if you like."

She handed me the cover, and we both lay on the carpet and listened to the whole album.

"Even if I get a guitar, I'll never be able to afford lessons."

"You should be able to pay for one lesson a month with your tips."

"I guess."

"I used to play the harp."

"I can picture you doing that."

Ezza began to cry.

"What's wrong?"

"I used to do a lot of things. My life is filled with used-tos." She sat up and picked up a glass of water from the coffee table. "You have to go now. I need quiet."

"Can I stay a while longer? I don't wanna go home high."

"I want to be alone." She retreated into her bedroom.

Ezza got upset like this almost every week, but she'd let me hang around as long as I didn't disturb her. I'd listen to some tunes, take a few hits from my pipe, and if she didn't come out after an hour went by, I'd leave.

I went home and played through all the Robert Johnson songs until I fell asleep. It was the only record on my turntable for the whole week. I never listened to any piece of music with such intensity, and I could recall each note and chord even though I had no knowledge of music theory. When I closed my eyes, I imagined myself on stage, playing my own guitar. My ability to visualize seemed so real that I sometimes lost my sense of time and space. After hearing Robert Johnson, I knew I had to get a guitar. All I needed was ninety-nine, ninety-nine, and the M.I.J. would be mine.

Spilled Coffee and Rain

Stirred with a Gibson SG

Where wolves and ti - gers and pan - thers creep. _____ I close my

With the police more than likely looking for me, I decided to stay away from my car. I tied my hair back, threw on my newsboy cap and cautiously walked along Bleecker Street. No matter how many times I traversed this neighborhood, it never got old. Each store, café, and jazz club was like a loyal friend to me, always available to cheer me up when I needed it. My mother was correct; familiarity is comforting. It's a companion when you're lonely, a mood when you need inspiration, and a connection when you need grounding. All you have to do is absorb it into all your senses until it becomes a permanent fixture.

In the early a.m., no matter how many people are out here, there's this odd sense of isolation. It's as if everyone is wandering aimlessly, trying to conquer some inner-demon or on their way to creating a new one to talk about at work the next day. My loneliness typically subsided during these after-hour jaunts, but tonight the street life rhythm made me all the more lonely because I wasn't a part of it anymore. I was a dead man walking.

I thought about what Gus said about my father being the kidnapper. I took the subway to Astoria and ended up in front of the house where he grew up and now lived in with his new bride. My cellphone rang, and the kidnapper's synthesized voice wasted no time tormenting me.

"Tick-tock, tick-tock, our deadline is nearing, and it seems you got yourself in a spot of trouble. The NYPD is looking for you because of the misguided stunt you pulled at Jake's. You better not get yourself arrested before it's time to pay up."

"All the more reason for us to get this over with."

"Ready for the final challenge?"

"Tell me all about it…*Rumplestiltskin*."

"Where are you right now?"

"Why are you asking? You've been following me."

"I want to hear you say it."

My father's house exuded a dark, magnetic force that pulled out all the memories I've been fighting to keep inside. "At my father's."

"How does that make you feel? Knowing he got away with his crime? Did he pay enough for what he did?"

"He can never pay enough."

"You can make him pay. You can knock on your father's door and execute your own justice. I'll bet that's what you're thinking right now."

"Since you're so smart, you should consider ending this and avoid a jail sentence. Return Jessie, and I'll forget this night ever happened."

"I can't let you off so easily. However, I can offer you this one last challenge…kill your father, and I'll let you go free."

"What would you get out of it?"

"I'm not here to answer your questions. Rest assured, I have my reasons for making you this offer. Do you accept my challenge?"

I scanned the street for activity. No one was around.

"I'll bet your father's playing your new stepmother like an old out-of-tune guitar, turning her pegs until she sounds exactly how he wants her to sound."

"He plays everyone like that."

"He's got everyone fooled. Everyone except you."

"How do you know so much about me?" I asked.

"Find me, and you'll have your answer."

I clutched the grip of the gun in my pocket.

"Are you going to accept my challenge?" the kidnapper asked.

"I'm thinking about it."

"Don't take too long to deliberate. Time is in constant motion, and so am I." He hung up.

I marched to the front door and rang the bell with my other hand still wrapped around the handle of the gun. A dog barked, a light turned on inside, and a powerful shock thrust out from behind my sternum. I picked up my guitar case and ran off to hide behind a van parked in the driveway. My father opened the door, and I aimed the gun at him as he turned his head from left to right. My finger was positioned against the trigger, ready to fire when my new stepmother came outside.

"Who is it?" she asked.

"Probably a neighborhood prankster."

"It's cold out tonight."

"Luckily, I got my love to keep me warm." He kissed his wife.

After watching the typical newlywed display, I knew my father wasn't the kidnapper. My anger intensified anyway. I redirected my aim towards my stepmother. In that instant, I hated her for receiving the affection that should have gone to my mother, who was treated more like a servant. Stunned by my desire to kill someone I never met and who never did anything to me, I ran off.

I sat on a bench in a subway car with my cellphone pressed against my ear.

"You're a coward," the kidnapper said as the car pulled away from the stop.

I didn't answer since I agreed with him.

"While you constantly replay what he's done to you, he's having the time of his life with his pretty young bride. His house will soon be filled with little brothers and sisters who'll probably get everything you were deprived of."

"I hope they do."

"Where's the justice if he's rewarded?"

"My father is immune to justice."

"Only because you led him to do what he did."

"I led him nowhere!"

A homeless man asleep on one of the benches awoke and grunted.

"It was all your fault, Markos. And you better admit to the truth before you die."

"Why? What will you gain from all this? After I die, you'll still be a loose string, and no amount of peg turning will bring you in tune."

"Look at the reflection in the window. If you're honest with yourself, you'll see who you just described. The next time we speak will be when this is almost over." The kidnapper hung up.

I got off on Christopher Street and walked around some more, playing back the events of the whole day. All my actions failed to bring me closer to finding Jessie. I had nothing else left to do but stop resisting. I'd have to pay the ransom. It started to sink in after I freed Leda, but now I knew I was nearing the end. My surrender brought on a level of comfort you wouldn't expect in such a circumstance. I was about to die, yet the night seemed like any other night. What did this translate into? I had no answer. An admission like this would normally depress me; instead I found relief. This was my way of escape, my liberation from my misery. The kidnapper was correct. He was giving me what I wanted all along…an excuse to die.

I passed by a late-night cafe where Cro was in the middle of sketching a young couple that looked as though they came from the Mid-West. Cro was the ideal person to have a final conversation with. I sat at a sidewalk table and drank an espresso while I waited for him to finish.

⁂

Cro pulled out a chair and sat. "Stella came 'round looking for you earlier on. She told me about Jessie."

"What did you say to her?" I asked.

"Same thing I'm gonna tell you now; everything's gonna be all right as long as you keep the faith."

A waitress came over and gave Cro his coffee.

"Are you waiting around here for the drop?" Cro asked.

A police car passed by, and I concealed the side of my face with my hand. "Got nowhere else to go but here."

"Stella's scared."

"She's got Teddy and Leda with her."

"But she wants you with her."

"Did she say that?"

"Not directly. But it was what she didn't say. She didn't say she didn't want you around."

"Can't argue with your logic." I sipped my espresso.

"Why are you still stationary?"

"I like the atmosphere."

Cro wagged his finger at me. "Let me tell you something, Markos, your song is *way* overplayed. Stop acting like a whiny, self-centered prima donna. There's a frightened woman who's worried sick about her child. You should be with her, not sitting around here drinking espresso and rapping with the Cro. You only get one chance at this life, so don't blow it."

I eyed Cro with concern. "What's wrong?"

"Ain't nothing wrong with me." He waved his hand in front of him. "You're the one who can't seem to deal with reality."

"Is this about your brother?"

Cro turned away from me.

"Cro…talk to me."

"I don't wanna bring none of this up. You got bigger problems."

"Not big enough for me to turn away from a friend in need."

"He's dead." Cro grabbed his forehead, and his elbow knocked over his coffee.

I wiped up the spill with a napkin.

"He had leukemia. Late stage. Happened about a year ago. I should've looked for him sooner."

The waitress came over and refilled Cro's coffee cup.

"Don't wait too long to say what you wanna say," he said. "You may not get another chance."

It began to rain on my walk to the subway station, and I barely noticed. The only thing on my mind was Stella and Jessie and what Cro said about getting only one chance. I spent most of my time worrying about every detail of my life, from the way I looked, to the way I talked, to the way I thought everyone perceived me. It took up so much of my energy that I had nothing left to give back. I inherited this wonderful dysfunction from my father who was always on me about everything from my appearance to my grades. I wasn't his son; I was a project.

I stopped in front of Music Man and Flipper's old music shop. A row of guitars sat behind the display window. Playing guitar was the only thing in my life that came easy. I never thought beyond the song I was learning. Everything else in my life seemed synthetic and forced by comparison. As I fixated on a Gibson SG, I thought to myself: *if I played myself the same way I played my guitar, my life would move along as smoothly.* Sometimes it only takes one sentence, at the right moment, to bring you to a profound understanding. And this one little sentence connected to what Leda told me about trusting what I receive without judgment. Putting the two together made me see the clearest I'd ever seen in my life. I laughed, and it was the first real laugh I had in years. It intensified when I glanced back at the guitar that led to my recent liberation: a *Gibson SG.* The experience made me see Gibsons in a new light.

A homeless man passed by and gave me the Gray Pines, but I didn't care anymore. Life was good on the eve before my death.

Playing Our Song

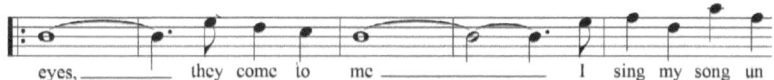

eyes, _____ they come to me _____ I sing my song un

I slipped an envelope in a public mailbox. Inside were two letters addressed to Stella and Jessie. I glanced at my watch. In three hours, I'd be no longer, but I never felt more at peace in my life. It's impossible to explain how I could feel this way when my daughter was still missing. I've read about how people had spiritual awakenings after the most traumatic experiences of their lives. They sounded nuts to me back then but not anymore. There's this inner-awareness in you where you just know things. The religious call it belief in an outside force. I saw it as an intuitive understanding that switched on when I paid close enough attention.

With only a little time left before I had to pay up, I went to Stella's. I wanted her to see the new me so that after my body was taken away in an ambulance, her last memory of me wouldn't be of a delusional man who dealt with his problems by over-medicating. After she read my letter, she'd understand I left my life embracing it. I needed her to know that, so that she could tell Jessie her father died happy and that he gave his life for her without the slightest hesitation.

Stella opened the door in a panic. "What happened? Is Jessie all right?"

I put one of my arms around her, grabbed her hand and danced into the foyer. Okay, so I might've come off as slightly loony-tunes for doing this, but I figured she'd understand my reaction after I was gone.

Stella pushed me back. "Did you find Jessie?"

"I found everything." I entered the living room, lay my guitar case on the coffee table and took out Ezza. "I remember Teddy telling me how a crime scene is like a puzzle, and how he had to put it all together one piece at a time to recognize the whole picture." After a quick tune-up, I started swinging to "Sometimes I'm Happy."

"I followed his advice when I started playing, picking one note at a time. I wouldn't attempt the next note until it became automatic. By the time I mastered the last note, my fingers were playing without me telling them what to do."

"Now is not the time for a concert. The way you ran in here I thought you found Jessie."

"I was able to play freely because I heard the whole song rather than individual notes placed on a staff." I stopped playing. "I had to come over and tell you I see the whole now. Before tonight, my nightmares kept me locked inside my own head, keeping me from seeing what I had with you and Jessie."

"Markos, I..."

"Let me finish. I've been silent long enough." I played "Our Love Is Here to Stay" nice and slow to accompany my admission. "I blew away any chance we had of being happy together. I can't ever make up for what I did, but I can at least accept my responsibility over messing things up. Let's start over, right here, right now."

I wish I had a camera to snap a picture of Stella's reaction. The only time I saw the look she now had on her face was when she found the ruby engagement ring in her wine.

I walked over to Stella and took her hand in mine. "I don't want you to be scared. Jessie will be back with you tomorrow morning, and the days that follow will only get better for the both of you. That makes me happy, and I want you to know and remember that always."

Stella leaned up, removed my cap and kissed me. It was the type of kiss that told me she still loved me. What killed me was the knowledge that I still stood a chance with her again, but I wasn't going to be around to experience a reconciliation.

After playing through one of my original tunes, I went to check what was keeping Stella. She thought a hot bath would help relax her, and I wanted her relaxed. I planned to give her the locket. When I got to the bedroom door, I heard Stella talking quietly. I picked up the phone in the living room and listened in. Teddy was on the other end of the line.

"He seems calm. Too calm considering everything that's going on," Stella said. "I think he may have taken too much of his medication. The pressure is getting to him."

"I'm down the block. As soon as he leaves, I'll be right behind him."

"Any news on Gus Barras?"

"Not yet."

"You don't really think Markos killed him, do you?"

"I honestly don't know what to think anymore, Stella."

"And the kidnapping?"

"Everyone is a suspect until we find out for sure. Call me when he leaves."

When they hung up I returned to the couch, grabbed Ezza and played the same song from before but with a different attitude. I thought Stella wanting me to stay meant she trusted me. Now I wondered if the only reason she kissed me was to keep me from leaving. I wasn't angry with her or Teddy. I couldn't blame them for thinking I killed Gus. Even Dottie seemed terrified of me tonight.

"Everything okay?" I asked when Stella came out with a towel wrapped around her hair.

"Not really," she said.

"I know what might help."

I plugged into the stereo speakers, and Stella and I grooved to "You'd Be so Nice to Come Home To."

"Sing," I said.

"Not tonight."

I sang, and Stella closed her eyes to connect to her musical space. I then scatted the next time through.

It seemed Stella had calmed until she fumbled over a few notes. She stopped playing. "This is wrong." She walked over to the sofa and sat. "Our daughter is missing, and we're jamming. We both must be crazy."

I sat next to Stella. "Being stressed out won't change what's happening. Better to deal with this calmly."

"Nothing will calm me until Jessie comes home safe."

"She will."

"Wish I had your faith."

"Faith has nothing to do with it. Once I pay up, Jessie will be released. It's how these things usually work."

"It's the *usually* part that has me worried. What if the kidnapper changes his mind?"

"No what-ifs. It's almost time. I'd rather leave with optimism. It's all I got left."

"You have us." She held my hand. "You always will."

I placed my other hand over Stella's. "I overheard your conversation with Teddy, and I want to assure you, I didn't kill Gus."

"Now that you know, you can have Teddy go with you."

"The plans haven't changed. I go alone."

"Why? This could be dangerous for both you and Jessie. You'll have a better chance if you let Teddy help you."

"You already helped me tonight, along with a Gibson SG." Stella crinkled her forehead.

"Never mind that. It'll take too long to explain, and it's already five AM. I gotta go now." I stood and pulled her up with me. "I'm okay with everything, always remember that." I put on my cap, kissed her and left, thinking this was it. No more Stella, no more music and soon…no more anything.

Ezza By Moonlight

der a sha - dy ban-yan tree._____ A qui -et place where___ I can sta

The spring nights had been getting longer, which meant my time with Ezza was almost at an end. Even though she was years older than me, it didn't seem that way. We shared many common interests. From music and astronomy to politics and philosophy, we spent hours after my tutoring sessions talking and contemplating the meaning of everything.

The last night I spent with Ezza was meant to be our night. I planned to sing to her and then propose my love and devotion with a poem I wrote. I stood in Ezza's living room with my hair slicked back, dressed in my best jeans and Led Zeppelin concert T-shirt. I think I might have even ironed my clothes. Yeah, I was in love. My heart gushed out of my voice when I sang, "Kind-Hearted Woman." I even managed to pull off a falsetto voice as in the Robert J. version. During my performance, I kept my eyes closed, and by then I was comfortable enough with the blues progression to scat my own guitar solo. I then went on to sing the melody and poured everything I had into it. This was the first instance I vanished into the mystical world where nothing outside of music existed. When I opened my eyes, Ezza leapt off the couch and clapped her hands.

"Wow! You sounded incredible, Markos! You're a natural."

"I listened to the music all week."

"I think you may have perfect pitch."

"What's that?"

She grabbed both my hands. "Just as your eyes recognize colors, your ears can identify notes by how they sound."

"Thought everyone did that."

"You have to do something with your ability. It's a gift."

"Come on. Are you serious, or are you playing me like Dottie when you told her that her blue eye shadow made her look ten years younger?"

Ezza pointed to her eyes. "Do I look like I'm playing you?"

I examined her face for a few moments. "It's gonna take me forever to get a guitar. I don't make much money bussing."

"Your birthday is coming up. You can ask your parents."

"My father thinks music is a waste of time."

"How about your mother?"

"She agrees with everything he says."

I went through Ezza's albums and pulled out B.B. King.

"We have to figure something out," she said.

"We?"

"After what I heard tonight, I'm going to talk to your father."

"He won't listen to you."

"He listens to me when I tell him you're doing well in math." Ezza crossed her arms. "You haven't told me yet."

"Got a C," I said as I read the back of the album cover.

"That's it?" She tossed her hands in the air. "Well, at least you didn't fail."

"I'm okay with it, but my father isn't. Nothing you say will make him change his mind."

"You need to get better grades."

"School isn't my thing."

Ezza snatched the album from my hand. "Make it your thing. Do whatever it takes to get a guitar…except steal one."

⚜

We lay in our usual spot on the rooftop, and I took a hit from my pipe.

"What are your plans for the summer?" Ezza asked.

I moved closer towards Ezza. "Rob a few houses to pay for my new guitar."

She slapped my leg. "I told you no stealing."

"You told me not to steal a guitar. Some of the seniors are hitting this house where they got a lot of expensive electronics. They said I could go along."

"You're not seriously considering it, are you?"

"I'm thinking about it."

"Ask for more hours at the diner."

"I hate working there. I spend enough time with my father at home."

"You have so much potential. Don't waste it."

The way Ezza gazed at me killed all my inhibitions, and I tried to kiss her. She pulled away from me and giggled.

"What's so funny?" I sat up.

"Nothing, I…"

"You said I acted older than my age."

"But you're still only fourteen."

"I'm gonna be fifteen soon."

"You're real sweet, Markos, but I can't get involved with you."

"Why not? Your ex was old enough to be your father."

"That's different. We were both adults."

"Afraid you'll get arrested?"

Ezza placed her hand on my arm. "You still have a lot of growing up to do."

I pulled my hand away. "My father told me if we were in Greece during my fourteenth birthday, he would've hired a prostitute for my present."

"We're not in Greece."

"Eighteen is only three years away. What kind of magic will turn me into a man between now and then?"

"You'll be legal."

"I won't tell anyone."

"It's more complicated."

"What? Are you an alien from another planet that has to fly back to your home world tomorrow morning?"

"Sometimes I wonder about that." She laughed.

"Is everything a joke to you?"

"It has to be."

"Why?"

"When I'm not laughing, I'm crying, and I don't like to cry."

I got up and parked myself on the ledge. Ezza followed and sat beside me.

"It would show poor judgment to go with you, and I don't want to hurt you." She put her hand on my thigh. "You have your share of problems, and I won't add to them. I already did enough damage by letting you get high here."

"You did nothing wrong." I tried to kiss her again.

Ezza stood. "Didn't you listen to anything I said?"

"Why do you look like you want me to?"

Ezza laughed again, which infuriated me. I went to leave, and she clutched my arm.

"I'm not laughing at you. It's flattering that you'd want me when I'm almost old enough to be your mother."

I retracted my arm and peered into Ezza's eyes that I still see when I think about that night. She wanted me to stay and be the friend she desperately needed. But I was unable to hear her over my own disappointment, so I left. I tossed my poem in a sewer. I tried to recapture the mood in a new poem several years later, but it wasn't the same. Once experience overcomes naivety, it's impossible to duplicate the essence of your first love.

Ezza's rejection smashed my ego and going home would have depressed me further, so I met up with Flipper and Music Man. Flipper let me noodle around with one of the acoustics and then started to teach me some major chords.

"You're picking this stuff up fast."

"Ezza told me I got perfect pitch."

He got out his '72 Telecaster Thinline and played a C. "This is a C." He continued playing the remaining notes, naming them as he played them chromatically. He tested me by sounding them in random order, and I got most of them right.

"Yep, you got perfect pitch." He hung his guitar on the hook.

"But I missed a few of them."

"You never associated a note name with the sound before tonight. After a few more listens, you'll have them all down."

I handed Flipper the acoustic, and he examined me for a moment. "Something's wrong. You seem a little off."

"Had a joint on my way over."

Flipper shook his head. "You're fast on your way of becoming Music Man." He hung up the guitar and wiped off a few smudges with a lint-free cloth. He turned around and cleared the counter of papers and emptied out the ashtray. "I keep telling Music Man not to smoke out here, and he never listens." Flipper spritzed some Windex onto the glass and wiped it down. He then stared up at me. "Surely, you must have more fun things to do than watching me clean?"

"I don't wanna go home."

He narrowed his eyes. "Your problem is bigger than reefer." He thought for a moment and then slapped the counter. "You got girl problems."

"How did you know?"

"At your age, it's always over some girl...and when you grow up you'll find it's *still* over some girl."

"She thinks I'm too young."

"How old is she?"

"Thirty."

"You really aim for those high numbers."

Flipper invited me into the back room to listen to some tunes. When I entered, a thick haze of pot smoke almost knocked me out. Music Man was in the middle of reading something and didn't acknowledge our presence.

Flipper waved his hand in the air and coughed. He then picked up a can of air freshener and sprayed the room. "How many times do I have to tell you to open the door when you light up?" Music Man remained focused on his reading, and Flipper opened the back door.

I headed over to a large box that housed Flipper's record collection.

He walked over to me. "I know what will take your mind off of...what's her name again?"

"Ezza."

"Strange name."

"It's short for Esmerelda."

"That's beautiful."

"I think so too. But she hates it. And if you call her that, she'll go nuts on you."

"I can understand why you love her. The tougher they are, the harder you fall."

Flipper rifled through the albums. After several minutes he found what he was looking for.

"Seeing how quickly you're learning, think it's safe to move you to some more intense sounds." He slid out the record and handed me the jacket.

"Wes Montgomery," I said. "Never heard of him."

"Wait till you hear what you've been missing." He put the record on the turntable and rested the needle on "Round Midnight." He turned up the volume. "Love how Wes makes this one swing."

When I heard Wes play, I had a similar reaction to what I felt when I first heard Robert J. I sat behind Flipper's desk, closed my eyes and pictured Wes playing in some smoky jazz club. "Ezza told me jazz is big in Paris."

"And Japan," Flipper said.

"I wanna learn how to play so I can visit all those places and get paid while doing it."

"You have to practice a lot to get a gig like that."

"How long?"

"Many, many, many years."

Music man slammed his book shut. "According to Vilfredo Pareto, twenty-percent effort produces eighty percent of your results."

"So if you go past twenty percent, what happens?" I asked.

"You lose your momentum, and all you're doing is wasting your energy."

"Don't listen to him." Flipper closed his eyes and smiled. "Listen to how Wes plays. To play like him takes years of practice. I'd give up pool for a lifetime if I could play like him."

Music Man glanced at Flipper. "Tchhhh. You still wouldn't be able to play more than three scales. You barely have time to practice with all that cleaning you do." He took a hit from his joint and returned to his book.

Music Man had focus. If he applied his twenty percent to music, he probably could've been the next Mozart.

"Tchhh yourself," Flipper said. "You'd probably remember where the notes on the fretboard are located if you didn't smoke all that pot, you goon."

Music man shot Flipper his middle finger without looking away from his book.

"Goon." Flipper shook his head.

I laughed, and Flipper put his hand on my shoulder. "Observe, absorb, integrate, and experience all you can here," he said. "Drugs can hold you back, so don't do them."

"He's right," Music man said as he took a drag from his joint. "Drugs suck."

I raised one of my brows and faced him.

"Except for pot. It's natural."

Flipper turned my head to face him. "Do you want to end up like him? And I'm not any better. Sure, I take care of my health, eat a low-fat organic diet and avoid everything with artificial flavors, MSG and GMOs, but I still got nothing else going on for me other than this store. If I did apply twenty percent of my time to my playing, I probably would've been playing concert stages across the world."

"You guys aren't so bad."

"If you want to master the guitar, you need to live, breathe, and think music. Leave Esmeralda and all that petty shit you've been worried about behind."

"You're starting to sound like a public service announcement," I said.

Flipper removed the record, put it back in the sleeve and handed it to me. "My advice comes free and without any conditions. You can either take it or leave it." He looked at Music Man. "Have anything to add to that?"

Music Man put his book down and pointed his joint at me. "Don't be one of the crabs in the bucket." He returned to his reading.

"What's that supposed to mean?" I asked.

Flipper gathered some magazines on the table and neatly piled them up. "If a crab tries to crawl out of a bucket, the others will climb over it, preventing it from getting out. In the end, they all end up on someone's dinner plate."

"I still don't get it."

"I'm not finished explaining." Flipper picked up a can of furniture polish and spritzed the tabletop. "A lot of folks go through life not living up to their potential. They become unhappy and try to cheer themselves up through their vices. But vices never fulfill them, and they spite everyone who has what they're missing in their own life." He wiped off the polish with a rag. "They spend all their energy bringing other people down. You can either be the type of person who drags people down or lifts them up. The choice is yours to make now. Don't let your circumstances turn you into one of the crabs in the bucket."

"What about the people who don't give a shit either way?" I asked.

"You don't want to be like them either. They're the worst of them all. They're zombies. They feel nothing, do nothing. They might as well be dead." Flipper sighed. "When I look around this store, that's how I feel sometimes. But I'm too old to fix myself." Flipper pointed at me. "You aren't."

I took the record but not the advice. I went home, listened to Wes, got high and wrote a few angry poems over my humiliation with Ezza. Happiness, sadness, confusion, and anger vied for control of my brain. I picked up the phone and dialed Ezza's number to get rid of the conflict going on in my head. After one ring, fear overpowered my emotional quartet, and I hung up. I fell asleep to my mother singing church music downstairs.

An Appointment to Keep

Sit   with   my   friends and ____   play   all   day. __

Teddy was waiting for me outside of the brownstone. My lack of surprise disappointed him. He prided himself over his stealth maneuvers that led to the arrests of some of the most dangerous drug dealers.

"Don't have time. Got a deadline to meet." I looked around, hoping the kidnapper wasn't nearby.

"I'm coming with you."

"I can handle this myself."

"You didn't keep up your end of the bargain. You got no choice."

I took out the gun and aimed it at Teddy. "I know you've been following me."

"Holy anchovy, where did you get that?"

"If I'm not where the kidnapper tells me to be, he's gonna kill Jessie."

Teddy edged towards me.

"I'll shoot if you don't back off."

He stopped and stretched his hands to the side. "I'm only here to help, Markos."

"Who else is with you?"

"No one."

"I know all about the tracker."

"Why didn't you remove it?"

"If I did, you would've gotten all of your buddies involved."

"You're damned right I would have."

I retracted the hammer of the gun.

"I helped raise you and kept you from traveling the same road as your old man. Now's not the time for a drive back through the old neighborhood."

"You have to leave now, and keep an eye on Stella."

Teddy approached me again, and I shot the sidewalk, near his feet.

"Ask yourself how Jessie will feel when she finds out her father lost his mind while saving her life."

"Tell her I lost it way before tonight. You wouldn't be lying." I tapped my head with the gun. "You should hear the crackpot music this thing's been playing since last night."

"Stop and listen to how you sound. And what kinda stunt were you trying to pull at Jake's?"

"I won't be responsible for your death." I retracted the hammer again.

"Your concern for me is touching, but why don't you let me worry about my own life?" Teddy removed a pack of cigarettes and slid one out. "I'm coming with you." He lit the cigarette and took a drag. "And then afterwards, I'm taking you in to answer for what happened at Jake's. I told you to call me when you ran into Barras."

"There wasn't enough time."

"Did you get any information?"

"The kidnapper called while we were together."

"That being the case, I'm involved now."

I opened my mouth to respond, and Teddy thrust his cigarette at me.

"I don't wanna hear another word. Either shoot me, or tell me I win again. Thanks to you, I'm back up to a pack a day, and your sister will probably be a widow soon because I'm going against my doctor's orders."

"You may not even last that long if the kidnapper finds out you're here with me. He said he'd kill you if I told you about what was going on."

"The only person pointing a gun at me is you." Teddy tapped his shirt. "And I'm nobody's fool. Got my vest on."

"That won't help if he shoots you in the head."

"Standing out in the open makes me an easier target. Let's get out of here."

I kept the gun aimed at him. My hand was shaking and then I realized it was my whole body. "Leave now, Teddy. Please."

"We're on the same side."

"What if he kills you both? I can't live with that. I can't live with losing the both of you."

"The ransom is what's motivating him to do this. He won't risk losing the jackpot." Teddy sidled toward me. "Come on. Let's go get Jessie. Don't let her come home to a father in the middle of another breakdown. She's gonna need you more than ever when she comes home."

While I was mulling over what to do next, a car pulled over to the side of the road. The radio was tuned to a station playing Mel Tormé's version of "Stardust." Time around me seemed to slow, and all I heard was the song until Teddy waved his hand in front of my face.

"Thought you were in a rush."

I seized his arm, still disconnected. "I'm not gonna be around for her after this, Teddy." The sound of my voice seemed to come at me as though it were being echoed back.

The person in the car shut off the radio, and I became lucid again. I no longer had the gun in my hand. Teddy snatched it from me while I was unplugged.

"What's that supposed to mean?" Teddy asked.

"I'll tell you after I answer the next phone call."

Crazy They Call Me

Trust in me and fol - low a - long, when ev - er you hear m

Teddy and I took the elevator to the roof. When we stepped outside, the wind blew my cap off my head and over the ledge. I brushed my hair away from my face and Teddy said, "Stop fussing, you're gorgeous."

I flashed him my middle finger as my cellphone rang. I hopped onto the ledge and answered.

"Have you figured it out yet?" the kidnapper asked.

"You won. Congratulations."

"What did he win?" Teddy asked.

"It's time for you to give me my prize," the kidnapper said. "At exactly 7:30 a.m., you'll fulfill the terms of the ransom and jump off the roof."

I peered at the street below. All the cars went by as though this were any other morning. A garbage truck pulled over to the side to empty a bin, and the lights in the deli across the street turned on, reminding me I hadn't eaten since I left my mother's. A bagel with everything, smothered with cream cheese and washed down with a cup of coffee sounded like the perfect last meal. "You couldn't come up with something more original? It's been done before."

Teddy's eyes expanded. "Holy anchovy, he's not asking you to…?"

I cupped the phone and whispered, "Quiet down. I'm supposed to be here alone."

"I already know your brother-in-law is with you. He's been following you all day. The only reason he's still alive is because he thinks you're behind Jessie's disappearance, and for good reason. You've been crazier than your old man since our game began."

"Right there alongside you."

"For the terms of the condition to be met, you must be declared dead on sight."

"At least keep Jessie away from all this," I said.

"I'll escort her to the back of the building so she won't see the mess you're going to leave on the sidewalk. After that, I won't be able to guarantee her safety. The city is filled with psychopaths. Pass these instructions on to your brother-in-law and have him ready to receive your daughter after payment is made."

"Since I conceded, can I talk to Jessie one last time?" I closed my eyes. "Please." I hated how desperate I sounded.

"I'll contact you when it's time." The kidnapper hung up, and I put away my cellphone.

"I'm not letting you do this," Teddy said.

"I've got no choice."

"We'll figure out a way to make it look like you jumped."

"It's too late for that."

Teddy pointed his finger at me. "It wouldn't have been if you told me what was going on from the beginning!"

"I thought I could handle this on my own, and I didn't want anything to happen to you."

Teddy shook his head. "I've gotten you out of every scrape you were in since you were a kid. But I don't know how the hell I'm supposed to get you out of this one."

"There's nothing you can do. If I don't jump, Jessie dies."

Teddy paced back and forth. "For the first time, in a very long time, I'm not sure of the right thing to do. This all sounds crazy, like some twisted nightmare that I'm gonna wake up from."

"I felt that way too, but I'm okay with everything now. I made my peace." I waved at some people in a balcony across the street.

"Get your ass down here! You're making me nervous."

"When there's a crowd, it's hard for me not to put on a show. I should've brought Ezza. I could've put on my last concert here."

"What the hell is wrong with you, Markos? You're about to commit suicide, and you're acting like you're at a party."

"I don't want you to worry about me, Teddy. If I have to die tonight, I'd rather die happy." I sat on the ledge and hung my legs off the side. "After all I went through tonight, I can't look back feeling sad anymore. Jessie's gonna go home to Stella, and everything will be as it should be."

Some press vans pulled to the side of the road and parked.

"Too bad I won't be around to read the headlines," I said.

Teddy sat next to me.

"I know you think I'm behind this," I said.

"You're about to kill yourself in the same way as you tried to last time. Can you blame me for being a little suspicious?"

"I wouldn't believe me either, but what I'm telling you is the truth."

"Convince me I'm wrong. Why would anyone want you dead?"

"I still have no clue. The only two people who had a strong enough motive to want me dead led me down a dead-end street."

"If you do this, how do you know the kidnapper will let Jessie go?"

"I don't have any other choice."

"Are you sure?"

"If you got a better alternative, tell me now."

Teddy lit up a cigarette.

"Whatever it takes…remember?" I said.

"Why are you up here?"

I swung around and faced Stella. I threw an accusatory glance towards Teddy. "You should've kept her out of this." I glanced back at Stella. "I'm here to pay the ransom."

"You're not taking the easy way out again."

"It's not easy this time. I don't wanna die."

Stella squinted her eyes at Teddy.

"The ransom is his life."

"Is it true?" She asked me.

"Think I'd make something like this up?"

A vision of Jessie holding the red lotus came to me. "Take it, Daddy."

I ignored the vision and kept my eyes on Stella. "I've known the outcome since all of this started; it was either me or Jessie. The choice wasn't a difficult one to make. She's my daughter and more deserving of life than me."

Stella and Teddy glanced at each other and then at me.

"You have to stop this now," Stella said.

"If I do, Jessie will die. Is that what you want?"

Stella and Teddy said nothing, and I couldn't take their Gray Pines stares any longer. I stood up and threw both my hands in the air. "What do I have to do to convince you this is real?"

My cellphone rang. "He's got great timing." I answered. "Let's get this over with."

The only response that came was the sound of fire crackling.

"What's he saying?" Teddy asked.

After a few more tense moments, Jessie began to sing. Her voice broadcasted from all around.

"Can you hear her?" I asked.

"Hear what?" Teddy said.

"Jessie. She's singing."

"I don't hear anything but the wind," Teddy said.

"Where is she, Markos?" Stella asked. "Where did you hide our daughter?"

I placed the receiver to my ear, and the kidnapper was laughing with his real voice. I recognized it immediately, and it was the most terrifying sound I could have ever imagined. The voice laughing back at me was none other than my own.

Lost Friends

sing my song.   Hear my call, you'll ne-ver go wrong,   as   long as you hear my   song.   I

I had spent most of my hours after school listening to Wes Montgomery and Robert Johnson. Flipper also turned me on to other guitarists like Joe Pass and Django Reinhardt. I dug them both, but Wes and Robert J. remained my mentors who visited me from the other side. I'd sing all their guitar lines in my head, and whenever I'd hit a wrong note, they never let me get away with it. Being able to visualize them so clearly is what I think made me pick up the guitar so fast. When you can imagine yourself being observed by two musicians you idolize, you'd be surprised how hard you'd work to impress them. Think it has something to do with the subconscious mind not being able to distinguish between the truth and lies we tell ourselves. I used this particular feature to my advantage…with my playing, at least.

I rarely hung my coat at home on weekends. After Ezza turned me down, I spent most of my Saturday nights at the local skating rink. The loud music and cute girls skating around in their short skirts made it the perfect place to forget about Ezza for a few hours. I had a pair of skates, but I hardly used them. I mostly hung out by one of the tables smoking cigarettes and catching up with my friends, who eventually became lost to me either through a jail sentence or graveyard plot. The few of us who survived past these rough years went on to lead disparate lives. We were like oil and water, and none of us ever made the effort to shake the bottle and mix us back together.

The only time I bothered to skate was when I found a girl I liked. I'd take her around for a couple of laps, and we'd usually end up at one of the dark corner booths. The spinning lights and retro disco spheres could even make the most unattractive girl enticing.

On my last visit to the rink, Blonde Girl sat beside me at my regular table near the snack bar. I can't remember her name. I was drawn to her as she had similar features to Ezza. Beyond the extrinsic package, they shared nothing else in common.

"There will always be wars," she said in response to one of my lost friends who was talking about how the Illuminati started most of the world wars. "Doesn't matter if it's the Illuminates or the presidents of the world, you can't do anything to stop them. They have the power to do whatever they want to do."

My friend and I looked at each other and both sniggered at her mispronouncing the word *Illuminati*.

Blonde Girl never noticed and continued on. "Why worry about something you can't change? If the world is gonna end with a big explosion, I'd rather go out partying."

"Not me. I gotta know what's going on in the world," I said.

"Why?"

"If you're ignorant, you're easier to control," I said trying to sound as studious as Ezza. "Our leaders want us to be like sheep."

"No one can control you unless you let them."

"But what if you can't tell you're being controlled?" I asked.

"I think I'd know if someone was trying to control me."

"How can you be sure you're not being controlled now?"

"Because I can do whatever I want."

"You really think so?"

"I know so."

"I heard on the news that in the future the government's gonna put cameras up to monitor all the city streets in America. Did you hear about that?"

She yawned. "I don't watch the news. It's boring, and they're just being paranoid. Nothing like that would ever happen. No one would go along with it."

"What if there's an asteroid about to hit the Earth? Wouldn't you want to know?"

"Don't they usually interrupt television shows for those kinds of announcements?"

"The emergency broadcast system," my lost friend said. He died the following year after smashing his car against a telephone pole.

"Yeah, that's it," Blonde Girl said. "They always play that annoying beep in the middle of *General Hospital*. Hate when that happens."

"So, television is more important than global annihilation?" I asked.

Blonde girl laughed. "You're funny."

"Wasn't trying to be."

Blonde Girl stared at me seriously for a moment and pointed at me. "The way you just looked at me reminded me of Scott Baio. You look a lot like him."

"That's a first," my lost friend chuckled.

I desperately needed a hit after that conversation. Lost Friend and I went to the bathroom where we numbed ourselves enough to deal with the emptiness of our lives. On our return trip to the table, a thick trail of smoke flooded my nostrils. It seemed everyone smoked back then, and no adult told us to stop. We owned the rink.

"You don't look so well," Blonde Girl said as she met up with us.

"Wanna get outta here?" I needed fresh air to get rid of my nausea.

My stomach ached for a plate of fries with gravy and melted American cheese, a favorite after-skate snack of mine. On our walk over to Jake's, Blonde Girl prattled nonstop. She mentioned a soap opera my mother watched with Mrs. Barras, and I would have ditched her had I not caught sight of the Jake's Diner sign flashing ahead of us. Half a block later, I forgot about the plate of fries when I saw a man leave his car and hurry out to put newspapers in a display case. I glimpsed at Newspaper Man, the car, Blonde Girl, back at Newspaper Man again, and the next thing I knew, I was in the car with Blonde Girl. I shut the door as she screamed out in excitement.

I never drove before, but I'd seen my parents do it often enough. I slammed my foot on the gas and pulled out, narrowly missing an approaching car.

"Woo-hoo-hoo!" I yelled out with an intense euphoric energy. I loved this feeling. Whenever I got it, I believed I was invincible.

"Where are we going?" Blonde Girl asked.

"I'll figure it out when we arrive."

"Have you ever stolen a car before?"

"This is my first time."

"Why did you do it?"

"Just felt like it."

"Do you always do whatever you want?"

I started to feel as though I were being interviewed for *Delinquent's Digest*. "Whenever I can get away with it."

"This is so awesome! Never thought I'd be in my own little road-trip adventure…like in that movie *Natural Born Killers*."

"Where do you live?" I asked.

"Why?"

"I'm taking you home."

"Why?"

I clenched the wheel. "Got anything more interesting to say?"

"Like what?"

"Science, art, music. Anything other than overly-hyped movies, and their unrealistic caricatures of today's youth."

Parroting Ezza's response to me after I told her I rented the aforementioned movie made me miss her more.

"I love Broadway music," Blonde girl said. "My mother signed me up for some voice lessons over at the community center."

"Address please."

"What do *you* do besides hang out at the rink with your druggie friends?"

Sirens screamed from behind us, and I glanced at the rearview mirror. A police car was flashing its headlights at me.

"Step on the gas!" Blonde Girl yelled.

"This isn't a movie, and I can't outrun the cops in a Pacer. The guy probably left the engine running cuz he wanted to get rid of it."

"My father is gonna kill me."

"You and me both," I said as I pulled to the side of the road.

My second visit to a police station almost led me to commit another offense. Blonde Girl sat beside me, and the pitch of her crying gave me a strong urge to strangle her. The police officer seemed equally disturbed as he kept shifting his eyes up to look at her while he was filling out his paperwork.

"My father's gonna ground me for life," Blonde Girl said.

"I thought you said you could do whatever you want?"

"I should've listened to my friends. They warned me about you. They said you're probably gonna end up in prison for the rest of your life."

"Pipe down," the police officer said to the girl. "Your voice is making my headache worse."

Teddy showed up and threw a folder on the desk. "Thanks."

"Anytime." The police officer moved the folder to the side and returned to his work.

Teddy looked at me. "Come with me…now."

I got up and followed him to an office. He motioned for me to have a seat.

"How's Leda?" I asked.

"She's doing great. Got herself an exhibit." He went to the coffee maker and poured me a cup.

"Black, four sugars."

"Leda told me." He handed me the cup along with four sugars. "Can't believe your old man lets you drink coffee at your age."

"It's a Mediterranean custom." I held the packs together and tore them open.

"I'm half-Italian. Never heard of such a thing."

"Your other half excludes you from our club."

Teddy laughed and sat behind his desk. "You should come to Leda's exhibit. She misses you."

"When is it?" I poured the sugar into the coffee and took a sip. One taste told me why the police frequented Jake's. I wanted to spit out the vile liquid.

"I'll tell you where if you tell me what happened tonight."

"I was in the mood for a ride."

"This is the second time you've been here."

"You were on the day shift then. Did they demote you?"

"Your sister got upset when she found out about your last visit here. I told my buddies to notify me if you were ever brought in again." He got out a cigarette and tapped the butt on top of his desk a few times. "And I was notified…by a ringing phone that woke me from a sound sleep." Teddy lit the cigarette and took a drag.

"Why didn't Leda come with you?"

"I wanted to talk to you alone. She agreed with me. Thought you'd say more without her hanging around."

The overhead lights were making my head hurt, and I yearned for another hit from my pipe to take my pain away.

"How are things for you at home?" He took another drag from his cigarette.

"Leda already filled you in. What else do you need to know?"

"Whatever you want to tell me."

"There's nothing new to add. My father's still the same friendly old man who pounded on your squad car window when he caught you making out with my sister."

Teddy rested his cigarette on the ashtray and crossed his hands on the desk. "I know you don't trust me yet. This is the first lengthy discussion we had since Leda and I got together. I can only imagine what your old man told you about me."

"He never said a thing."

Teddy jotted something down on a sheet of paper. "Your sister and I are here for you. If you ever need a place to stay for a few days, call us." He handed me the paper.

"My father's gonna be pissed when he gets here. Think I can stay with you guys tonight?"

"You can't leave here without your father's permission."

"Knew you weren't serious."

"You're free to call when you get home. I'll come pick you up."

My father walked into the room, and I shoved the paper in my pocket.

"You're not alone. Your sister wanted me to remind you of that. Remember…call us anytime."

The words were gratifying to hear, but they didn't lessen my anxiety. My father's face unveiled the fury he was going to release on me when we got home.

My father grasped my shirt and shoved me onto the couch. "You low life piece of garbage!"

My mother grabbed my father's arm, and he pushed her. He lifted his hand, and she put her arms in front of her face in a defensive posture.

"Go away. You're making things worse."

"I'm not leaving you when you're this angry," my mother said.

"What do you think I'm gonna do, kill him?"

"I don't want you to hit him again."

"He needs discipline."

"He needs a father."

"A father's job is to discipline, and that's what I'm doing now. Our son is on the verge of becoming a career criminal. Going easy on him won't help." He pointed his finger at me. "And how dare you disgrace the family name in front of your sister's loser boyfriend."

"You saw Teddy?" My mother asked me. "Was Leda with him?"

I shook my head.

"Did he say anything about her?"

My father's voice calmed. "Give me some time alone with the boy, Maria. I'll let him answer all your questions later."

She nodded and left us. My father looked around the room and fixed his gaze on my video-game console. "You've left me with no options." He tore the plug from the outlet, picked up the console and smashed it against the wall. "You're no longer allowed to go to the rink. When you come home from school, you'll go straight to your room to study. You can only leave the house to go to church, work, counseling and tutoring sessions."

"School's almost over. I don't need any more tutoring."

"You're not even close to over. You should've asked Ezza to help you with science and history. You flunked them both. I told her you'll be continuing your studies with her for the rest of the summer." He sat on his recliner. "I've lost Leda, and it looks like I'm on my way to losing you. I don't know what else to do. I've tried to teach you things I was forced to learn the hard way. My father was always drunk and never around. I had to figure things out on my own. If you don't stop your destructive actions now, you'll lose everything."

"I don't have anything to lose."

My father shook his head. "Why are you so ungrateful? I work my ass off to give you the upbringing I wish I had."

"All I ask is for one thing, a guitar. And you always tell me no."

"A guitar will not put food on your table. You need to study so that you can get into a good college and get a degree. It's too late for Leda now. She's already corrupted. But it's not too late for you."

"Leda got her own exhibit. Teddy told me."

"I don't care what the old cop told you. In this house, I'm the boss and what I say goes."

"Ezza told me I got talent. She said I have perfect pitch."

"So do I, and it didn't make a difference in my life."

"Why can't I have the same chance to figure things out like you?" I asked.

"I was smart enough to understand I had to get a real job. The bills piled up, and I had to take care of Leda and your mother." His eyes drifted away for a moment. "It was a nice dream. But I eventually had to wake up and see that life was more than a string of gigs that kept me on the road and away from my family."

"What makes working in a diner more real than being a musician?"

"I'm not getting into a philosophical debate with you over this. You need to improve your grades if you don't want to grow up and turn tonight into your full-time career."

"What if I do everything you ask? I'll study everyday and even work on my Greek. If I do all that, can I get a guitar?"

"If you do all that and get nothing lower than a B, I'll buy one for you myself."

"For real?"

"If you can manage to pull it off, you'll have earned it."

I was so happy with the deal I struck with my father that I leapt up from the sofa and hugged him. "Thanks, Dad."

I went up to my room and started to read a chapter in my science book. I lost my focus and fell asleep. I started to take my meds on school nights to get my homework done. On weekends, I'd surreptitiously spit them out. I liked the way my mind raced from one thought to the next. Lying in my bed late at night, a rush of energy would force me up to write a song or a poem. I disagreed with my doctor's diagnosis. I did my best work during what I called an artistic rush. I learned to trust this manic surge of inspiration even though my father wanted it obliterated from my personality. He commanded me to accept his programming, but I wanted to make waves and live life my way. I was lucky to have friends like Flipper, Ezza and Music Man who insisted nothing was wrong with me. For all their faults, they steered me towards music. Without them, I would have more than likely become one of the lost friends.

I Died for You

home   when the moon is   high. _____   I can-not stay be - cause my mom :

"I overestimated you," my own voice said back to me. "I thought you'd have figured it out by now."

"Who are you?" I asked, not able to accept what I was hearing.

"That's always been your problem, Markos. You hear, but you still don't listen."

"Who are you!"

"…You."

I dropped the cellphone.

Stella picked it up and held it to her ear. "Hello?"

After a few seconds, she repeated the greeting and gave the cellphone to Teddy who did the same and then hung up.

Teddy extended his arm to me. "Step down, Markos. You don't wanna do this. Jessie needs her father."

"Does she?" I asked.

Teddy grabbed my hand, and I pulled it away. He stepped back. "Easy."

"Where is she?" Stella yelled. "Damn it, Markos! Tell us where she is!"

"I don't know."

"What do you mean you don't know? You promised you'd bring her back to me! You promised! Goddamn you, Markos! I could push you off the roof myself!"

Teddy pulled her back. If he didn't, I believe she would have pushed me off. I never saw Stella that furious.

"You were both right," I said. "All of this is my fault."

"You can make things right by telling us where Jessie is," Teddy said.

"I would…if I knew. I'm so confused right now, I'm not even sure I'm having this conversation…or if any of this is actually happening."

"It's happening, Markos," Stella said. "Try to think. When was the last time you saw her?"

"When she came over for dinner, over two months ago." I faced Teddy. "Did I play last night?"

"You played, and you were incredible."

"What song did I open up with?"

"Reflections."

"Where did I come from before the gig?"

"You told me you spent all day practicing."

"Tell me about the woman I met."

"Samara Moon. You dug her because she reminded you of Sean Young in *Bladerunner*."

I looked at Stella. "Did I come to your lecture the night before Jessie disappeared?"

Stella placed her hand on her hip. "Right in the middle of it."

"Did I mention a dream I had about Jessie?"

"Yes. But what does that have to do with the kidnapping?"

"Something about this is all wrong."

Jessie began to sing again. Her voice seemed to come from all around me.

"You can't hear her, can you? It's all in my head. It's always been all in my head."

Sirens blared from the street below, but Jessie's singing overpowered them. I cupped my hands over my face. "I can't take this anymore! She won't stop singing!"

"She will…if you put an end to all of this now," Teddy said.

Stella looked around as though confused. "Something feels off here."

"I agree." I pointed to myself. "I'm more *off* than I've ever been."

Stella slowly walked toward me. "If this is a lie, you can stop this now and tell me what we're doing here."

"I don't know anymore. I…"

A vision came to me. Jessie held out the red lotus. "Here Daddy, take it. Take it now!"

"I can't do this anymore." I stretched out my arms to the side, wanting everything to end.

Teddy ran to me, and I let myself fall backwards. During my free-fall, everything around me slowed. I gazed a few blocks over and noticed a building on fire. Jessie returned in a vision and yelled, "Open your eyes, Daddy! Open your eyes!" She tried to hand me the red lotus, and I refused to take it. Time then accelerated, and I hit the ground. Death came, and I welcomed it with a smile.

Flashes, Clicks, and Commentary

dad will cry. ____ chil - dren have par-ents to go home to. ____ Out in

The night I'd attempted suicide wasn't worse than any previous night. All my nights were equal in their gloominess. It was Sunday, and I was hosting my show. After a mock interview with Jellyroll Morton, a caller asked me to read one of the poems from my book. I recited "The White Orchid in Her Hair." After that, I had trouble concentrating. On my break, I went up to the roof to have a smoke as I'd always done. I looked down at the street, watching the motion of the city. Life went on. All the tiny people that walked along on the sidewalk lived their own individual stories, some happy, some not, while some were simply going through the motions. None of those applied to me. I believed I had my own category. When you're depressed, you think you're unique, that no one else is suffering except you. I spent years perfecting my guitar skills so that I could play a few gigs and cut some records. I got what I wanted and traveled the world, but my family was broken. I was broken, and I didn't know how to fix myself.

Without Stella, I was missing a counterforce. I didn't do well alone. My mind drifted to places I didn't want to revisit. Donnie once told me that even though his wife drove him crazy, it was nice to have someone to come home to after a gig. He was right. After I sang the song with a similar title, I laughed and jumped off the ledge. I should have died, but an updraft cushioned my fall. A man with dark scraggly hair and a beard looked down on me and I remember thinking, *Shit, I can't even kill myself the right way*. I chortled as I mused over my father's likely response. "That's because you never plan ahead. Don't you listen to the Weather Channel? Oh that's right, you're too busy staring at yourself in the mirror to bother with the news, Elvis."

"Hold on to your sense of humor a while longer," the scraggly-haired man said as I continued to laugh in my hysteria. "An ambulance is on its way."

A rabble of people huddled around me until the medics arrived with the media close behind. When they found out I was a musician with a few releases out, I was surrounded by a fleet of flashes, clicks, and commentary. A celebrity was born, my hair was a mess, and I was still alive. I laughed all the way into the ambulance.

Stella sat on the chair next to my bed. She didn't say a word. I don't think she knew what to say.

"How's Jess?" I asked.

"I didn't tell her."

"Better tell her soon. I'm all over the news."

"If you're so concerned about Jessie, why didn't you think of her before doing this? If you succeeded, your pain would've ended, but her's would've been with her forever."

I looked away from Stella. I felt unworthy of being Jessie's father. "I wasn't thinking."

"Obviously, you weren't."

"Sorry if I'm *inconveniencing* you."

"You can act like such a child at times."

"What do you expect me to say?"

"I have no expectations of you."

"Why are you here?"

"I still care about you," Stella said.

"Then why did you leave?"

We watched a news clip of me getting rolled towards the ambulance while giving the cameramen and photographers the thumbs-up.

Stella shook her head and then faced me. "I still love you, Markos. But I just can't live with you."

"Think things will work out better with Phil?"

"Jessie told you. Is that why you did it?"

"Don't flatter yourself."

"I tried to make things work. It was you who let us go."

"Save the empty dialogue for Phil, and leave me alone. You're nothing to me now."

Stella cried.

"Get out. You're bringing me down, and I can't drop any lower than I did last night."

"See if they can prescribe you medication to get your heart to start beating again." She ran out of the room.

After I was released from the hospital, the press wouldn't leave me alone. I checked into Gray Pines where I remained for three months. I spent most of the time in my room listening to music or playing my acoustic until I could sort through whatever issue was discussed during my therapy sessions. In the midst of my self-inquiries, I'd often come up with a new song that I'd record on my digital recorder.

I put on a concert in the dayroom two times a week. The nurses loved it. Music helped cheer up the patients. Their enthusiastic reaction, especially from the ones who would more than likely be committed for the rest of their lives, motivated me to play. One kid who had suffered a breakdown after coming back from Iraq asked me to play John Lennon's,

"Imagine." In the middle of my performance, he broke down and cried. It was difficult to watch, but my doctor told me it was beneficial to release pent-up emotions. These performances fulfilled me, made me feel as though I was giving back something and making a difference in people's lives. I continue to play at Gray Pines to this day. Some of the faces are familiar, and the rest are always changing. I always leave feeling lucky to have met them.

Three days before I was released, Stella brought Jessie over for a visit. Stella was still mad at me and waited in the cafeteria while we talked.

"Are you cured, Daddy?"

"Don't worry about me. I'm fine."

"Are you sure?"

"Of course I'm sure." I pulled her onto the bed and hugged her. "I'm gonna be here for you until I'm a hundred. I promise."

"How can you promise something like that? Sometimes people die because they can't help it. Like in a plane crash or from getting sick."

"True. But I'll make my best effort to stay alive. It'll be at the top of my list of things to do."

"Even over playing the guitar?"

"Even over playing the guitar." I hugged her tighter.

After I got out, I refused to deal with Stella. My anger was so consuming that I believed distancing myself for a while was the best thing I could do for Jessie. An absent father was safer than an angry father.

Smack Dab in the Middle of

Who Knows Where

jun - gle   that   still   is   true.

The man with the scraggly hair from the day of the incident looked down at me, and I said to myself, *Shit, I can't even kill myself the right way*. Then I remembered this wasn't the incident. This was something entirely different.

"Hold on, an ambulance is on its way," the man said.

"I don't need an ambulance. My daughter was kidnapped. I have to know if she's okay. The kidnapper told me she'd be left in the back of the…"

I stopped myself when I recalled the conversation I had with myself on the roof.

Everything started getting weird the night before Jessie's kidnapping when I found myself standing on the ledge after my alarm tone rang on my cellphone. I had no idea how I got up there, but I recalled everything after that.

"Try and stay still," the man said. "You had quite a fall."

Jessie emerged from out of the crowd. "Daddy!" She kneeled down next to me.

"Jessie! You're okay!" I wanted to reach up and hug her, but I was in too much pain.

"Why did you do it again, Daddy?" Jessie cried. "You promised me you'd never do it again."

"I did it to save you."

"Why can't you hear me?"

"I hear you, Jess. I hear you."

Jessie held my hand and began to sing her song. Stella showed up and stared down at me as though entranced.

"She's here, Stella! Jessie's okay!"

"Where?" Stella looked around. Her head seemed to move in slow motion, along with everything else around me.

"She's next to me. Can't you see her? She's singing to me." I laughed from elation. "She's okay."

"Where? I can't see her."

Medics arrived and asked if I could feel various portions of my body. I felt every inch of me and requested drugs so I wouldn't have to. They hoisted me onto a gurney, and Jessie moved out of the way.

"Go to Mommy," I said.

"Where is she?" Jessie asked.

"Behind you," I said as the medics rolled me away. "Wait for my wife and daughter," I said to one of the medics.

Stella peered at me solemnly and then walked away.

"Stella, where are you going?"

She continued on without looking back.

"Stella!" I yelled. "You can't leave! Jessie's all alone!"

The medics lifted me into the ambulance and shut the doors. I tried to sit up and screamed out from the pain. One of the medics slowly eased me back down.

"I can't stay! My daughter is out there all alone! She was kidnapped. She was—"

"Please sit still," one of the medics said. "You have a concussion."

"I said I'm okay!"

The other medic placed an oxygen mask over my mouth, and I lost consciousness.

Perpetual Contest

Close your   eyes,   and dream a   dream.   A   hap - py   lit -

When I'd returned to work on Saturday, I did my best to avoid Ezza. I was relieved to find Jake's more crowded than usual. A football game over at the local high school had ended, and the victorious home team was tapping their utensils against their glasses. When they started to sing "Eye of the Tiger," I left the dining room to save my ears from the torture. They couldn't seem to agree on what key to sing in.

Staying away from Ezza was easy, but not so easy with my father who kept complaining about how slowly I moved. I wanted to drop the bus tray and tell him to clean the tables himself, but my desire for a guitar forced me to deal with the humiliation as he yelled at me in front of the waitstaff. When a swarm of customers overtook him at the register, I slipped out to have a smoke.

Ezza followed me out. "Why have you been avoiding me?"

"Didn't know you were here. It's packed, in case you haven't noticed."

"Sorry if I hurt your feelings."

"You didn't." I lit my cigarette and took a drag.

"Why did you steal a car?"

"Who told you?"

"Your father. He asked me to tutor you in science and history."

"I don't want your help."

Ezza sat on a milk crate and lit a cigarette as Dottie came out for her break.

"What did I miss?" she asked.

"Ezza not minding her business."

"What's bugging you today?" Dottie asked.

"All these questions."

"Your father is being a little tough on you today. I'm gonna throw you some extra cash for your troubles."

"Count me in," Ezza said.

"I don't need charity," I said.

My father opened the door and pointed at me. "What the hell are you doing out here?" He spotted the cigarette I tossed on the floor when I heard the door open. "Is that yours?"

"It's mine," Dottie said.

"You should know better, Dot."

Dottie picked up the cigarette and extinguished it in the ashtray.

My father threw a dish towel at me. "Leave the flirting for after work, and get back inside. There are four tables that need to be bussed, and I got a line of people waiting to be seated."

I put my apron away and went to get my tips from the waitstaff. When I approached Ezza, she walked off.

I followed her into the kitchen and extended my hand to her, palm up.

"I'm not paying until you listen," she said.

"If I'm late, my father will give me hell."

Ezza reached into her pocket, and I noticed track marks on her inner elbow. She handed me my money.

"I'm thinking of having a party," Ezza said.

Dottie walked over. "What's the occasion?"

"Just an appreciate-your-friends party."

"Sounds like fun. You going, Markos?" Dottie asked.

"I'm busy."

"I never told you the date," Ezza said.

"My father grounded me."

"I'll have it next Friday night. I'm tutoring you then, so you'll be there anyway."

"I already told you I'm not coming."

"Stop being rude," Dottie said. "You're starting to sound like your father."

"If I was my father, you'd both be fired for nagging me too much." I walked away.

I spent the rest of the afternoon over at Flipper's. He taught me some chords on the guitar and played me a few records in the back room where Music Man was reading a book on Carl Jung.

Flipper put on a John Coltrane record. "If I spent all these years practicing rather than hanging out playing pool, I'd probably play guitar as perfectly as Coltrane played sax."

Music Man shifted his eyes away from his book. "Pool isn't your problem. You spend more time polishing the counter than practicing the only three scales that you know."

"And if you weren't always high on something, you wouldn't keep screwing up the first chord in the chorus of 'Smoke on the Water,'" Flipper said.

Music Man flashed him the finger, and I laughed.

Flipper glared at me. "There's nothing funny about murdering a Deep Purple classic." He threw a jazz fake book at Music Man. "All the Jungian philosophy will never reproduce the brain cells you lost." He turned to me, and put his hands on my shoulders. "Observe, absorb, integrate, and experience all you can here. Music Man has an IQ of one-seventy-five, and all he does is sit in this room, read, and get high. I'd shoot myself if that was me. I don't know how he does it."

Music Man put his book on his lap. "It's *because* I have a one-seventy-five IQ that I do nothing. While the rest of the conformist sheeple kill themselves over some job so that they can make lots of money, I do what I want because I don't care about any of that shit. That's all it is…shit. Shit, shit, shit. It's as worthless to the body as money is worthless to the mind. In the end, we all die and take nothing from this ball of vacuous tomfoolery with us." He returned to reading his book.

Flipper shook his head. "Always makes sense when he says that. But man, if I was him, I still don't think that would be enough for me." Flipper picked up an aerosol can and re-spritzed the room.

I thought a lot like Music Man. All the effort we put into our life knowing we're eventually going to die made working seem pointless. Most people seemed to want to leave some kind of legacy thinking that'll somehow make them immortal, but they'd still be dead in the end. I didn't want to wait until I died to be remembered. I wanted to live and experience as much as I could before I died.

The customer bell rang. Flipper got up, and I followed him out. I had to get home and study to honor the deal I made with my father.

Gus stood at the counter holding a pack of guitar strings. He didn't seem pleased by my presence. "What are you doing here?" he asked.

"Listening to some tunes." I knew Gus lied about hanging in the back with Flipper and Music Man. They told me they never met him before. Gus was easy to forget if you didn't know him.

"You can come back tomorrow if you like," Flipper said to me. "I'll start teaching you the minor chords."

Gus paid for the strings and followed me out.

We sat on the swings in the playground near our houses, and I wanted to do a hit, but I didn't trust Gus. I suspected he'd probably run straight to my father.

"I don't get it. You stole a guitar from them, and they invite you to hang out?"

"I'm not as annoying as you."

"What do you do back there?"

"Thought you hung out with them."

"I haven't for a long time."

"Flipper said he never met you."

"No surprise. They're stoned all the time. It's hard to believe Music Man remembers where he keeps his guitar."

"Flipper doesn't touch drugs, and I like Music Man. We think alike."

"How would you know that? He never talks."

"He does to me."

"Whatever. I don't have time to hang out with those losers because I don't have time to waste. I'm learning how to play jazz so that I can try out for the jazz band next year. They say whoever gets in wins a music scholarship to college."

I hated to be copied, especially by Gus who wanted to be the next Yngwie Malmsteen before I played him the Wes Montgomery album Flipper lent me.

"That's the kind of music I'm gonna play when I get my guitar," I said.

"It's going to take you years to get to my level. You'll have to learn the basics first."

"Flipper says I pick things up fast. I got perfect pitch."

"You have perfect pitch?"

"Yeah. Don't you?"

"I got relative pitch. You don't need perfect pitch to be a good musician."

"I know. Flipper told me that too."

"It'll help you learn songs faster, but it can make you lazy and think you don't need to learn music theory. I can teach you the modes when you get your guitar. If you learn all of them, you'll be able to solo over everything."

"You'd do that?"

"Of course I would."

"Thanks, Gus."

There were rare moments Gus could be friendly, and this was one of them. He really meant it when he said he wanted to help. Despite that, his smug attitude about me having to take years to get as good as he was lingered on my mind, and it made me want to prove him wrong. The contest between us started that day and never ended because neither of us stopped competing.

Flowers and Flames

sum-mer in my jun-gle dream._____ Where no one ev - er_____ has to sle

I tried to move my body, but it wouldn't respond. Pain surged in my abdomen with such ferocity that I wanted to scream, but all I could do was accept what was happening. I cried, but I don't think I produced any tears. Certain parts of me still worked. My breath entered and left through my nostrils, and my heart beat so hard that I thought it was going to bust out of my chest. A breathy drone entered my ears, but I couldn't recognize the pitch. It terrified me enough to reconsider my belief in hell. A wave of intense heat followed, and I breathed in deeply. When I exhaled, I pushed forward by sheer will with the intent of propelling myself out of my body. The movement was fluidic, intense and felt as though I was applying physical force. On each subsequent exhale, I'd push a little more. I did this until I lost complete sensation of my body. I pumped out my final breath until my lungs were expelled of air. I was liberated from my prison body after a loud explosion made my ears ring in F-sharp.

I opened my eyes with my ears still ringing. Jessie knelt beside me with her red lotus and sang to me.

"Thank you for staying with me," I said, thinking I was dying.

"Keep listening, Daddy."

"I will."

She began to sing again.

Steve showed up and stared down at me. "For Pete's sake Markos, what's it gonna take for you to understand what I'm telling you?"

Steve opened a small box and from out of it flew a firefly. It flew over me and spun around, expanding into a large golden spiral of light that descended and surrounded me. The glow was so bright that I closed my eyes. A baby's cries made me open them again. I was now lying in bed staring at Stella's backside.

"Your turn to change her," she mumbled half-asleep.

I sat up and stared at Jessie's bassinet. "Am I dead?"

"No, but you will be if you don't get up now. I've been up four times in a row already, and I have to get up in three hours."

I walked over to the bassinet and looked down at Jessie. I picked her up and nestled her in my arms, slowly forgetting everything that happened to me. After I changed her, I lay Jessie next to me on the bed.

"Put her back in her bassinet, Markos."

"I will."

"Don't fall asleep with her on the bed. It's dangerous. You can roll over her."

"I won't." I pulled Jessie close to me and kissed her cheek.

After she fell asleep, I placed her back in the bassinet and returned to bed. I put my arm around Stella and as I was about to fall asleep, I was thrown onto my back. I opened my eyes and Samara Moon was on top of me, kissing me. I was going along with it until I smelled flowers. I rolled on top of her and yelled, "Where am I?

"Why did you do it?" she asked. "Seems like you have lots of positive things happening in your life."

I sat up and gasped at the scene all around me. Red flowers of every imaginable type filled the room. Orchids, lotuses, and many other types of flowers I couldn't identify were everywhere, on the dresser, floor, windowsill, and a vine of roses carpeted the ceiling. It was both eerie and stunning. *You're not in New York anymore, Markos. You're dead.* You'd think I would have figured this out way before now, but it took a room full of flowers to make me recognize the obvious. Death is funny that way. And now that I figured out the song, I had to learn how to improvise over it.

Samara was no longer in the bed, and Stella was gone. I wasn't surprised. I was the one who was dead. I took a moment to survey the florist shop from the other side, and a poetic line came to me: *Red flowers awaken my mind. I smell the life I left behind.* I went to inspect the bassinet. A red lotus lay inside, and I picked it up. A strong floral scent entered my nostrils, and the room erupted into flames. They quickly dissipated, and I found myself standing on the ledge of my apartment with my cellphone alarm tone playing "Crazy People." This was exactly how everything started two nights ago, and I wasn't in the mood for a rerun. One name came to my mind again: Gus. He was somehow connected to what was happening. I thought this whole elaborate setup might have something to do with making amends for the past. I was dead, and I couldn't think of any other reason he would show up in my afterlife.

I got off the subway at Christopher Street and when I made it to the street level, the sidewalk was jammed with pedestrians.

I laughed to myself as I thought, *The night is young, the moon is full, I'm dead, and the Metropolitan Transportation Authority is fully operational.* The city not only never slept; it never died. Two more lines came to me as I walked: *Each step toward my end, my soul will ascend the dream.*

I laughed at the religious reference. I never believed in a soul. Even after my purported death, I didn't believe in the afterlife. Whatever happened to me seemed like a natural process, and I surmised that what I perceived as my identity was residual energy that would soon dissipate. Such a thought didn't scare me, but I was stricken with grief over not seeing Jessie again. Was she abducted or was the kidnapping an intricate hallucination? I couldn't answer one way or the other. Drivers honked their horns on the street, pedestrians crossed the road, and patrons sipped their coffees at their tables as if it were any other night. I couldn't figure out why they didn't disappear like my injuries. Why such a serpentine production? I stopped in front of a store with a pink neon sign that read, *Psychic Readings*. It reminded me of my one and only visit to a psychic.

Kyria Thassoula

Where wolves and ti - gers and pan - thers creep. _____ I close my

While our mothers were engaged in their coffee talk, Gus and I played rummy 500. He'd spent most of the game bragging about a new acoustic his father promised to buy him for Christmas.

"You should see it. It's got seven strings," Gus said.

"Sounds cool, but it won't make *you* cool." I chuckled as I picked up a card.

"You won't be laughing when we're all grown up. You'll be living on the streets while I'll be playing on all the big concert stages of the world."

"In your dreams. No one would pay money to watch a nerd play guitar. Remember what happened at the school talent show? Barely anyone clapped after you finished."

The comment hurt Gus. I could see it in his face, and I regretted saying it, but I didn't apologize. Taking jabs at each other was the norm for us. I was meaner than usual that day as I had left several messages for Ezza on her voicemail, and she never called me back. I missed her companionship, the way she laughed, and even the way she slapped her hand on the table to get me to pay attention.

When I heard the opening theme to *Oprah Winfrey* I threw my hand, face down, on the table. "I'm getting out of here."

"You'll do anything to get out of losing."

I showed Gus my hand. "Three aces and two kings, and I only need thirty more points to get to five-hundred." I slammed the cards on the table and pushed back my chair.

"Where are you going?"

"To shoot some pool."

"I'm coming."

On our way to the PAL, we stopped in front of a psychic walk-in shop run by Kyria Thassoula, an old one-eyed Greek gypsy who kept to herself. Most of the people within our community feared her. If they met her on the street, they'd walk in the opposite direction to avoid her. The patch over Kyria Thassoula's right eye ignited superstitions and frightened the older women of the church who believed she had a demonic eye. They insisted she covered it to keep her identity as a witch a secret. If Kyria Thassoula lifted the patch in your presence, you'd be cursed for life.

My mother had the evil eye symbol everywhere, on her jewelry, on her keychain, over the headboard of her bed, and one even hung from her rearview mirror. She believed people turned demonic once they allowed themselves to succumb to envy. My mother once told me, "Envy is the root of evil. It'll rot your insides if you don't cure it in time. And it works both ways. You can be the giver or receiver. I don't want you on either side, so don't act like a big shot. Always be modest about your successes."

Gus was never modest about his successes, which is why I relished watching him tremble as he stood in front of the door of Kyria Thassoula's storefront. He hesitated to enter, believing in her witch persona. I pushed Gus out of the way, opened the door and went inside. He crept in behind me. A red bulb lit the reception area, and in the corner of the room sat a pot filled with a small tree. Evil eye symbols hung from the branches.

"Your mother would love that," Gus said.

"Don't give her any ideas. Our house looks more like a church than the church."

"Want to get a reading?" he asked.

"Got no money on me, and even if I did, I wouldn't give it to Kyria Thassoula. She's a fake."

"How do you know?"

"My father told me about her, and I've seen her at Jake's. She sits at the counter and talks to her coffee cup. She even puts her ear over it cuz she thinks it's talking back to her."

"Who cares if she's a fake? I always wanted to get a reading." Gus turned his head up to the sign that read *$5.00 per reading*. "I have a twenty on me. I'll pay if you want."

We walked up to the counter, and Gus tapped the call bell.

"*Ena Lepto, parakalo,*" Kyria Thassoula called out. She came out through a beaded curtain. Her fire-red hair cascaded out from underneath a black scarf adorned with small decorative gold coins. "I know you," she said to me with a thick Greek accent. "You're Simon's boy, Markos. I've seen you working at Jake's." She faced Gus. "I have no idea who you are." She rubbed the palms of her wrinkled hands together, and the bangles on both her forearms jangled. "What can I do for you boys?"

"We want a reading," Gus said.

Kyria Thassoula stretched out her bony fingers to receive her payment. Gus handed over the money. "I'll go first." He followed her into the reading room.

I sat on a stained velvet couch in the reception area. Think it used to be yellow. It reminded me of the garish furniture in my grandmother's house, minus the plastic slipcovers. The wall was filled with Greek scenic photographs. My eyes stopped at a picture of the tower in Thessaloniki, the city from where my parents' family originated. I missed Greece. I was given more freedom whenever we visited. My parents permitted me to ramble outside late at night as they weren't afraid I'd be abducted. On weekends, I'd hit the amusement park on the waterfront with my friends. We'd always hook up with some local girls and hit a cafe afterwards. We wouldn't get back until past midnight. I was even allowed to have a beer with my dinner. The moment I returned home, the late-night jaunts and beer became a distant memory.

"When in America, we do as the Americans do...we lock our children in the house to keep them safe from all the perverts," my father would always say. I found it amusing how he classified Americans as being different from himself even though he was born in America.

While I waited for Gus to finish his reading, I flipped through the only English magazine I found: A five year old edition of *Muscle & Fitness*. As I drooled over a picture of Cory Everson, Gus walked out with Kyria Thassoula.

"Do I get a refund?" Gus asked.

Kyria Thassoula pointed to a no refund sign on the wall and snapped her finger at me. "It's your turn."

I followed her into a small room in the back. She had a candle lit at the center of the table. The smell of myrrh permeated the room and made me feel as if I was in church.

"Give me both your hands," Kyria Thassoula said.

"Why?"

She waved her hand quickly towards herself, and her bangles clanked together. "Come on, come on. I do not have all day."

I did as she asked, and Kyria Thassoula clamped down on my hands with her cold, damp grip. She closed her left eye and remained silent for about a minute and then cleared her throat. "You will travel the world with a girl whose name starts with *S* or *J*."

"I don't know anyone with a *S* or *J*."

Kyria Thassoula's eye shot open. "I did not tell you when. This can happen when you are all grown up. Now *shhh*. I do not like interruptions while I am reading." She closed her eye and continued her reading. "You will find success with *S* or *J*, but an accident will follow."

"What kind of accident?"

"I see an…*P.*"

"How can a letter cause an accident?"

"Shhh! *Skase esi!*" Kyria Thassoula opened her eye. "That is what I see. Now be quiet, or I will stop reading." She closed her eye again. "A woman will help you through this difficult time, and she will die, but you will be stronger for knowing her. *Much* stronger." She squeezed her eye tighter. "I see…a red flower." She pulled her hands away and made the sign of the cross.

"What do you see?" I asked in anticipation.

"Nothing else."

"What a rip-off." I got up.

Kyria Thassoula pointed at me. "You must humble yourself. Do not let pride destroy you."

I sat back down.

"I see many good outcomes for you, but I also see many bad ones."

"Can the future be changed?" I asked.

"If you can stop and take the time to think before you act, maybe you can miss some of the bad outcomes." She blew out the candle. "We are finished."

"Why do you wear a patch over your eye?" I asked.

I expected Kyria Thassoula to tell me to mind my business. Instead, she slowly lifted the patch to reveal a yellow eye that resembled a cat's eye."

"It is easier to wear this. I do not like when people stare at me or when children laugh." She placed the patch back over her eye.

"Next time you come to Jake's, I won't laugh."

"You are a good boy, Markos."

"I still don't believe in any of this."

"Then why did you come here?"

"This was Gus's idea."

"Your friend is empty. I have seen empty containers before, and I do not trust them. Be careful. The empties look to the full containers to help fill them, and they can sometimes take too much and steal your soul."

The pronouncement rattled me. Kyria Thassoula had a way of delivering a reading that made you believe her as she spoke to you. Her spell was broken after I left the reading room and met up with Gus.

"What did she tell you?" Gus asked.

"Nothing anyone couldn't have made up, but she did show me her eye."

"Really? What did it look like?"

"A cat's eye."

"Wonder why she hides it."

"She doesn't like people laughing at her."

"What else did she say?"

The way Gus peered at me made me feel sorry for him. "Nothing."

After a few games of pool, I went home and waited for Ezza to call, but she never did. Even her cheery greeting message never came on. I sneaked out after my parents fell asleep and headed to her apartment. Either she wasn't around or wasn't answering the door. I spent the next couple of hours tootling around the Village. I got Ezza a mood ring I planned to give to her in my next tutoring session. A party sounded like a fun way to make up. I also got tired of smoking my dope behind the bleachers, talking about rock bands I no longer had interest in, with lost friends who depressed me more than I already was. Back at home, things weren't any better. I felt as though the walls were closing in all around me. The smell of my mother's cooking even depressed me. All the familiarities that once comforted me became reminders of a life I found unsatisfying.

Ezza was the only one I knew who could pull me out of this mood. That looked less likely to happen when I showed up to work the following weekend.

"Ezza quit last night," Dottie said. "She walked out in the middle of her shift."

"Stop with the gossip Dot, and get back to work," my father said. "Thanks to Ezza, we're minus one waitress." He glanced at me. "And a tutor. We'll have to find someone else to help you."

If I thought my father would understand, I would've told him to forget about finding another tutor. Ezza was irreplaceable. She became more than a tutor to me. She opened my mind to new music and philosophies and made me want to learn. Before that, I never cared about anything beyond playing Donkey Kong over at the Fun Palace. Now she was gone, and I felt all alone again.

Ghost of a Chance

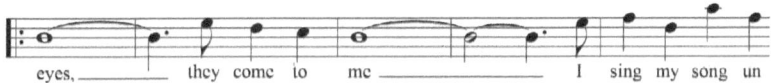

eyes, _____ they come to me _____ I sing my song un

Gus wouldn't open the door to his apartment, so I got out my credit card and let myself in. When he saw me, he ran behind the couch. "Get away from me! You're not real, you're not real, you're not real," he said in a triplet-beat.

I plodded through a heap of newspapers. "You should think about getting a housekeeper."

"You died. I saw them take you." Gus edged back towards his desk. "What do you want from me? Why are you haunting me?"

"I need you to come back down to Earth, or wherever we are so that we can have a talk."

"You're a ghost."

"I know."

"You have to be a ghost."

"I said, I know."

"I can't think of another explanation."

"Stop talking for a minute and listen to what I'm saying."

"You should be dead."

"I am dead."

"Why can I see you?"

"I don't know. I'm not even sure I'm seeing you."

Gus waved his hand. "Here I am."

"Maybe I have to make peace with you."

"I thought the same thing, but now I…" He slapped the top of the desk. "No! That still doesn't sound right!"

"Did you take Jessie?"

"I told you I had nothing to do with your daughter's kidnapping."

"I need to know what's going on here. Was she taken, or am I making all of this up?"

"Are you saying you don't know why you're haunting me?"

"I was hoping you could answer that for me."

"I'm not saying another word until I know for sure what you are." He opened a drawer, pulled out a gun and aimed it at me.

I reached in my pocket to grab the gun I took from Teddy, but I no longer had it. "We don't have to do this."

"I think we do." Gus shot me, and I fell to the floor. He paced back and forth. "Question answered; you're dead."

Blood spilled out of a wound on my abdomen. "Then why am I bleeding?"

Gus pushed his gun casually towards me. "You're not bleeding."

I pointed to my abdomen, now unsure of my current status. "What do you call this?"

"The output of an active imagination. No wonder you were so good at improvising, and why I struggled so hard and failed to sound as original. Pagels said I was a great technician, but I had to loosen up more in my solos. I couldn't trust the chaos. Couldn't trust myself to restructure the notes into a beautiful solo."

"Can we put our competition on hold until an ambulance gets here?"

"There's no one you can call to get you out of this one, Markos. You jumped off the same building twice and died this time around."

I leaned against a recliner and hoisted myself to my feet.

"How long will it take you to figure it out?" Gus asked. "Then again, I'm no better. Is that why you're here? To get me to admit I was wrong about you? Fine. I admit it. Now go away."

He walked to the door and opened it, but I wouldn't budge. *Am I haunting Gus? Am I a ghost?*

"Why aren't you moving?" he asked.

"I can't leave until I know what you want from me."

"What I want? You're the one who's haunting me. Go back to wherever it is you exist." He pointed to the hallway.

"I would if I could. This is worse than when we were forced to hang out together."

Gus lifted his gun and pressed the barrel against the side of his head. "If I can't get rid of your ghost, I'll get rid of myself. It's not like I have anything to lose. My father was right about me. I'm a failure."

I ran to Gus as he pulled the trigger. The gun fired, but he remained unharmed.

I stared down at my now uninjured chest and Gus staggered backwards, almost tripping over the recliner. "No…" he cried. "It can't be true." He touched the side of his head where the bullet should have entered. "I'm dead too."

"Nice try. I'm not falling for any of this."

"Who else do you think you're speaking to?"

I probed Gus, attempting to ascertain if it was him, but I had no way to verify anything here.

"No, no, no. I refuse to believe any of this," Gus said.

"Do you know how I got here?" I asked, not believing Gus's claim. "Why am I haunting you?"

"Don't have time. I'm going to be late for work."

I crossed my arms. "If you're dead, you don't have to go to work."

"Remember when I told you there's nothing to ponder in produce?"

"Yeah."

"There is tonight. And in the event that I'm wrong, and I'm making all this up, I don't want to get fired. I have bills to pay."

"Can we discuss this after you get off?"

"Sure." He tossed his hands in the air. "Why not?" He headed to the door. "There's a box of my mother's cookies in the kitchen. Help yourself, but don't eat them all." He left.

I thought about all my interactions with Gus since the night he turned up at my gig, along with all the possible ways we could have ended up here together. I came up with nothing and was forced to admit that Gus wasn't any more real than the flowers in the bedroom. He was a phantom, like everything else in this netherworld. Unsure of what to do next, I ate all the cookies and waited for inspiration to hit and tell me where to go next. A poem came to me instead. I sat at Gus's desk and jotted it down. After I finished, I laughed at the notion of publishing another poetry book. Death is funny that way.

What a Difference My Death Makes

der a sha-dy ban-yan tree.＿＿＿ A qui-et place where＿ I can sta

I got tired of waiting around for Gus's phantom and figured I'd pass the time by visiting my usual hangouts. I came across Cro who sat at a sidewalk cafe watching people walk by. It was his select method of finding inspiration. I pulled out a seat and joined him.

"What's up, bro?" he asked.

"I haven't the slightest clue."

"You'll figure it out, I'm sure."

"I'm not so sure. Meeting up with you should've given it away."

"You're as fast as a bullet on guitar but slow as snails when it comes to seeing the obvious."

"If you don't mind, I've had enough criticism tonight."

A waiter brought me a coffee and set it down in front of me.

"What do I do now?" I picked up four sugar packs and tore them open.

"Whatever you want."

I poured the sugar into the coffee and stirred. "Is this heaven?"

Cro laughed.

"Hell?"

"Thought you were an atheist."

"I am…was…" I rubbed my forehead. "I'm not sure what I am anymore."

"And you're never gonna figure things out by talking to dead people."

"But I am dead."

"Mmm. Sort of."

I shook my head. "I'm getting nothing here tonight. I might as well be talking to myself." I sipped my coffee.

"If I was a game-show host, I'd declare you a winner for that answer."

"I am…talking to myself?"

Cro tilted his head to the side and shrugged his shoulders. "For the most part."

I took another sip of coffee and examined the cup. "This is no different from the coffee I've had when I was alive."

"Death is funny that way." He fluttered his eyebrows.

Considering I said the same thing to myself only a while ago, I had to assume I was talking to myself. What I couldn't figure out was when all of this began. When did I die and how did it happen? I still didn't know if Jessie was kidnapped. Not knowing her fate either way made me more anxious than before.

I gazed at Cro. It had been years since our last conversation. He became despondent after he found out about his brother and stopped sketching. He got evicted from his motel room for not paying, and each time I tried to offer him assistance, he'd push me away. He wouldn't even accept money or shelter from me. A police officer on horseback found his body on a park bench in Central Park. He froze to death in the middle of the night. It was good to catch up with Cro again, even if it was my own representation of him.

I watched my sister paint. As in my previous reality, her eyes didn't wander far from the canvas. While she created art, I played "Lulu's Back in Town" on my guitar. After I finished the song, I stopped and surveyed the room. "I'm either dead or insane. I never considered that one." Something sounded strange about my voice. It sounded higher in pitch.

Leda stopped painting and stared at me. "What do you see?"

"Light rays sent to my brain tell me I'm watching my sister paint."

Leda continued working. "Every time I complete a painting, I sit in awe. Not of my work, but of the place from which it came. An image pops into my mind, and all I have to do is get my brush and paint what I see. I never attempt to alter it into something other than what's presented to me because if I do, the picture disappears, and I never get it back."

I appraised Leda's painting. It was another one of me. I was looking into a guitar shaped mirror. The reflection staring back was a younger version of myself with a cross painted on my face.

"Seeing things as they are is like looking at one of those pictures within a picture," Leda said. "When your eyes finally adjust to the hidden image, there's a sense of recognition."

I clutched my forehead. "Even in death your art confuses me."

"See yourself through your eyes." Leda pointed at the younger version of myself. "Not his. You'll find your peace then." She turned to me. "Now get out. I got work to do."

The painting hypnotized me, and I couldn't move.

"Why are you still here?"

"I don't know where to go." Immediately after I said that, I knew who I had to visit next. And if she was home, I'd have a clearer understanding of what happened to me.

S

Something's Gotta Give

Sit   with   my   friends   and   play   all   day.

My father entered my room while I lay on my bed listening to Wes play "Out of Nowhere." He sat close to me, which made me uneasy. The only other time he'd done this was on the day my maternal grandfather died of a massive stroke. I was closer to him than my father. On Sundays after church, he'd take me to the neighborhood park and tell me about the good old days. He used to manage a night club where a lot of the famous big bands played, and he had personalized autographs from Duke Ellington, Gene Krupa, Count Basie and Buddy Rich. I envied the time he lived in. The way he'd describe it made me think I was born in the wrong era. "Back then men were men and ladies were ladies," he'd always tell me. "These days, you sometimes can't figure out which one is which."

The frown on my father's face told me my birthday was going to be a day of mourning.

"I'm afraid I have some sad news about Ezza."

I couldn't speak as I sensed what he was about to tell me. I pictured the track marks on Ezza's arm when she gave me my tip.

"She died last night," my father said.

"How?" I tried to hold myself back from crying, but I failed.

My father hugged me. "It was a drug overdose." He leaned back. "Has she ever done drugs in front of you?"

I shook my head, and my father put his hand on my shoulder.

"I know you and Ezza were close. She thought you were a smart boy and was very proud of you for all the hard work you've done."

"She said that?"

"And also that if you applied yourself, you could accomplish anything you set your mind to."

"Is there gonna be a funeral?" I asked.

"Not here. It'll probably be held in her hometown, wherever that is."

"Corvallis."

My father got up. "If you need to talk, I'll be downstairs."

He left, and I cried all day, took a break for dinner and then continued until I fell asleep.

I spent the next few days high and in bed. My father must've grasped I wasn't handling Ezza's death well. He eased up on our deal and let me sleep as much as I wanted. My mother brought dinner to my room each night, and I'd finish it off with a few hits from my pipe. I'd blow the smoke out the window, but I didn't care if I got caught. I didn't care much about anything. I got lost in a thick fog of narcotics to keep myself from cycling over my last conversation with Ezza and how I wished I said yes to her party invitation. Ezza once told me if a person dies before you have a chance to make amends, it's therapeutic to visualize a conversation with him or her. "Imagine you're talking with them," she said. "Then, depending on your situation, you can tell them you forgive them, that you're sorry, or both."

In the next few drug-induced hallucinations, I pictured Ezza's large eyes peeking at me through her librarian glasses.

"Markos Adamidis, you did this to yourself. All you had to do was say yes to my invitation, and you wouldn't have needed to call me."

"I'd still miss you."

"True, but you'd get over me the next time another pretty girl tells you what a handsome and brilliant guy you are."

"I'll never forget you. You'll always be on my mind."

"Guess that sort of makes me immortal. In Greece they built statues of their goddesses. How will you honor me?"

"I'll figure out a way."

"You better. I put up with a lot of shit from you."

"Not too much."

"Why are we doing this?" she asked.

"You told me this would make me feel better."

"Is it working?"

"Not really?"

"Why?"

"I know it's not really you."

Ezza would never have said any of the above, but in my videogame imagination anything seemed possible. Although I thought the exercise didn't work, I caught myself laughing during the exchange.

I continued the internal dialogue for a few more days because when I was lucid, I didn't know what I wanted anymore. Even music seemed trivial. Maybe Music Man had a point. Why bother with anything if we're going to die anyway? I thought back to the track marks on Ezza's arm and wondered when she started shooting. The marks didn't disturb me when

I saw them. Even more troubling was the fact that they made me want to try shooting. It was something new to do to get me out of my chronic boredom.

Lots of people say they're bored, but there's a point where it becomes pathological. I was bored with drugs, bored with girls, bored with video games, bored with life. On the day of my fifteenth birthday, I felt as old and tired as my father. Death, boredom, my depressing home life, and my unrealized dreams all cycled through my mind, and I couldn't find an off switch. No matter what direction I searched, my thoughts trapped me somewhere between melancholia and mediocrity. A lackluster existence that made me constantly ask myself, *is this it?*

On the seventh night of my grieving, before I drifted off to sleep, I decided to run away to some place warm, maybe near a beach. I closed my eyes and could smell the salty air, the warm sand under my bare feet and waves crashing on the surf. I kept the imagery in my mind until I fell asleep.

I woke up to my mother singing her choir music. She always sang while she cleaned the house. After I almost fell back asleep, she entered my room and ripped off my covers.

"Rise and shine Sleeping Beauty, today is a brand new day for you."

I pulled the covers over my face, and she pulled them off the bed.

"I'm still tired," I said.

"Tired? You slept for seven days and seven nights. Are you a sleeping prophet?" My mother threw the sheets on the floor and sat down on the bed. "You can't stay here forever."

"I won't."

"When will you be getting up?"

"Soon."

"When is soon?"

"Tomorrow."

"Why is tomorrow more special than today?"

"I still have things to sort through."

"How about the bookshelf downstairs? It can use some organizing."

I glanced up at the ceiling and traced the cracks with my eyes. More seemed to have formed since I last counted them the night before.

"A package came for you," my mother said.

"I'll open it later."

"It's from Ezza."

I sprang out of bed like a jack rabbit and ran out of my room.

"Wish you would move that fast with your chores," she yelled.

❖

I stared at a large, rectangular-shaped box.

"Hurry. The suspense is killing me," my mother said.

"In a minute." I nervously stared at the package.

"You may not be curious"—my mother handed me a knife —"but I am."

I cut a slit through the packing tape and lifted up the flaps. My heart almost jetted out of my chest when I removed a white Vintage '76 Fender Strat from the box. It was in mint condition.

"She must've spent a small fortune on this," my mother said with tears in her eyes.

I read the attached card aloud. "You sang the blues so well, I can't wait to hear you play them. Happy birthday. Love… Ezza." I spilled a few tears as I held the guitar in my hands. It embodied the relationship between Ezza and me. She truly cared for me, and I had no idea how to thank her, how to honor her for everything she'd done for me.

"Why couldn't I see you as she did?" My mother cried.

"It's okay, Mom."

"No, it isn't. I have perfect vision, but I'm blind when it comes to you and Leda."

I hugged my mother, but she remained troubled. She went up to her room, refusing to come out until the next moring. It didn't seem like such a big deal at the time, but my mother was on her own journey, and her destination would bring us to places we never imagined we'd visit.

I'll Never Be the Same

Trust in me and fol-low a-long, when ev-er you hear m

I knocked on the door with a burning anticipation in my stomach. It erupted into a wave of bliss when Ezza opened the door.

She embraced me. "I'm so glad you changed your mind."

I picked her up and carried her into the apartment. She was heavier than I anticipated.

"You're a strong kid."

"Who are you calling a kid? I'm older than you now."

"Maybe in dog years."

I put her down and inspected myself in the wall mirror. A fourteen-year-old version of myself was staring back at me. I glanced back at Ezza. "Are you really you?"

She eyed herself in the mirror. "Sure as hell looks like me."

"Am I dead?" I stared at my youthful face as though I expected an answer to come.

"If you were dead, we wouldn't be talking," Ezza said.

"If I were alive, I'd be a lot older than I am now." I studied my reflection, unconvinced by my assertion.

"Did you dream you were in the movie *Big* again?"

"Again? I never had that dream."

"Oh…right. My dream, only in reverse."

"Either I'm engaged in one of my bizarre drug-induced dialogues with you or…" I clasped Ezza's arm and probed her elbow. There weren't any track marks.

"Are you high?" Ezza asked. "Because if you are, I want you out of here."

"I'm not high." I walked over to Ezza's record collection and picked up a Styx album, *The Grand Illusion*. "I'm not here. None of this is real." I slipped the record back in its proper place. "I get all that now." I stared in the direction of the mirror, afraid to peer into it again. "But why do I look like I'm fourteen years old?"

"You *are* fourteen."

"I'm really fourteen?" I asked. *This is all a hallucination, Markos, caused by a heavy intake of drugs. You're still fourteen. Everything that came after never happened.* I smiled in relief and slumped onto the couch.

Ezza sat beside me.

"I missed you, Ezz."

"It's been less than a week."

"A week is a lifetime to a kid my age." I reached into my pocket and pulled out my pipe.

"What do you think you're doing?"

I laughed. "You ought to know. You got me started."

Tears emerged from out of Ezza's eyes. "I didn't want this for you."

"I know. You keep saying that." I took out my baggie of dope.

"You can't smoke in here."

"Come on Ezz, you always say that, and you end up letting me."

"Not this time."

I unzipped the baggie.

"If you open that, you're going to have to leave."

"If you're out, I can give you a hit."

"I don't do drugs."

"Since when?" I peered into her eyes until the picture within a picture finally cleared into a distinguishable image. I glanced down at my empty hands and said with a deeper voice, "Guess dope doesn't exist in the afterlife."

"Why did you come over?" Ezza asked.

"The last time we met, I wish I told you how I felt about you. How I was lucky to have met you."

She smiled at me. "Why are you so hard on yourself?"

"You saved my life, and I should've been around to save yours."

"You can only save your own life, Markos." She pointed her hand towards the door. "It's time you go and do it."

"I don't want to go just yet."

"Sometimes the choice isn't up to you."

"I'm making it mine now." I grabbed Ezza and kissed her, and she pushed me away.

"This isn't what you want," she said.

"It's what I always wanted."

"And then you grew up."

"I never forgot you. I even named my guitar Ezza."

"That's very flattering."

"But I much prefer the real one. We couldn't be together alive, but there's nothing holding us back now."

"How about everything that came afterwards? Can you forget all that?"

I gazed up at the mirror and saw Jessie singing to me.

Close your eyes and dream a dream.
A happy little summer in my jungle dream.
Where no one ever has to sleep.

Where wolves and tigers and panthers creep.

"I cared about you a lot, Markos, but I don't recognize you anymore," Ezza said.

I stood and examined myself in the mirror. My age returned along with all the memories and desires I amassed through the years. Ezza came over to me, and I hugged her. "Thanks, Esmerelda." I kissed her softly on the lips and left.

Dancing Flames

sing my song.   Hear my call, you'll ne‑ver go wrong,   as long as you hear my   song.   I

I stood in front of what used to be my home and contemplated whether I should visit Stella. The light in her bedroom glowed as though beckoning me to the front door. Memories of the time I lived here awoke. Crickets sang in the trees, Mr. and Mrs. can't-remember-their-name were in the middle of their weekly screaming match, and the neighborhood dogs barked for no particular reason other than to keep me up at night. Cats fought nearby, and I recalled how their screeches sounded like music to my ears during my first heroin high. I would have enjoyed playing a part in this death theater during that period of my life. Without any sign of a director here, anything seemed possible. When one experience ended, another one presented itself in random order. If there was a pattern present, I couldn't detect one. Discerning between reality and fantasy was now impossible. Even my own death was a mystery. Was I dead, or was this a new reality I shifted into?

After a few more attempts at talking myself out of hooking up with a phantom version of Stella, I ended up knocking on her front door. When she answered, I didn't care that she wasn't real. In her flowing white nightgown, which intensified her warm brown skin, she appeared more like an angel than the mere mortal I fell in love with. *This is definitely not hell, I* thought. *And if it is, I'm staying.*

Stella set a tea tray on the table and sat next to me. "I'm glad you came over."

I picked up a cup, smelled the spices and took a sip.

"I now know you're well enough to take care of Jessie."

"You wouldn't be saying that if you heard about all the crazy stuff that happened to me today."

"How crazy?"

"I'd rather not get into all that again." I sipped some more tea. "I want to spend the rest of my time here with you."

Stella smiled and poured some sugar into her tea.

"You're having an easy time dealing with all of this." I laughed to myself. "Why wouldn't you? You're not hanging out on Night of the Walking Dead Street."

"Is that one of your new songs?"

"It should be."

"Everything is as it should be." Stella placed her hand on my thigh. "Despite your dreams, I was right to trust you. You'd do anything to save our daughter, and that's what matters most to me."

"I wish this was real, then I'd know you were okay. It would make this so much easier to deal with."

"It's real, Markos. That's why you're here with me...to assure me Jessie is going to be all right. And she will be. I'm not sure how I know this, but I'm going to trust in what I'm feeling for a change."

"Care to pass some of that along to me? I'm not sure of anything anymore."

"Do you love your daughter?"

"You know I do."

"Sounds like something you're sure of."

I put my arm around Stella.

"Did you want to tell me something?" she asked.

"Only that I'm glad I'm here with you."

Stella lay her head on my shoulder, and I lost myself again. I would've volunteered to remain in my delusion for an eternity, but even in death change comes, whether you want it to or not.

I sat on Jessie's bed, reminiscing over each item in the room. Stuffed animals lined up on the bureau in a neat row. In the center rested the porcelain doll Phil had gotten for Jessie. He was more than likely with Stella now, comforting her and Jessie over my death. Stella would probably marry him, and Jessie would have a new father. Phil was a decent guy, and I hated to admit that. There were many things I hated to admit to that night.

On the wall hung a portrait of Stella, Jessie and me taken during happier times. It was one of the few family portraits she had of me. That Jessie chose to have it displayed here told me more than an "I miss you, Daddy." While I was alive, I wanted to die. In death, I wanted to live for my daughter and for myself so that I could become the father I wished I had. I owed that to Jessie.

Smoke pulled me out of my chimera. I got up and ran towards Stella's room. The doorway was overcome by flames, and the only way in was from the window. I ran towards the front door and stopped when I recalled what happened at Gus's. *I'm already dead. What am I running from?* I stared at the flames that moved silently without the crackling. They danced as if to a silent melody. I strolled through them, digging their tranquil groove that transmitted Sarah Vaughan's rendition of "Midnight Sun" to my radio brain.

I opened the bedroom door, and Stella stood in front of me with her mouth agape. I extended my arm to her, but she entered the blaze without acknowledging me. She waved her hands within the flames and then extended her arms out to the side, slowly spinning with a beguiling smile on her face.

"I never believed in angels, until now," I said.

Stella glared at me and stormed out of the room, leaving me alone in the flames.

You Stepped into My Dream

It was my turn to stand with my mouth open as I watched Stella jam to "Just in Time" on her baby grand.

"Stella…"

Stella ignored me. Her eyes were closed, and her whole body swayed with the music.

"Stell—"

"Not now, Markos. I got the groove back."

I leaned on the piano. "You never lost it."

"That's because you never listen to anyone's song but your own." She stopped playing and gawked at me. "Just when were you planning on telling me you died?"

My mouth stretched out so wide that I thought it would tear apart my jaw. "It's…really you?"

"Who the hell else would I be?"

"Not Stella. Stella didn't die."

"I'm dead."

"You're not dead."

"Then who are you talking to?"

"Myself."

Stella got up and slapped my face.

"Why did you do that?"

"To convince you I'm here." She raised her hand again. "Convinced?"

"I'm convinced." I rubbed my cheek, which was still stinging. "When did you find out you were dead?" I asked.

"After you told me Jessie was okay, I looked for her but couldn't find her. I thought you finally lost your mind until I recognized the man who was talking to you. He was in the picture with you after your suicide attempt. I remembered him because he had the strangest name, Jasper Brown."

"Yeah, I remember that too. I thought his name had a nice ring to it. When he found out I played jazz, he came to a few of my gigs."

"After the paramedics rolled you away, he said he couldn't wait to hear you play again. I asked him when was the last time he saw you. He said, 'Another time, another place.'"

"Why did you leave me when I called out to you?"

"I wasn't absolutely certain I was dead yet. And when I finally figured it out, I still couldn't remember how I died. How about you?"

"I have no memory of what happened. How did you know I was dead?"

"Seeing you here, acting like the husband I always imagined you'd be disturbed me. I came in here to be alone and sort through everything I was feeling. When you entered the room, I knew you were dead."

"Because I walked through the flames?"

"When I first realized I was dead, I noticed I could manipulate my environment. It's like lucid dreaming, which I practiced for many years. I tried to get you to leave, but you weren't responding to my thoughts. I was grateful that you were still here after I tried to tune you out. When you compared me to an angel, my senses returned."

"Was that when you decided to come out here and play 'Just in Time?'"

"I don't want you to be dead, Markos."

"And I don't want you to be dead."

"Did the kidnapper ask you to kill yourself?"

"The kidnapping happened?"

"You don't remember?"

"I do, but I was hoping that was another hallucination."

"It wasn't. Did you pay the ransom?"

"I don't remember jumping, but I'm here, so I probably did…I think. Can you add another piece to this puzzle?"

"I had a migraine and went to the bedroom to meditate." Stella glanced at her bedroom door. "That's the last thing I remember. I must have fallen asleep or passed out from the pain. It was intense."

"There was this medium on a recent episode of *Behind the Curtain AM*. She said ghosts hang around places they lived in when they don't know they're dead. Do you think it works the same way when you don't remember how you died?"

"The only thing I do know is Jessie is going to be devastated. She lost the two of us on the same day."

"Teddy and Leda will take good care of her."

Jessie started to sing softly as if to comfort me.

"Jessie's singing," I said. "She sounds beautiful."

"You hear her again?"

"Right now."

"I can't." Stella cried. "Why can't I hear her?"

When I went to hug her, she pushed me away and ran to the bedroom.

Stella sat on the bed, leafing through a photo album of Jessie. I sat beside her with Ezza in my hands.

"Maybe I'm not really hearing her," I said. "I could still be delusional."

"I don't want to talk about this now," Stella said.

I played through one of my original compositions figuring Stella would talk to me when she was ready. It also helped calm me down. I still had trouble accepting she had died.

"I was diagnosed with Lou Gehrig's Disease six months before you moved out," she said.

I stopped playing. I knew the disease. I was a big fan of Stephen Hawking. Despite that, I asked the next question anyway. "Is it serious?"

"It *was* serious."

"I asked how your doctor's appointment went. You told me you were okay."

"Between your nightmares and the issues you had with your father, there wouldn't have been any room for my problems."

"I should have been there for you." I hugged her.

"Don't feel guilty. I was spared the suffering, and I now know everything I believed in was true. We go on."

"Can you fill me in? Even though we're here together, I can't get the atheist out of me. I haven't met any angels or demons yet. For all I know we could be on some alien hybrid ship plugged into some hallucination-making machine."

"Or our consciousnesses are here communicating together, and we evolve."

My eyes widened. "Have you experienced any missing time?"

Stella slapped the side of my arm and smiled. "I'm serious."

"I always envied your ability to commit to an ideal. I see too many variables."

"Like what?"

"What makes your interpretation of where we are more accurate than mine? Neither of us has ever died before, and we have nothing else to compare this experience to. For all we know, we're either dead, insane or fodder for aliens who are feeding on our hallucinations. There's no clear answer here, Stella."

Stella laughed. "Come on, Markos. Can't you ever be serious?"

"Not as long as I can make you laugh like that."

She turned to a picture of her brother and gazed at it reflectively. "I saw Joseph. He was always my light at the end of the tunnel. Our conversation felt so real, I forgot he died." Stella wiped fresh tears from her eyes.

"Same thing happened to me. I saw my mother. Wish we could've said the things we said when we were alive."

Stella placed her hand on the side of my face. "At least you got a chance to say them here."

"I saw Dot and Cro as well." I shook my head. "When Gus said Dot looked the same as she did when we were kids, I never put it together."

"I saw Cro," Stella said. "He told me he sketched the truth of us."

"He said the same thing to me. Do you think they were real?" I asked.

"I'd like to think so." Stella smiled. "Cro makes the perfect angel."

"So do you." The moment felt right to give Stella her belated gift. I reached inside my pocket, removed the box and handed it to her.

Stella opened the lid and removed the locket. "It's lovely." She draped the chain around her neck, and I clasped it for her.

"I was gonna give this to you on our anniversary, but we became history before that happened."

Stella opened the empty locket.

"I give you my heart, and you're the one who fills it."

Stella put her arms around me. Our lips then partnered and slow-danced for a while. The motion electrified my whole body, reminding me of the first time we kissed. I was dead and with the woman I loved. This was my definition of heaven.

SET 3

"I hope for nothing. I fear nothing. I am free." Nikos Kazantzakis

Afterglow

dad will   cry. ____   chil - dren have   par-ents   to   go home   to. ____   Out   in

We lay silently in each other's arms. I don't know what was on Stella's mind, but I was still trying to adjust to the reality of an afterlife. Whenever I heard Father Nicholas talk about death, he made it appear as if every question I ever asked would be answered in one profound moment. A profound moment of all-knowing would've been appreciated, but one never came. I had more questions than when I was alive. Death is funny that way.

Feeling restless, I picked up Ezza and played through "I've Got My Love to Keep Me Warm."

"How will we know if Jessie is okay?" Stella asked.

"I keep hearing her sing. Maybe that means she is."

"Is that what you heard on the roof?"

"She's been singing to me since all of this started."

"Tell me about your visions."

I stopped playing. "So now you wanna hear about them? Earlier you thought I was delusional."

"Under these new circumstances...let's just say I have a more open mind about why you're experiencing them."

"They always start off the same way. I'm lying on the sidewalk, flat on my back. Jessie is singing to me and holding a red lotus."

I got lost in my playing as I recapped the day's events, and the music seemed to echo from all around me.

"Anything else?" Stella asked.

"Steve shows up wearing his goofy hat and glasses."

"Steve?"

"Steve Pagels. He was my music teacher. He shows up and says, 'The truth can't be undone. We all eventually must pay.' My father used to always say that to me." I stopped playing my guitar. "I didn't figure out I was dead until after I woke up in our bedroom. It was filled with all different kinds of red flowers. I dug the ambience and how the moonlight shined on the petals. A poem then came to me. 'Red flowers awaken my mind. I smell the life I left behind.' After that, the whole room burst into flames."

"Like the fire in here?"

"There must've been a fire," I said.

"I can't remember."

"Neither can I. Except for the one at—never mind, I'm not sure if it happened."

"If what happened?"

"The fire at Steve's house. He and his wife were both killed. I hope I made all of it up, and that Steve is jamming at the Village Gate every week with an adequate replacement for me."

Stella snapped her fingers. "Could've been my breathing. I used to wake up in the middle of the night because I stopped breathing."

"The timing is too convenient."

"My symptoms were getting worse. I used to wake up at least twice a week, gasping for air."

"Dying on the same morning I pay Jessie's ransom? That's too much of a coincidence."

"I don't have any other explanation."

Jessie began to sing again with the crackling sound of flames accompanying her.

"Can you hear her now?" I asked. "Jessie is singing."

Stella wept. "I would do anything to hear her sweet voice again."

I put down my guitar and hugged Stella.

"What if we never find out what happened to her?" she asked.

"We'll figure this out."

"What if we don't? What if we never learn her fate? I can't bear not knowing."

"We'll find out...one way or another."

Stella continued to cry, and I held her until she calmed.

I leaned against the headboard playing "The Way You Look Tonight" while Stella lay on the bed staring up at the ceiling. I tried to cheer her up, but I knew nothing would help her until I could find a way to prove Jessie was all right. But how would I find her? It wasn't as easy as filling out a missing-person's report at the local police station.

I stopped playing when a shimmering golden mist shone through the window. Stella and I got up to have a look. The glow mixed within the night sky, and all the buildings and cars appeared dreamlike as they reflected the ethereal sheen.

"It's enchanting," Stella said.

I took her hand in mine and sang "The Way You Look Tonight." Tears streamed down her cheeks. I put my arms around her, and we danced. I managed to get the whole song out before Stella pulled away from me.

"Damn you for doing this to me now," she said.

"What did I do?" I probably sounded more like the little boy who stole the guitar rather than the man who grew up to play it.

"Why couldn't we have been like this when we were alive?"

"Didn't you always tell Jessie how we make mistakes so that we can learn from them?"

"I'm not so sure I believe my own advice anymore. With all my expectations gone, everything I strived for seems pointless."

"If everyone thought like that, civilization wouldn't exist. There'd be no buildings, no bridges, no music"—I placed my hand over my chest and gasped—"and no jazz."

"I'm starting to think that wouldn't be such a terrible thing."

"Gotta brace myself for this one." I sat on the bed and clasped the sheets with both my hands. "Did I just hear my ambitious wife, who on top of being a great mother, had the time to teach college, play piano, and travel the world, say laziness is the better alternative?"

Stella sat next to me. "I'm exhausted hearing you say all that. I think that's why I got sick…from doing too much. Our bodies aren't meant to deal with so much stress."

"So laziness is the cure?"

"We work all our life to become proficient in some skill, never thinking we can get sick and lose everything we worked so hard for." She turned and faced me. "For those of us lucky enough to stay healthy, we end up dying anyway. All the hard work and struggle…to what end? As I reflect upon my life, at this moment, my family and friends matter most, along with all the meaningful moments we shared together."

"Never in my strangest dreams—and I've had plenty of those—would I ever have imagined comparing you to Music Man. You sound a lot like him."

"Who's he?"

"He was the local pothead who owned a music shop with his buddy, Flipper. You would've loved them. Picture Cheech and Chong meets the 'Odd Couple,' and that's Flipper and Music Man. They were like my big brothers. They gave me advice and were the ones who turned me on to Wes."

"Don't forget about Robert J." Stella smiled.

"I'll never forget about Robert J." As an avalanche of nostalgia hit, I sat up and got Ezza. "Flipper gave me the idea of naming my guitar." I played "Everyday I Have the Blues."

"I would've appreciated if you brought up all these childhood stories when we were together." She covered the fretboard of my guitar with her hand. "Can we talk for a while without the soundtrack?"

"I'll try, but it won't be easy." I put Ezza down, crossed my hands over my lap and twiddled my thumbs.

"Why do I remind you of Music Man?"

"Music Man was definitely an interesting individual. He always hung out in the back room with some book in front of his face. He said something similar to what you said before about how most people kill themselves over some job and after all that expenditure of energy, they die and can't take anything they've earned with them. Better to lie back, have fun and enjoy life. That was Music Man's philosophy."

"Not sure if I like reaching the same conclusion as a pothead."

"Unlike us, he's still alive and doing well. After Flipper died he wrote a literary novel about their lives together. It sold really well and even made it into Oprah's Book Club. He went on to write more books and eventually sold his shop. He's running a farm in a small community outside the Himalayas. I was thinking of stopping over to say hi to him next year."

"Sounds like a lot of work to me."

"It's not work when you love what you do." I picked up Ezza and played an old Greek folk song my grandmother used to sing to me.

"You really love what you do."

"Don't you?" I asked.

"I liked what I did, but I never had what you have. I don't think I've ever seen you without your guitar in your hands."

Stella glanced at the window. "I always searched for a way out of my life, which is why I think I traveled a lot."

I stopped playing and lay my guitar next to me.

"I resented you," Stella said, "for having such a strong passion for something. It made me realize what I lacked in my life."

"But Stella, you've got so much talent. The first night we played together at the Piano Bar, I saw it."

"My tempo was off," Stella said.

"Your tempo was fine."

"No, I was off a little."

"Didn't notice."

"You squinted your eyes when we got towards the end of 'Round Midnight.'"

"I always squint my eyes when I'm playing." I laughed.

"I spent hours practicing, and I never got close to being as good as all the artists I grew up admiring."

"Is that why you refused to play out with me again?"

Stella nodded. "I couldn't even get into a decent music school. That's why I changed my major to anthropology. I knew I'd have a better chance at success."

"And you found it."

"Except for the passion. I wanted to throw myself into something where I could completely lose myself."

"You're like that with Jessie."

"I wanted something that belonged only to me." Stella rubbed her eyes. "I thought I was being ungrateful to want more for myself. I interpret things differently now. If I found my true passion, I would've been able to show Jessie, by my example, how she could live her dreams and have a family. Neither is mutually exclusive."

I placed my arm around Stella.

"I planned to take her to India for her tenth birthday," Stella said. "We were going to start off in New Delhi, work our way to Agra to see the Taj Mahal and spend the last week in Kanha National Park for a guided safari. Jessie was so excited when I told her it was the part of India that inspired Rudyard Kipling to write *The Jungle Book*."

"I was excited when she told me. I wanted to invite myself to go with you."

"I would've said no."

"And I would've probably booked a flight and showed up anyway."

"You wouldn't have."

I smiled. "Not even you could keep me away from *Rikki Tikki Tavi*."

"That's what I miss most about you," Stella said with a smile.

"What?"

"You can cheer me up when I'm at my worst."

The gold mist now entered the room and made everything appear almost transparent.

"I wanna walk with all this stuff around us. It's very romantic." I put Ezza in her case and extended my hand to Stella.

She shook her head. "We're dead, and I'm still playing second fiddle to your guitar."

Stella took my hand, and we headed towards our destiny, wherever that was.

Anthromarkosophy

jun - gle   that   still   is   true.

A translucent golden glow filled Times Square. The buildings could've been a part of one of Leda's paintings. This was definitely her style. I hummed another song that came to me. The composition ended up on my sixth studio release. Every song on that album came from this night, a night that existed only right now, beyond time.

"Sounds beautiful. Is it a new one?" Stella asked.

"Only a few minutes old."

"Got a name?"

"Roaming with Stella."

She pointed at my case.

"You know me well," I said.

"Go right ahead."

"In a while." I held Stella's hand. "I wanna take in a little more of the scene."

"Death certainly has changed you."

"Hopefully for the better."

Stella squeezed my hand. "For the better."

Everything was oozing out almost perfectly, but perfectness here was an illusion created by Stella and me. I guarded my emotions, afraid to let go because of a nebulous future and Jessie's undisclosed fate. Death failed to enlighten me any more than life did. If a grand purpose existed, I wished for a light to shine down on me now and show me the way.

We stopped in front of a travel agency. On the door was a poster of Paris that reminded me of our honeymoon. Stella and I spent seven days in Paris. We enjoyed exploring all the narrow roads and sidewalk cafes and thought about moving there.

"I loved the view from the Eiffel Tower," Stella said.

"The catacombs were my favorite."

"You always had an eye for the macabre."

"Death as art to be viewed by people hundreds of years later is proof the French were always in vogue."

"Not us. We're going to be buried underground."

"Not this body." I pointed to myself. "I gave Donnie and Snaps implicit instructions to sprinkle my ashes in the ocean while playing, 'How Deep Is the Ocean.'"

"I sometimes find it hard to tell when you're serious."

"Oh, I'm very serious. My ashes might now be adrift somewhere along the Atlantic."

We continued along our walk, and Jessie sang again. I kept it from Stella so as not to upset her.

"Now that we know we're dead, we're probably moving on to a new level of our test," Stella said.

"This is a test?"

"I believe we're in a bardo."

"What's that?"

"According to Tibetan Buddhism, it's the intermediate state between life and death where the consciousness experiences karma-induced hallucinations."

"I always knew marrying a scholar would come in handy. If you weren't here, I'd think this is my forever."

"If that's what we're experiencing, how we handle ourselves during this process will determine our next life. We'll probably have to judge ourselves before moving on."

"Have you ever read about two people experiencing the same bardo?"

Stella shook her head.

I stopped to survey a large monitor in Times Square playing a commercial for Apple Computer, but the slogan read: *Think Unique.* "After all this is over, we probably won't remember anything about our lives together. I'll forget all about Robert J., Wes, the catacombs, my secret baklava recipe, how to play guitar, Jessie and—"

The ground violently rumbled beneath our feet, and we both fell. We held on to each other as the ground shook and quaked.

"I was never good at tests," I said.

Several seconds later everything settled, and we got up. The building in front of us was replaced by two transparent screens about fifteen feet tall. All the buildings on either side of us remained as they were. As we approached the screens, a low hum reverberated off the buildings and ground.

"I'm surprised you didn't make a pitch reference," Stella said.

"I have no idea what it is."

Behind the screens were other screens lined up as far back as I could see. As we stood in front of the first ones, they switched on. The screen on the left portrayed a scene that could've come from the days of Ancient Greece or Rome. A woman poured wine from a carafe into her husband's cup. After he took a sip, the wife smiled in a way that suggested she knew something he didn't. After a few moments, the man grabbed his chest, collapsed onto his back, and his wife emptied out the remaining wine from the carafe. There was something familiar about this woman. I knew this woman. No...*I was this woman!* Whether out of remorse, embarrassment, or both, I kept this admission to myself. "Are we here to be tested or watch movies?" I asked.

We walked to the screen on the right where a posse on horseback chased a Native American, also on horseback. They shot him in the back, and he fell from his horse. Stella appeared troubled and walked away.

"What is it?" I asked.

"I shot that man." She went to the next screen where a man was fox hunting with his son. Stella pointed her finger at the screen. "I remember this," she said. "I took Stan to hunt on his sixteenth birthday. I was so proud of him. He had the highest grades in his class."

"Are you saying you're…the man?"

"We're observing our past incarnations. The screens lined up on the left appear to represent your previous lives, while the ones on the right are from my own past."

"I knew it. We're in a computer simulation, like in that movie, *The Matrix*."

"Or the information is presented to us in a way we can understand. We live in a computer-dominated society, so everything we observe here would be familiar to us."

"If only I could be as optimistic as you."

"Why do you have to have a definitive answer? Accept there are some things we'll never understand, and all of this will be easier for you to deal with."

"But we don't know anything, other than we're here, and we don't even know where here is. Wish someone would come out and tell us if this is a bardo or a holographic simulation aboard an alien ship."

"Why does everything have to have a name?"

"I'm not asking to know everything, Stella. I just wanna grasp what this all means so that I can brace myself for whatever is coming. I don't like not knowing what happened to Jessie, not knowing how we died, not knowing where we are, not knowing where we're going, not—"

Stella clutched both my shoulders. "Try to recognize yourself in these screens. They'll help ground you."

"How will knowing I murdered my husband in Ancient Whatever Land make me feel better?" I squeezed the handle of my guitar case. *Did I just say husband?*

"You're not her anymore."

Stella covered her mouth with her hand to hold back her laughter, but I caught on.

"You're not any of those people on the screens," Stella said, "including who you used to be in your recently completed life."

Stella waved her arm to the screen in front of us. "This is exactly what I told my class. We're pure potential. With each life comes a new interpretation of that potential."

"So if I'm not me anymore, who the hell am I now?"

"You." Stella winked her eye and smiled.

I followed her down Past Life Lane where we continued to watch different versions of ourselves. Some of the screens showed Stella and me together, others depicted us apart. Every imaginable epoch was displayed for us along with some I didn't recognize from any history book. Technology I had never seen before, beings that weren't human, and ships that flew through space seemed more like well-produced science fiction movies than lifetimes I lived through. Although they were familiar to me, I would have dismissed them all as hallucinations if Stella wasn't with me. Nevertheless, I still couldn't rule out the possibility that they weren't.

We came upon a screen that peeked into my life from Ancient Egypt. A young soldier stood near the edge of the Nile River, flexing his biceps as a girl giggled.

"Which one is you?" Stella asked.

"I always was and always will be an alpha male."

Stella giggled and pointed to the following screen, which showed a prima ballerina on pointe doing a perfect spin. "Now I see where you got your rhythm."

"And I never lost it." I winked one of my eyes. My moves were impressive. Mikhail Baryshnikov would've agreed had he seen them.

Stella and I separated to observe our personal screens. When I witnessed Steve's house on fire I sensed what was coming next, and I wasn't ready to bear witness to one of the most tragic nights of the life I recently left behind. I went to check out what screen Stella was watching and halted when I saw her kissing Phil. After a kiss that took way too long for this ex-husband to feel comfortable watching, Phil stepped back and handed Stella a small box. She lifted the lid and removed a gold bracelet with two heart-shaped rubies.

"It's beautiful," Stella said.

As Phil clasped the bracelet around Stella's wrist, I recalled the day she told me she bought it on sale at Fortunoff's.

"When are you going to tell him?" Phil asked.

"He's having a hard time now. His father just got out of jail."

"You told me it's always something with him, and time is a luxury we don't have."

"I can't leave him until I'm convinced he'll be okay on his own."

"I realize I'm being a little selfish here, but I want to spend whatever time we have left together."

"I'm still struggling to accept all of this. Other than a couple of falls, I don't feel any different."

"None of this matters to me. I love you."

"But it does to me. I'm not ready to leave Jessie alone. Markos isn't capable of handling her on his own."

"You can always fight for full custody."

I cleared my throat. "I'm usually good at predicting what happens next in a movie, but I was way off with this one. I thought the wife was faithful."

Stella turned to face me. "You're not seeing everything."

"Tell me what I'm missing."

She took too long to answer, which infuriated me.

"I don't wanna see your face for the rest of this bardo or whatever the hell it is! I want us to be over with so that I can forget all about you and the lies that broke apart our family!" I turned to leave, and Stella clutched my upper arm.

"Please, Markos. You have to give me a chance to explain. There's not one simple answer I can give you."

"I don't need you to explain anything." I pointed at the screen. "I can see it in full color. Why couldn't you be honest and tell me you wanted out?"

"I still loved you."

"You had a strange way of showing it." I observed the screen that looped back to where Phil was kissing Stella.

"We both did, in our own ways," Stella said. "We need to talk about this." She took my hand. "We have to make things right between us before this is all over."

What was happening on the screen made Stella's words sound hollow. I wanted to yell some more, but the fresh tears running down Stella's cheeks shut me up. *She's the one who cheated, and I feel like the bad guy?*

"I'm not in the mood to talk." I walked away.

Milestones

Close your   eyes,____   and dream a   dream.____   A   hap - py   lit -

After I'd tuned the strings on my guitar, I practiced some of the chords Flipper had shown me. Other than a minor intonation problem, the guitar was in excellent shape. I practiced all night, into the next day and stopped when I heard my mother shouting.

"Stop crowding me! I need to breathe. Can't you tell I'm suffocating?"

I went to see what was going on. In all my years living at home, my mother never raised her voice to my father.

"All I asked is what's for dinner," my father answered weakly.

I crept towards their bedroom and pressed my ear against the door.

"That's all you do. Ask, ask, ask!" my mother yelled. "I had enough of your demands. Climb down from your Mount Olympus, Zeus, and make your own damned dinner!"

"You know I can't cook."

"Learn!"

I cheered on the inside. I wanted my mother to speak up for herself for the longest time.

"All right, I'll order a pizza from Antonio's, but you better get over whatever's bothering you by tomorrow, or I'll—"

"Or you'll what? Punish me? Hit me? Torture me? You've already done all the above, and I'm not gonna take it from you anymore."

"You're talking like a crazy woman."

"That's what you turned me into. I feel crazy, in addition to being a failure." She cried. "A stranger knew my son better than me because I kept my mouth shut all these years. I'm not doing this anymore. Do you hear me? You don't own me. I'm in control of my own life."

I heard a slap followed by another slap.

"I can hit back too!" my mother said.

Then came another slap.

"I'll come back when you're calmer," my father said.

I ran back to my room, picked up my guitar and started playing "Highway Star." My father knocked once and opened the door.

I stopped playing. "I didn't steal this."

"I know." My father's voice sounded weak. "Your mother told me."

"I'm starting my homework now."

"I'm glad you've decided to cooperate because our deal still stands. If you want to keep that, you have to maintain your grades."

I rested my guitar on the bed.

"I'm ordering a pizza. Your mother has a migraine."

He left the room, and I picked up my history book. I fell asleep somewhere in the middle of the Spanish Inquisition.

I brought my guitar to Flipper the next day. He examined the neck. "I told her you'd like it," he said.

"She bought it here?"

"I handed her the M.I.J. special I was holding for you, but when she asked me what I thought you'd like, Music Man showed her this. He restored it himself." Flipper started playing. "I can see why you fell for her. She's pretty cute. If you weren't so into her, I would've hit on her myself."

"She died…ten days ago."

Flipper stopped playing. "That's real tough, kid. I know she meant a lot to you. How'd it happen?"

"She OD'd." I sat behind Flipper's desk.

He shook his head. "Hate hearing stories like that." He plugged my guitar into an electric tuner.

"Does she have a name?"

"Not yet."

He plucked a string and checked the tuner.

"That's good. This isn't something you should rush." Flipper picked up a screwdriver and adjusted the bridge to correct the intonation. "Did you ever hear the story about how B.B. King named his guitar?"

"Was it named after his girlfriend?"

"B.B was never that predictable. There were these two guys fighting in the middle of one of his gigs. They knocked over a burning barrel of kerosene. They did that to heat places back in the day. The bar caught on fire, and everyone ran outside." Flipper plucked another string and eyed the tuner. "B.B. went back inside to get his guitar. A cheap thirty-dollar Gibson."

"Is that really true?"

"Yeah, it's true."

I shook my head. "I'd never risk my life for a Gibson."

"Two people died in that fire." Flipper adjusted the bridge and moved on to the next string. "The following day B.B. heard those two guys were fighting over a girl named Lucille. He named his guitar, along with all the rest of his guitars, Lucille to remind himself never to do anything stupid like run into a burning building to rescue a cheap guitar…or fight over a woman."

I examined my guitar and without hesitation I said, "Ezza."

"Good choice."

And so I named my first guitar, and all the rest of my guitars, Ezza as a reminder never to touch heroin again or turn my back on a friend. I'm proud to say I kept both promises to this day.

After I got my guitar, music became my drug. Every song I wrote, every gig I played, every recording I completed gave me a buzz unmatched by the poison in the needle that stole Ezza's life. I was lucky to have found direction at such a young age. While most of my friends continued to hang out at the rink and arcade, I stayed at home and worked at being the next guitar god so that I could travel the world with a string of female groupies close behind. It didn't matter my motivation was immature. I moved forward and for that reason alone, Ezza deserved to be immortalized. She was my angel whose death wasn't in vain. Each time I thought about smoking dope, I only had to remember what Ezza did for me to get me back on track.

My mother didn't come out of her room for three additional days, and my father left her alone. I guess he was scared of her. On the third night, in the middle of our third pizza, my mother came down with a large smile on her face. My father beamed, probably from thinking a tray of spanakopita or pastitso would soon be in the oven.

He hugged my mother. "I'm glad you're back."

"I was never here."

"What do you mean you were never here? Who am I married to?"

"The new and improved me." She cradled his face with her hands and kissed him. "I love you, but things won't be going back to the way they were." She walked to the cabinet. "I'm going to make some baklava now…because I want to."

I watched my father slump into his chair in a heap of humiliation. I chomped on my pizza and relished every moment of my mother's victory. Whatever transformed her made things a lot better at home. I no longer had to go to counseling, and my father was less confrontational. He even complimented me when he heard me playing, "Living in the Past." He was a fan of Jethro Tull.

During the next six months, I left my room only to eat, go to school, and attend mass. The rest of the hours I spent practicing guitar and listening to Robert J. recordings until I could play all his songs by memory. The Faustian myth behind his playing inspired countless stories about coming face to face with the devil and being offered Robert J.'s playing ability. In each scenario, I took the offer mostly because the devil had no idea I was a closet atheist. So after I struck the deal, I got what I wanted, and the devil vanished when I told him he didn't exist.

Robert J. visited me from the other side and gave me a high five. "Yeah, that'll show that nasty ol' devil a lesson. You can continue to borrow what I got so long as you give it back after each gig."

I accepted the offer, and after each gig I gave back what I borrowed as promised. I did the same with Wes until the night of my last gig when I played without my mentors. I never told my parents about my deal with Robert J. They would've sprinkled holy water on my bed and had Father Nicholas bless my room out of fear I was possessed by some demonic force.

Life kept getting better. After my mother listened to me sing and play "Terraplane Blues," I didn't have to beg for lessons anymore. She argued my case to my father and won, and I began my studies with Steve. Unbeknown to me, my mother's path was about to run parallel to my own.

Opa!

sum-mer in my jun-gle dream._____ Where no one ev - er_____ has to sle

I entered the Jazz Room. It was odd to find the place empty. I switched on the stereo system and scanned through the MP3 playlists. Before making my selection, I contemplated my mood, which was in need of some cheerful music. I chose Ella Fitzgerald. Her soulful, pitch-perfect voice could make even a sad song sound hopeful, and I needed a little of that for myself.

When the music began, I hopped onto the pool table, lay on my back and tapped my feet to "The Lady Is a Tramp." I was feeling better already. You just can't be depressed when you listen to Ella sing, even when you're dead.

Stella showed up and peered down at me. "Are you going to give me a chance to explain?"

I didn't want to leave my pool table fantasy world yet, so I ignored her and started to sing along with Ella. Stella flipped out by the time I sang the part about not bothering with people I hate. A large crash extracted me from my reverie and into the fury of a very irate ex-wife. I sat up, and Stella held a bottle of wine in her hand. Think it was a merlot. On the floor in front of her was the bottle she smashed to pieces.

"Go ahead," I said. "I won't stop you, but I'm not cleaning up."

Stella threw the bottle at the mirror behind the bar. Perhaps it was Ella or the sound of breaking glass that I loved since I was a kid that put me in a jocose mood. I jumped off the pool table and strode over to the dartboard.

"Are you going to talk to me?" Stella asked.

I removed a few darts from the board. "Maybe after I finish up this game." I stepped back and threw one of the darts, which hit near the bullseye.

Stella smashed another bottle, and I felt left out. I walked over to the bar and got a half-empty bottle of Jack Daniels. I untwisted the cap, took a big swig and flicked the glass with my finger. "G-sharp."

Stella crossed her arms and glared at me. I slammed the bottle on the bar and got a baseball bat from the shelf beneath the cash register. I smiled at Stella and whacked the bottle of whisky with the bat. The crushed glass splattered along half the length of the bar. "Oh yes! I get why you like doing this." I grabbed two more bottles.

Stella snatched the bat from me, nabbed a bottle of wine and plunked it on the bar. "Everything is a game to you!" She batted the bottle, and I hopped to the side to avoid being struck by the flying slivers of glass. My reflexes apparently failed to realize I was dead.

Stella next aimed at a row of bottles on the shelf. "You never listen to me! But maybe you will now!" Stella swung the bat, smashing the bottles. Shards of glass rained all around us.

I set the two bottles onto the bar and pointed to them. Those poor bottles never sensed what was coming. Stella pulverized them with one long sweep of the bat.

I sat on a barstool and leaned my elbows on the bar. "Impressive. Is there anything you're not good at?"

Stella took aim at the cocktail glasses hanging overhead. "Managing time. I've wasted enough of it with you, worrying about your mental health while neglecting my own." She swung the bat and more glass splattered everywhere. "I'm not apologizing for Phil. He was there for me when you weren't. You were either drunk and feeling sorry for yourself or globetrotting with *the guys.*"

I grabbed the bat from Stella. "Justifying your actions doesn't make them right."

"Are you talking from experience?"

I walked to the front of the bar and smashed the window. "As of right now, I'm done with all the excuses." I dropped the bat. "I was a jerk, but I never lied to you."

"How would I have known that? Whenever you were home, all you did was drink. We never talked anymore."

"I can't give you an answer you'll find acceptable because I'm not like you. I don't analyze my behavior and get all *introspective,* although I've been doing a lot of that since arriving here. Give me more time to assimilate everything. This is all new to me."

"I'm not asking you for a drawn-out explanation. All I want to know is why you always kept me at a distance? Why didn't you trust me enough to tell me what was bothering you?"

"For the same reason you didn't tell me you were sick. Neither of us trusted each other."

"I trusted you. And even after all that we've been through, I still loved you."

"I find that hard to believe. You left me the day after the second-worst night in my life."

"I had no idea you wanted me around. From my perspective, I thought you used the bottle to find your way out of your problems…Jessie and me."

I shook my head. "After all these years, you still don't know a damned thing about me. Not a damned thing."

"Then tell me."

I turned to leave. This sounded too much like conversations I had with my father. He always expected the worst from me.

Stella grabbed the sleeve of my shirt. "There you go, running away again. Why should I have bothered to stay?"

"Because you were my wife."

"What does that mean to you?"

"For better or for worse." I picked up my guitar case. "You walked out on me when I was at my worst."

I left the bar, and Stella followed behind me.

The flashing Jazz Room sign reminded me of a life left behind. All was quiet outside. Not even a pedestrian or car traversed the avenue. The emptiness of the city now seemed more post-apocalyptic than heavenly.

We walked within the gold haze in silence. As I was sorting through everything Stella told me, she began to sing "Amazing Grace." I never felt anything when I heard the song in the past, but as Stella sang, her voice lured me in. *Perhaps it's not too late for a wretch like me to be saved. It happened once before.*

Buhinduanity

Where wolves and ti - gers and pan - thers creep. _____ I close my

We ended up on a bench in a small neighborhood park. The evening breeze and crickets beating their wings in quarter time would've made me forget where we were had it not been for the golden mist. My memory seemed to fade, and it became difficult to focus on what made up my identity. Was this how we came to our conclusion? A little piece of us removed until we were unrecognizable even to ourselves? I once longed to fade into nothingness but after everything I had just been through, I wanted to continue. To be ripped from my body and discover I can exist without it and then to be stripped of my awareness seemed diabolical. I could accept aliens torturing us like this but not a god from any of the world's religions.

Things were a lot less complicated when I never gave death much thought other than I knew it happened. I couldn't do anything to stop it, so why worry? I had always thought that one day death would come, and it would be like I was asleep. My awareness would vanish, and I'd be no longer. This notion haunted me as a kid, but as I grew, so did my acceptance of the inevitable. If I died without having experienced this bardo, purgatory, computer simulation or whatever it was with Stella, it wouldn't have mattered. I never expected my consciousness to survive after death.

Thinking came easier while I played my guitar, so I got Ezza out of her case and started to play my new song. While I jammed through my existential crisis, Stella sat in silence. She stayed still, like a sculpture. Another song came to me as I studied each curve, blemish, and line across her face. After I committed my song to memory, I forgot the reason I was troubled. I stopped playing and basked in the silence with Stella. When I listened beyond the street sounds and crickets, I heard it. The silence seduced me and took away the pain that accompanied my life. The apprehensive voices that never ceased to chatter within my hyperactive mind eased, and my breathing ceased. Hours may have passed, yet time seemed nonexistent. The usual anticipation of what I had to do next evaporated until Jessie appeared to me in a vision. She extended the red lotus to me and sang.

I opened my eyes in a panic and turned to Stella. She started to look a little too much like everything else around here. She was disappearing right before my eyes. I shook the side of her arm. "Stella, wake up."

She had this beautiful smile upon her face, and I didn't want to erase this moment by waking her. However, I grew concerned over my lapsing memory. I had an eerie feeling that if Stella didn't wake up, she'd be taken from me. "Come on, babe. You can have your nap after this is all finished." I caressed the side of her arm.

Stella opened her eyes and gazed at me almost as though she didn't recognize me. "Markos?" She gasped. "Oh my God, I almost forgot you!" She hugged me so hard that I could feel her nails dig into my skin.

"We should keep talking to each other before we completely unplug."

"I almost forgot I was here."

"Same here. If I didn't hear Jessie sing, I don't think I would've pulled myself back in time."

"In time for what?"

"I'm not sure. But we should keep a close watch on each other so that this doesn't happen again."

"It's getting harder to remember things."

"For me too." I took her hand.

"I'm not ready to leave you yet, and we still haven't found out what happened to Jessie."

"That's gotta be why I'm having these visions. Maybe they're the key to letting us know Jessie is okay."

"I won't let go without her. I won't let go until I know my baby is okay," Stella said.

"How about we take a walk? It'll help calm us, and it'll be easier to stay alert if we keep moving."

We ambled quietly down the road, and I drew spiral patterns in the mist with my index finger while pondering the notion of unbecoming.

"It's like Etch-a-Sketch." Stella drew a smiley face and giggled.

"It's great to see you like this."

"It's great to have control over my legs again. I feel as if I can walk for an eternity."

We continued our stroll, and I whistled "Manhattan."

"I miss this so much. I could exist in this moment for an eternity."

"Be careful what you wish for around here. You just might get it."

Stella halted in front of a poster of two cyclists in a race. "Remember the last time we went bike riding?"

"You fell and broke your ankle."

"My balance had been way off that day. That was my first symptom of ALS, but my doctor told me I pushed myself too hard and needed a rest."

"Seemed like an accurate diagnosis at the time. Between taking care of Jessie and me—whenever I was around—you never had much of a break."

"When my illness started to affect the quality of my life, I refused to acknowledge it. It was easier to ignore my symptoms than face my own mortality. I drove myself hard to avoid thinking about my illness and spent extra hours on campus writing more articles." She laughed. "I even started to plot out a new book. I was busier after I got sick than I was previously."

"In a way, I did the same thing. There were lots of things I didn't and still don't want to deal with."

"I was very judgmental of you."

"Not as much as you were on yourself."

"You know me well."

"I tried to avoid anything that had to do with judgment, except when it came to Steve and my father. Other than those two, whenever I made a judgment call, my reason for doing so would hang around my mind until I resolved whatever issue caused it. Most of the times I found my judgements came from assumptions. And the thing about assumptions is they can be way off. My father's were." I surveyed the street with that understanding. "There's always more than one way to perceive things."

"That was the basis of all our troubles," Stella said. "You saw possibilities where I saw only absolutes."

"As I always use to say…"

"One person's right is another person's I'd-rather-not-say." Stella smiled. "You said that to me on our second date, after I asked if you believed in God."

"When I told you I was a recovering Christian and you told me you went to church every Sunday, I was certain you'd never want to see me again."

"I seriously thought about ending it with you."

"Why did you stick around?"

"I was already in love with you."

My lack of faith caused some tension during our early years together; however, after a trip to India, Stella became obsessed with Hinduism and Buddhism. I welcomed her foray into the Eastern philosophies. She no longer made an issue of my atheism and even told me having no belief system made it easier to see the world as it truly is. According to Stella, a believer and nonbeliever can and should coexist since everything is made up of the same stuff, and if she judged me, she was judging herself. I liked the sound of that a lot, even though the judging continued. Nevertheless, she never took an issue with my atheism again.

Stella incorporated Hinduism and Buddhism into her faith while still attending church. It was as if she formed her own religion. I even gave it a name, which Stella took offense to at first. But when "Buhinduanity" ended up on my third studio release, she gained a new appreciation for the term and even identified herself as a Buhinduian at the parties we attended. When she got into Taoism, I couldn't figure out a way to include that, so Buhinduian remained.

Stella and I found a small neighborhood playground. I regressed back to my frolicsome years and crossed the monkey bars. After two rounds I bopped over to Stella, who had been sitting on a swing. I took the one next to her.

"I was just thinking about my mother," Stella said. "I saw her before, but like Joseph, I forgot she had died."

"Thinking my mother was alive when I talked to her made the transition easier...after I figured out I was dead. Before that, it confused me. My mother never cooked vegetarian meals for me."

"I believed having a career would give me the strength I thought my mother never had. She depended on my father for everything. After he died, she didn't have any skills to take care of us. She worked as a housekeeper. When she'd come home after a twelve-hour shift, she'd tell us to get an education and work hard until we achieved our dreams. What I failed to notice is it took a great deal of strength to do what she did. She managed to put food on the table and keep a roof over our heads."

I reached to the side and took Stella's hand.

"I did what my mother expected from me, but I was still afraid of turning out like her, of relying on a man to take care of me. I put every ounce of my energy into my career, never allowing myself enough time for a break." She wiped her eyes. "That's why I got sick."

"Working can't make you sick, Stella."

"It can. The stress I put on myself, it was too much. And I told you about my schedule after I got sick. I was terrified of dying, so I worked more, never realizing I was killing myself inside. On top of all that, I was scared of leaving Jessie behind and didn't want to think of what would happen to her after I was gone. I wanted to spend as much time as I could with her...just the two of us. For those brief periods, I was at my happiest. It hurts me to admit this aloud. You were right. I left you when you needed me the most because I needed to be happy more, especially after my diagnosis." Stella squeezed my hand. "Please forgive me."

The tightness of her grip on my hand spoke to me more than her words. "You really do love me."

"Of course I do."

"I never believed you until today."

"Why?"

"You never asked me to stop touring."

"Would you have listened if I did?"

"I'd like to think I would have. And not because you're pretty persuasive with a baseball bat."

"You should see me with a bowling ball."

"I can picture it in my mind clearly, and it scares the hell out of me."

Stella giggled. "I haven't laughed like this in a long time." Her expression quickly darkened. "It feels so wrong...to be happy with Jessie missing."

"It's not. Think that's why we're here together. So much has happened, and we never discussed the unresolved issues between us. Laughing about them beats avoiding them by you visiting some exotic place with Jessie or me running away by going on tour."

"We're finally visiting an exotic place together."

"I'm not sure I'd call this place exotic"—I waved my hand through the golden mist—"but it's definitely inspirational."

Stella got off the swing. "I wish I could tell Jessie to live for the sake of living rather than become someone else's definition of success. I'd tell her to chase after her dreams and be happy. Ultimately that's all that matters, and it's the only thing we can take with us."

"Along with the memories."

"*Pleasant* memories preferred."

I thought back to my current life screen and couldn't have agreed with Stella more. That's one memory I wish I could have left behind, but I knew I had to face it to move on. I wasn't in a rush. I'd stretch my time out with Stella as long as I could get away with it. If it was that important for me to move on, whoever ran the show had to make the first move.

Music Teacher

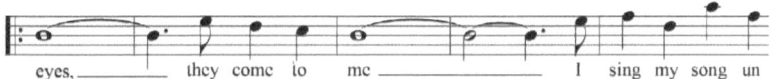

eyes, _____ they come to me _____ I sing my song un

My stay at Gray Pines had given me lots of time to think about my parents. I told my doctor that my mother had kept a journal. Leda tried to get me to read it once, but I refused. I also mentioned the CD Leda kept trying to give me. My doctor told me both would help me confront some of the unresolved issues I had. I didn't think reliving my childhood would help my condition, and I continued to resist. If I had a journal, I wouldn't be comfortable with people knowing my secrets. Reading my mother's deepest thoughts seemed like an invasion of her privacy.

I changed my mind a week into my hospitalization. My nightmares worsened, and I was willing to try anything to get rid of them. I told Leda to bring my mother's journal next time she visited. Each page I read drew me into a part of my mother I never knew, the part that was as unhappy and as unfulfilled as I was.

The days go on with no end. Even though I'm not a prisoner here, I might as well be one. I'm afraid of the responsibilities that come with freedom. I got Markos to take care of, and I have no skills to get a job where I could support him. My mother said I can stay with her, but the economy in Greece isn't good. It would be even harder for me to find a job there. I was a fool to listen to my father and not go to college. "You're getting married. What do you need an education for?" he told me, and I obeyed like a good little Greek girl whose father had the perfect man lined up for her. I should've had the guts to stand up to him, and now my children are suffering because I was a coward. The nights are the most difficult for me. I go to sleep wishing I won't wake up the next day. I have a bottle of pills in the medicine cabinet to deal with my stress. I have to fight myself every night against the urge to take them all and get my miserable life over with. Think I'm going to throw them away. I'm not so sure how long I'll be able to resist the temptation to liberate myself from this hell.

Simon's snores keep me awake and remind me he's sleeping next to me. I find everything about him disgusting. His attitude, his breath, his voice, his body—I can't find anything attractive or redeeming about him. It takes every ounce of my strength to remain civil, and I'm so tired. I pray to God, each night, to take me rather than Stephanie's daughter who's dying of lymphoma. Life isn't fair. She's young and has so much going for her while I've done nothing but waste my life.

I hadn't thought about Stephanie in years. She was in my Sunday school class and kept mostly to herself. She took Greek dance classes with my mother who encouraged her to dance for the festivals. Stephanie went from being shy to one of the best dancers in the church. The news of Stephanie's illness devastated my mother. She went to Stephanie's house at least twice a week to cook, clean and help out in whatever way she was needed. During the late stage of Stephanie's illness, my mother was on call twenty-four hours. All this happened shortly after my mother started to challenge my father. He was still getting used to the "Americanized Maria," as he called her, and he didn't appreciate his dinner's late arrival on the table.

"It's a shame about Stephanie, but you got your own family to take care of," he'd say on more than just a few occasions.

"Quiet or you'll be eating at Antonio's Pizza from now on," she'd say.

The threat of take-out never failed to shut my father up. Reading through my mother's journal reawakened my hatred for him. How he could put what he did behind him was beyond my comprehension. If things worked out the way my Sunday school teachers taught me, my father would still have been in jail. From the way reality presented its ugly self, the good got punished, and evil brought home the prize. And the more sinister the deed, the higher the award. One of the last entries in my mother's journal started to put things together for me.

Simon told me we could no longer afford to pay for Markos's guitar lessons. I feared I'd have to tell Markos he'd have to stop, and I didn't want to do that. Since he started playing, he stopped hanging around at the rink and getting into trouble. Markos's music teacher, Steve, told me he's a prodigy, and I believe him. Markos gets up two hours before school to practice and continues when he gets home from school, only breaking to eat his dinner. On more than one occasion, I had to bring a plate of food to his room because he forgets to eat. His grades have also improved, and all this came from his love of music. Simon is impressed with the progress Markos made, and the two haven't argued in months. I've never seen my son so committed to anything, and I'm afraid if I stop his lessons, he'll go back to the way he used to

be. That's unacceptable to me, and I tried to think of alternative ways to pay. The only thing I could offer was my cooking, which Steve seems to like a lot. Whenever we had leftovers, I'd send Markos to his lesson with a plate of whatever I made for dinner. Steve told me it was always the best meal of his week. Poor man. He lives all alone, and all he eats is Chinese take-out and frozen dinners. It's a shame for a kind man like him to live like that, so last week I offered to make him a tray of spanakopita for each lesson until I could afford to pay him again. I was relieved when he told me he'd rather take the food than the money. I'm so glad Markos can continue his lessons. I only wish I could've recognized his talent sooner. It's something that still hurts me because it reminds me of how my father completely dismissed my own love of singing. How did I not recognize this sooner? I failed as a mother. It may be too late to make peace with Leda, but I plan on making it up to Markos, and I think I'm off to a promising start.

After I got out of the hospital, I went to visit Steve. As I thought about what I'd say to him, the motion-detector lights betrayed my presence, and Steve opened the door.

"Still doing lounge gigs?" I asked.

"And weddings." He opened the screen door. "Welcome to my hole in the wall."

"Does it still lead into the dimension of jazz and blues?"

"In here, nothing else exists."

I went in and was surprised to find that Steve's studio appeared almost exactly like it did when I had my last lesson. It was surprising as this wasn't the same building.

"I'll never do another wedding again," I said.

"Heard about your one and only experience."

I probed the pictures Steve had on the wall of the various bands he played with. My favorite one was of him jamming on a large concert stage with Joe Cocker.

"Who told you?" I asked.

"Dreg." Steve stood in the middle of the room with his hands crossed in front of him. He always did that, and it made him look uptight.

"You know Dreg?"

"I subbed for his band a few times," Steve said.

"Dreg hired me for my *one and only* wedding gig. He praised me after the first set and cursed me soon after the groom tossed the garter belt."

"He told me that because of you, the Golden Manor banned him from playing at their establishment."

"I did Dreg a favor. That place has no respect for privacy. What kind of business hangs a security camera in the dressing room?"

"But with the bride?" Steve smirked. "That was so cold, man."

"We dated each other in high school, and we were both drunk on booze and nostalgia." I searched through Steve's massive collection of vinyl. It would've taken me into the next week to appreciate all the album covers. "I felt bad afterwards and told Dreg I'd play a few gigs for free. He turned me down."

"Dreg can hold a grudge," Steve said.

I removed an Etta James album and read through the credits.

"I checked out some of your releases," Steve said. "They're pretty good."

"Thanks." I placed the album back where it belonged.

"Except for the one with the remake of alternative tunes." He shook his head. "'Lips Like Sugar?' What were you thinking?"

"The president of my fan club loves it."

"Is she the only member?"

"Probably." I picked out a John Coltrane record. "Can I borrow this?"

"If it'll help bring you back to our side, keep it."

"I never take sides. It's too limiting." I glanced up at a picture of Steve playing on stage with his band. "Why did you stop recording?"

"I lost my momentum."

"Your fiancée should help awaken your inspiration."

"She already did. I wrote a few songs since I met her."

I faced Steve. His scarred face was still hard to look at. It brought the night his injuries happened into full view, and I didn't want to remember. I spent years hating Steve almost as much as my father, but now all I saw was a man as broken as me. "Mr. Pagels, I…"

"Think you're old enough to call me Steve."

"Steve…I'm not sure why I'm here."

"It's weird for me as well." Steve searched through a few stacks of CDs and pulled one out. "When words fail." He handed me the CD.

"Heard it while I was in the hospital."

"I thought my songs were awful. She brought them all to life."

"Is that how you?—"

"We didn't want to hurt you. She wanted to wait until after she talked to your father."

"You made her happy, Steve. I know that now. You saved her, and for that, I'll always be grateful."

"She saved me too."

I pointed to Steve's favorite guitar that hung on the wall. It was a Gibson. "We should play some time."

"I'd like that a lot, Markos."

I returned home and listened to Steve's music that was a mix of blues and country. My mother's soprano voice was beautiful. Her phrasing was relaxed, and the way she slid her notes at the end of each phrase reminded me of Dinah Washington. After the first listen, I came up with arrangements for the songs and programmed some accompanying electronic drum beats on a sequencer. I had recently gotten into trip hop, and the style suited Steve's music. I played them for him, and he intuitively got where I was going with the sound. We decided to put out a joint release and mixed in my mother's vocals. After only one month of rehearsals with Snaps and Donnie, we cut the album in under two weeks. Although I was starting to feel better, I still avoided Jessie. I didn't want to be around her until I fixed myself. I never got that we're always a work in progress.

On the Retro Side of the Tunnel

der   a   sha - dy   ban -yan   tree._____   A   qui -et   place   where__   I   can   sta

We strolled along a narrow street and halted when we viewed a tunnel up ahead.

"Don't remember that being there," I said.

We approached the entrance, and we could see through to the other side from where a bright light emanated.

"Let's go in," I said.

"I want to know where I'm going before I leave."

"We can't stay here forever. If we blank out like we did back at the park, we may not wake up again, and I'd rather finish things up on our terms."

"But what if we're not supposed to go inside?"

"I have a strong feeling we should enter."

"How can you be sure?"

"I can't. But I think it showed up for us."

"While you're new at introspecting, I'm new at trusting my instincts. That was always your strength."

"You're not alone, Stella. I'm here with you."

I took her hand, and she reluctantly entered with me. Once we were inside, a low hum reverberated against the walls and the ceiling. I could even feel my feet vibrating inside my boots.

"Name that pitch." Stella said.

"I can't."

"Two in one night. You're fading fast."

"Don't remind me."

We continued to walk but weren't getting any closer to the light. The tunnel appeared to extend infinitely.

"We have to get out of here," Stella said. "I can't take that sound anymore."

"Soon as I figure out where here is, I'll get you out."

Stella pulled my arm. "Let's turn back. I'm not ready for this."

I glanced back from where we entered. It was pitch black. "I don't think we can."

Stella wept. "If we're approaching the proverbial light at the end of the tunnel, that will be the end of us. I'm not ready to say goodbye." She hugged me. "I don't want to lose you, and we still don't know what happened to Jess—"

A chord sounded on top of the hum, and the ground started to vibrate beneath us. The chord never settled on any particular combination of notes. As they changed, the hum remained constant. I can't effectively explain what produced the tone. Imagine a string and wind instrument combined, and you'd get the idea but never the actual sound in your head.

A surge of electricity shot up through my body, paralyzing all my limbs. "Tell me you felt that."

"I felt something."

We were lifted off the ground, and Stella clasped my hand as we were drawn towards the light. Once outside, we were released from whatever held us. Looming ahead was an illuminated triple-helix contained within a glowing, semitransparent pillar of light. It stretched up to the sky until it disappeared from view. Small pearls of light glimmered as they shot up through each of the strands.

I slowly walked towards it. "Either I'm on some really intense drugs in a psych ward or…" I took another step closer and was knocked to the ground by some strong imperceptible force.

Stella kneeled beside me. "Are you okay?"

"That was weird. It felt like someone pushed me away."

We got up, and Stella attempted to approach the pillar.

"Be careful."

Stella entered the pillar without any resistance, and her skin lit up like a light bulb. "Can you see it?" She swayed from side to side as though dancing to the rhythm of the pearls of light. "It's pure love!" Stella spun around in a circle and smiled as she had when she danced within the flames.

"Looks more like a large alien lava lamp." I craned my head to take in the vastness of the pillar. "Music Man would love this."

Stella waved her hand through the helix, and it produced a wind-chime type of sound. "Do you hear that, Markos?" She lowered her hand, and the chime rang at a lower pitch. When she raised her hand the pitch ascended. She swept her other hand into the helix, and a higher octave sounded. "It's like a theremin!"

"Can you play the theme from *The Day the Earth Stood Still* on it?" I laughed.

Stella dropped her arms to her side. "Not now!"

"I was only kidding. I know how much you hate science fiction."

Stella stepped out of the pillar with the most angelic smile I'd ever seen. "Along with their accompanying movie soundtracks."

"Wish you told me sooner. I would've played them with my headphones on."

"We're not finished yet."

"Did the hippie light display tell you that?"

"In a sense…yes."

The pillar collapsed into a small point of light and shot off into the heavens.

"Think I failed the test. The elitist floor-lamp doesn't believe I'm good enough to join heaven's country club."

"Maybe you haven't let go of everything."

"Would've been helpful if it gave me a hint before blasting off to who knows…"

During our discussion, everything around us had rearranged into a neighborhood I knew well. We now stood in front of Steve's house that I hadn't been to since I was sixteen.

"Guess I gotta go for a visit, whether I want to or not."

"Where are we?"

"Steve's place."

"Your music teacher?"

A car pulled in front of the building, and my mother got out.

"Who is that?" Stella asked.

"My mother." I ran towards the porch as she rang the doorbell and adjusted her orange knit cap. She never left the house without it when the temperature dropped below sixty-five.

Steve answered the door.

"Is Markos ready?"

"He never showed up," Steve said. "I tried to call, but no one answered."

"Sometimes I got a little restless and skipped lessons to jam with Flipper and Music Man," I told Stella. "It was the only time I could sneak in a visit. My father didn't let me hang out with them."

My mother entered Steve's home, and I followed.

"I'm coming with you," Stella said. "It'll be great to finally learn something about your mother."

"You may change your mind if this is going where I think it's going."

You're the Syrup in My Baklava

Sit   with   my   friends   and   play   all   day.

My mother watched Steve as he tidied up the couch that was covered with magazines and coffee-stained sheet music. She removed her cap, and Steve took a step back, nearly tripping over the coffee table. He dropped the papers and bent down to pick them up. My mother turned away from Steve to keep herself from laughing.

Steve threw all the papers on the coffee table and adjusted the rim of his hat in an attempt to look debonair. "Sorry about the mess."

"You don't need to clean up on my account." My mother sat on the couch. "You live alone." She smiled. "I understand."

Steve stared at her, entranced.

"Why are you looking at me like that?" she asked.

"I…I like how you're wearing your hair."

As Steve pointed to his head, I couldn't help but laugh again.

Stella slapped the side of my arm.

"He never wore his fedora inside," I said.

Stella furrowed her brows.

"He was trying to hide his bald spot from my mother."

"You should take a lesson from him."

"What kind of lesson? On how to be a successful klutz?" I chortled. "A decent hair weave would've been less conspicuous than the hat."

Stella hit me again.

As my mother fluffed up her hair, and Stella lectured me on how to act like a gentleman, I recalled my mother's journal entry about that night.

Why can't Simon ever compliment me on my appearance? I appreciate it when a man looks at me like Steve did. I told him I used to sing in the high school chorus and even had the lead as Maria in "West Side Story." The director told me if I applied myself, I could have a successful career on Broadway. That really made my day. I also took tap lessons and got pretty good with that as well.

It feels great to be admired by a man again, but it also makes me sad because it reminds me of what I lost with Simon. He hasn't said anything nice about me in years. To him I'm just a cook and a maid, but I'm not afraid to tell him off anymore. He's weaker than I imagined him as he hardly answers back to me anymore. While I'm glad he leaves me alone, the way he stares at me is more creepy than Kyria Thassoula. I don't trust him anymore. I have to find a way to get out of this marriage. Only then will I feel in control of my life again. I had lots of dreams before I got married. Now I got nothing but regrets. It hurts to admit that I wish I never married Simon. It hurts because that would mean I would never have had Leda or Markos. I love them dearly, but I'm so miserable I can imagine a life without them. God forgive me, I love my children, but I have to be honest somewhere.

My mother organized the sheet music on the coffee table into a neat pile and picked it up.

Steve stood like a statue with his hands crossed in front of him. "Why did you stop singing?"

"I got married." She shuffled through the sheet music. "Never heard of these songs."

"They're mine"

"Can you play me one of them?"

"They're not any good."

"I'll be the judge."

Steve got out his Gibson acoustic and started playing a slow blues piece. He sang, and I wished he'd stop. Not only was he out of key, which drove my ears insane, his voice lacked the flexibility needed for the blues. My mother was impressed. At first, I thought she was being polite.

"You got a lot of talent…for writing music."

"Can you sing one for me so I can hear what your voice sounds like? Markos is always telling me you have a beautiful voice. I'd love to hear it."

"Oh no, I don't think so. I only sing in the choir at church."

"Come on, give it a shot. You'll have fun. The verse is easy." He sang through a few more painful bars. "Try it."

My mother sang through the first line with her eyes closed. Steve almost rolled over his guitar as he listened. I had an equally strong reaction, and I'd already heard my mother sing this material.

"That was sublime," Steve said.

"Really? Or are you just being kind because you like my baklava?"

"I like your baklava, but you also made my music taste good."

My mother cried.

"Did I say something wrong?" Steve asked.

"You said everything right." She smiled. "Thanks."

Stella glanced over at me. "I can't believe it. Liquid spills out of your eyes." She touched the side of my face, probably in an attempt to verify if what she was seeing was real. Stella never saw me cry.

I detested public displays of emotions, but I needed to witness this interaction to understand the depth of what Steve and my mother shared. I don't think I ever saw my mother smile with the full length of her teeth showing, and that told me more than any of the entries in her journal. "So that's what happiness looks like on her."

Stella held my hand. I turned to hug her but kept my eyes on Steve and my mother.

"I knew there was a reason I met you," Steve said.

"What do you mean?"

"When you first came here with Markos, something about you stood out. And after tonight, I know why."

"All I did was sing a song."

"You did so much more. You brought my music to life."

"What now?"

"My friend has a studio. Would you be interested in recording with me?"

My mother's smile got wider. "You really think I'm good enough?"

"You're a natural."

"I gotta ask my husband first. He thinks music is a waste of time. He's all over Markos about it."

After he saw her out, Steve watched her until she got into the car and drove away.

Stella and I sat on the steps in front of Steve's home. I tapped my foot on the ground and strummed "This Old House" on my guitar.

"Are we finished here?" Stella asked.

"I want to say yes, but something tells me that whoever sent us here doesn't want to go easy on me."

"Tell me what happened."

I continued playing, and Stella covered the strings with her hand.

"You need to confront this," she said.

"Why now?"

"So we can move on."

"I don't want to move on yet. We just found each other again, and I'm not ready for us to end."

"Stop with the false sentiment, Markos. This isn't about me."

I got up and leaned against the porch rail. Stella came over and stood beside me.

"Is that what you really think of me?" I asked. "Because if you do, I want you to know right now there's nothing false about how I feel about you."

"I believe you, but what's happening here isn't about us." Stella put her hand over mine. "The time has come for you to stop avoiding whatever brought you here."

"I died. How can I possibly avoid that?"

"You're doing the same thing here that you did while you were alive. You kept everything inside you until you released it by a self-destructive act."

"Since I can't kill myself anymore, what other harm can I possibly do to myself here?"

"Misjudge yourself."

"This isn't only about me. It's about you, it's about my mother, it's about my father, it's about Jessie, but not necessarily in that particular order. And while we're sitting here watching my screwed-up childhood, Jessie's fate is still unknown to us. This is too much to deal with, Stella. I need time to think things through, but I can't seem to slow things down here. And you know how I hate to be rushed. It messes with my thinking."

My mother's car pulled in front of the curb. She got out and ran to the front door crying.

"Round two begins," I said.

"Why is she crying?" Stella asked.

Steve opened the door, and my mother went inside.

"Does this have anything to do with the fire?" Stella asked.

"Who told you?" I widened my eyes. "Leda. I knew it."

"I found out about everything on the internet. I kept hoping you'd trust me enough to confide in me, but you never did." She pointed to the door. "Is this the night?"

"I'm not sure, and I don't wanna stick around here to find out." I walked away, cursing the invention of the internet.

"You can't run away anymore, Markos!"

"Why not? It's not so bad here."

"I'll go in myself then." Stella opened the door and entered.

Not wanting her to get any wrong ideas about my mother, I went in after her. Stella knew how to operate me.

My mother took off her cap and rapidly began to organize the sheet music on Steve's coffee table. I tried to remember the night I had seen her this upset. She masked her emotions around me very well.

"What did he say?" Steve asked.

"I'm tired of my life," my mother said. "I've spent the last twenty years living for everyone but myself. I deserve a chance to live my dreams."

"He said no?"

"The selfish bastard called me an old lady and said I'd make him the laughingstock of the church if I was seen singing in a nightclub. He told me only whores sing in clubs. I'm tired of putting on the happy family act, and I told him that tonight. I told him if he didn't give me space to breathe, I'd leave him."

"What if I try and talk to him?"

"Oh no. That would make things much worse."

"I'm sorry to hear that. I was looking forward to gigging with you."

"He can't stop me. I won't let him treat me like his servant anymore." My mother gave Steve a quick hug. "I won't let you down. When I make a promise I keep it."

Steve took a step back and regressed to his statue posture. "If it'll make things easier, we can stick to recording tracks whenever Markos doesn't show up for a lesson."

"I'm gonna sing with you. I don't care what *Simon says* anymore."

After a few seconds of silence, my mother and Steve both exploded in a fit of laughter.

"Simon says, don't sing," Steve said.

"But I will…without asking for permission."

Steve grinned. "Your husband doesn't know how lucky he is to have you. I'd give up everything to have a woman like you in my life…even my musical talent."

"Do you mean that?"

"I do." Steve slowly approached her. "I wanted to tell you that for the longest time, but I—"

My mother threw her arms around Steve. They passionately kissed and then slowly faded away.

"My mother gave up her life to raise Leda and me," I said, "and it was slowly killing her. I couldn't see it. I used to get mad at Leda when she'd yell at my mother about being a martyr, but she was right."

"It was her choice," Stella said.

"It's not as simple as that. She was raised to be a wife and mother. Her own dreams were irrelevant until she partnered with Steve." I glanced at my mother's cap that was on the coffee table. "She told him she was gonna leave my father, and two weeks later…it happened."

The room ignited into an inferno around us, and a rock came crashing through the bay window. I grabbed Stella's hand, and we ran through the flames and out the door.

The Truth Can't Be Undone

Trust in me and fol-low a-long, when ev-er you hear m

I was in the middle of practicing my scales when my father had entered the room.

"Unplug; we're going for a ride."

"Go on without me. I'm practicing."

I continued playing, and my father snatched the guitar and slammed it against the wall. I shot up and grabbed my father's arm, but I wasn't strong enough to stop him from smashing Ezza against the wall again. He tossed her broken remains on the ground. "You're done! Now get in the car before I smash your head to pieces next!"

I followed him outside, trapped somewhere between shock and anger, feeling neither enough to commit to an appropriate reaction. Once in the car, my father started mumbling to himself. We drove around for over half an hour, and neither of us uttered a word. My father turned on the news station and got perturbed when he heard them talking about the economy. He switched over to an oldies station and drove for another thirty minutes. We ended up in a parking lot behind a high industrial-metal fence. I didn't notice where we were as my mind remained back in my room were Ezza lay broken on the floor. The image of her shattered body finally sank in. I took a lot from my father through the years, but tonight he started a war I was ready to fight. Music was synonymous to my life, and when my father destroyed Ezza, I took his attack personally. My father broke me like my Fender Strat. I was broken from all the beatings and insults he threw at me, broken from my inability to stand up for myself, and broken because I no longer had a guitar. There comes a point when you're broken into so many pieces that you can't break anymore. That's the condition I remained in until, but not ending with, my death.

"Blue Moon" came on when I realized where we were. From behind the fence, the second floor of Steve's home was visible. He lived on a one-way street, and some of his students parked in this lot to avoid driving around the block.

"Why are we at Mr. Pagels's house?" I asked.

"Your mother told me she was behind on payments for your lessons."

"I thought he preferred food?"

"He only said that to be kind." My father got out of the car and shut the door. He peaked through the window with a large smile that didn't appear natural.

"I'm gonna show Mr. Pagels how much I appreciate all that he's done for our family." He walked away.

My father is gonna pay for my guitar lessons? For real? He again made me feel as if I was in the wrong. My anger didn't seem justified anymore. Maybe my father metamorphosed into a new man, reborn out of the guilt he had over breaking Ezza. Sentimentality always made him uncomfortable, so he went to pay for my lessons to show me how sorry he was. This was like a miracle. The previous year, he didn't even want me involved with music. *If he's paying for my lessons, that must mean he's gonna get me another guitar.* Sometimes when you want an outcome bad enough, you can easily miss the reality of what's actually happening.

I flipped through the stations on the radio and stopped when "Manic Depression" came on. I sat back, closed my eyes and pictured myself jamming with Jimi. A few more songs played, and I wondered what was taking my father so long. I figured he and Steve were talking and getting to know each other better. We'd all be friends. Life was looking better until "This Old House" came on. I opened my eyes as an outspread of smoke billowed up from behind the fence. I got out of the car and raced to a padlocked gate that led to Steve's backyard. I climbed over the fence and when I touched down on the other side, the whole backside of the house was submerged within a wall of flames.

I ran to the front of the house where my father stood watching the blaze. His expression still haunts me to this day. I don't believe in demons, but if one existed he'd smile like my father did on this night.

"Did you call the fire department?" I asked as I watched the flames start to overtake the front side of the house.

"And the police...but by the time they get here, your mother will already be burning in hell." he said in a calm, detached voice. "Along with me."

That's when I noticed the gasoline can on the ground, and my mother's car parked in front of the house. The setting would have been glaringly obvious to a neutral observer. Admitting my father went nuts and burned down my music teacher's house wasn't an easy truth to admit.

"Mom's in there too! We gotta get them out!"

My father grabbed me by my shoulders and pulled me to face him. "The truth cannot be undone. We all eventually must pay."

I pushed him, ran for the door and tried to open it, but it was locked. I banged on the door, yelling for Steve and my mother. When I got no response, I picked up a rock and threw it at the bay window, shattering the glass. I took off my shirt and cleared the shards from the frame. I went to climb in, but my father pulled me out from behind.

"You crazy kid, you'll die!"

Fueled with high-octane rage, I freed myself and punched the side of his jaw with every ounce of my strength. My father charged me, but my fury easily overpowered him. I threw him to the ground. He tried to get up, and I kicked the bottom of his chin with the tip of my boot and ran back to the inferno.

The bay window was now overcome by flames, and I ran to the side of the house searching for another way to get in. Everywhere I ran, flames shot out at me. I noticed a light on in one of the upstairs windows and searched around for another rock to throw. I found one and threw it at the window with the light. The glass shattered, but even if Steve and my mother managed to get over to the window, there was no fire escape. They'd have to jump, but at least they'd stand a better chance of making it out alive. People survive falls, and I'm living proof of my assertion.

Sirens were nearing, and Steve opened the window I struck with the rock.

"Mr. Pagels, help's on the way!"

He stuck his head out.

"Is my mother okay?"

My father sneaked up from behind and knocked me to the ground. We rolled around until I got on top of him. I started to pound every inch of his face and chest.

"I'm gonna kill you. You bastard! Why the hell did you do that?"

"Go ahead, I deserve whatever you give me." He wailed. "I couldn't keep my family together anymore. I'm a failure."

I wrapped my hands around his neck and squeezed. My father stopped struggling. He *wanted* me to kill him, and I was willing to oblige. "Die you bastard! Die!" I kept repeating the words and pounded his head on the grass as I continued to choke him.

A light shone in front of me, but I couldn't shut myself off. It was as though my hands were under someone else's control.

"Freeze!" a male voice shouted.

I jumped to my feet, and a gun shot went off. I felt a burn on my chest as I fell to the ground. I woke up in the hospital with Leda by my side. According to the police, my father started the fire on impulse. He found the gasoline can in Steve's backyard and snapped when he saw my mother's car parked in front of his building. The police thought I started the fire and that I was about to murder my father. I understood the reaction of the cop who shot me, so I don't hold any animosity toward him. I would've killed my father if he didn't stop me. So in a way, I'm grateful I was shot. I didn't want to have blood on my hands. That night was my father's to own, and he owned it…until the state of New York told him he didn't need to anymore.

Siren Song

sing my song.   Hear my call, you'll ne-ver go wrong,   as   long as you hear my   song.   I

Stella and I silently watched the fire that had ravaged Steve's home. There was an eerie silence that contrasted what had occurred in reality. By now, there would've been a fleet of fire engines parked on the street, and my father would be on his way to the police station where he'd eventually be charged with murder in the second degree.

"One of the medics pronounced my mother dead in the ambulance," I said while still staring at the flames. "Steve survived, but he had third-degree burns on over fifty percent of his body. Their affair came out during the hearing. In his testimony, Steve said he blamed himself for my mother's death. If only he didn't leave the gasoline can out back. If only he kept up with the yard work, the flames wouldn't have raged out of control so quickly. I agreed with him. I thought he got what he deserved, and I blamed him for what happened to my mother as much as I blamed my father."

Stella took my hand.

"My father is now a free man, married to a woman younger than me. How can you reconcile your idea of god with such an inequity?"

"Your father may be okay for now, but he's going to have to go through all of this just as you did. He's going to have to bear witness and answer for what he did."

"He was a coward in life, and he'll probably be a coward in death. I'm sure he'll find an easy way out."

"Like you did before you died?"

"Don't you dare compare me to him! I played guitar to get away from my father. I didn't want to be anything like him. Music was the only thing that kept me going, kept me thinking I could be more than him, better than him, and he almost took that away from me."

"You got over the worst of it and survived."

"But we still don't know any more than we did when we first realized we were dead. Jessie's fate is still a mystery."

"When I entered the pillar, I connected to an inner peace I never had. I've come to accept I can't know everything. I don't like the feeling, but I have no other choice. I have to have the faith that she's okay."

I still found Jessie's unknown fate unsettling, but I didn't bring it up. Stella was at peace, and I didn't want to take it away from her. I was thankful that her faith was restored and hoped she had enough for the both of us.

She gazed into the fire as though entranced by it. "I always wondered why you kept this part of your life hidden."

"Not as hidden as I would have liked."

"From what I see, you fought back."

"I didn't fight hard enough."

"That's not the way I saw it."

"My father saw his position as head of the household slipping away." I stared into the flames, and they began to entrance me as well. The deeper I peered at them, the more disconnected I felt from my surroundings. I barely heard my own voice as I spoke. "He must've felt as though he lost everything. Leda left, and I admired Steve more than him. And after all that, my mother declared herself independent. That probably bothered him a lot, not being needed."

"That's still no excuse for doing what he did."

"I know…but seeing this with my own eyes makes it hard for me to hate my father. I don't love him either. I don't know how I should feel about him."

"I understand your confusion. I also went to visit my father."

"How did that turn out?"

"I still would rather not discuss him, but let's just say I don't hate him anymore."

The flames began to hum, calling out to me as seductive as a siren's song. I couldn't resist, couldn't reason. It seemed as though everything I was saying was directed to them. "I was lucky to have Steve in my life. He was always patient with me. Whenever I got full of myself, he'd make some comment about how no one likes working with a smart ass no matter how fabulous a guitarist he is. He made me see myself without talking down to me like my father. I owe my life to him as well as to Music Man, Flipper, and Ezza. I took them all for granted. I never thanked them for being there for me…for saving me."

The flame strands intertwined into a braid, rolled into a tight spiral and spun at such a high velocity that it sucked in Steve's home. The rate of the spin then slowed, pulsed, and widened into a bright vortex of energy. Airy music chimed and lured me towards the entryway.

"Where do you think you're going?" Stella grabbed my hand and pulled me back.

"I was into my own life. Never thought about anyone else's problems because I had enough of my own to deal with at home. If I took a step back far enough to realize what I was doing, I would've been okay, Ezza would've been okay, my mother would've been okay." I glanced at Stella. "We would've been okay, and Jessie would be safe sleeping in her bed right now." I pulled back my hand and stared back at the vortex that now seemed to be singing a song for my ears only.

"Don't do this," Stella said.

"I already did." I put down my guitar case. "Truth can't be undone. I must pay." I sidled towards the vortex.

Stella grabbed me hard by the sleeve of my shirt. "You have no right to judge that boy so harshly!"

Stella's voice hurt my ears. Everything hurt. I had this inner sense that if I entered the vortex all the noise would go away, replaced by the beautiful music that was calling to me.

"What did you expect to do?" Stella asked. "You were just a child."

"If I could go back, I'd kill him for what he did to us."

"Would you really?"

"A few hours before the ransom deadline, I stood at the door of my father's house with a gun in my hand. Since I was gonna die anyway, I figured I could make him pay for what he did to my mother. I wanted to pull the trigger, I really wanted to, but I couldn't."

"Why?" Stella yanked my shirt sleeve again. "Tell me now!"

I glimpsed at Stella, at the vortex, and then back at Stella again.

"Damn it, Markos, for once say what's on your mind!"

"I'm not like my father, but that doesn't absolve or change anything."

"You need to internalize what you just said so that we can get out of this hell we're creating for ourselves."

"Is that what we're doing? Thanks for *enlightening* me, Stella. I thought this was only one of my dreams that I'm gonna wake up from tomorrow morning and say, 'Hey Markos, that was a real crazy one. You should up the dose of your meds before you have another *incident*.'"

Stella never reacted well to sarcasm, but the woman was on a mission. Once she had something on her mind, she never stopped until she was acknowledged.

"You're about to judge yourself. Think before reacting for once. I doubt you can change your mind once you enter that…whatever it is."

I continued towards the vortex, spellbound and ready to accept my sentence.

Stella ran ahead and turned to me with her palm pushed forward. "If you go, I'll be right behind you."

"I enjoyed the sparring while we were alive, Stella. But now, it's just scaring me."

She put her hands on her hips. "How about I go first and tell you what it's like to be damned. Once you pass through we can compare notes."

I pushed Stella out of my way, and she seized me by the back of my shirt and violently pulled me towards her.

"I took your avoidance when we were alive, but I won't take it here! You're not going anywhere until you listen!"

Stella's voice came out loud and shrill. A stabbing pain in my ears almost knocked me to the ground, but I didn't want her to stop. She was freeing me from the grip of the alluring siren song.

"Do you honestly want to condemn a boy for being a victim? A boy whose only refuge was music that helped shelter him from his pain?" Stella stepped in front of me and cupped my face with her hands. "And when he grew up, music continued to mask his hurt. The more he played, the better he felt. He barely took a break between gigs because the silence forced him to listen to the voices from his past, voices he's been trying to record over ever since."

I felt the sting of tears in my eyes, and I could hear my father's voice saying, "Save the crying for the sissies and pansies." I never saw him cry until the night I almost killed him.

"It's time to stop playing and just listen to the music, Markos."

"I am, but I hate listening to the oldies station."

"The truth can't be undone, and you already paid." Stella took my hand. "And if you enter that thing…your father would've been right about you."

Hearing that pulled me right out of my trance. "I paid enough for his crimes." The music stopped, and the vortex collapsed into one of those cosmic fireflies I wanted to swat at since the start of this netherworld adventure. It flew away into the night sky.

"You always knew how to tap into my *alphattitude*," I said.

"I listened to your album with that title."

I hugged Stella. I didn't want to let her go, but another vision decided to interrupt our moment. As I lay on the ground Jessie tried to hand me the red lotus, and I refused. She cried as she sang her song. The sound of her voice kept me locked in, just like the music from the vortex. Jessie tried to give me the lotus again. This time, I reached for it. Just as I was about to touch the petals, the neighborhood did another round of rearranging, and we found ourselves back at the brownstone. The way Stella and I both stared at each other told me we were about ready to get off this ride.

Going Bananas

home   when the moon is   high.   I   can-not stay be - cause my mom

I sat on the curb playing "Funkimental," one of my rock instrumentals. I hoped my strumming would get Stella to stop pacing, but it only seemed to make her move faster. I segued over to "Wipeout," and a few measures later I was interrupted by another vision. I saw flames, Steve and Jessie, who again tried to hand me the red lotus. As she sang, I wanted to slam my guitar against the pavement. I was that on edge.

"What?" Stella asked.

I stopped playing. "I didn't say anything."

"You screamed so loud I thought someone was killing you."

"I didn't scream."

"'Funkimental,' 'Wipe Out,' scream. Happened exactly in that order."

"I didn't think you were paying attention."

"We have to figure this out before we both lose our memories."

"I know Stella. That's why I'm playing. It helps me think."

I played again, and Stella tried to grab my guitar. I pulled it back.

"It's time you stop playing and start dealing."

"This is how I deal!" I dramatically strummed "El Toro."

"I should've directed that statement to myself." Stella clutched her head. "I'm not handling this well at all."

I terminated my pitiful attempt at playing flamenco. "You're doing all right, Stella."

"No…I'm not. I have no idea of anything anymore. I romanticized the idea of death, and what it would be like. It's not as wonderful as I imagined it to be."

"What about your experience in the peace pillar?"

"Probably a hypnotic suggestion I gave to myself to make me forget about Jessie."

"I agree that death hasn't been a party, but you have a better grasp of what's happening here."

"What you more than likely did that brought you here proves you're stronger than you think. You made the ultimate sacrifice for Jessie."

"Does that mean you want me to put my cape back on?"

"I should never have told you to take it off. The world needs superheroes now more than ever."

I smiled at Stella's improved opinion of me. It wasn't her words as much as the way she looked at me when she spoke them. She respected me. "Now that our mess is cleaned up, we can concentrate on finding Jessie."

"We may never find out what happened to her. You need to accept that." Stella sighed. "I need to accept that."

"And I will. After I've explored all our options." I stared up at the brownstone and then at the fire escape and started to remember something. "You were upstairs, and I think I ended up back here, only I can't recall how. I was supposed to take a dive off the WXQX building."

"If the kidnapper wasn't Gus, who was it then?"

"Me," I said more to myself and remained fixated on the fire escape.

Stella cried. "I didn't want to believe it was true. I told Teddy —"

"Not the real kidnapper. Only the one here."

Stella squinted her eyes at me.

"Long story. I'd rather spend the time looking for Jessie." I got up and paced to clear my head. "Other than speaking to people who died long ago and the kidnapper being me, there has to be some truth to what we're experiencing here."

"If we have no memory of what happened, it'll be difficult to ascertain what is the truth."

"But not impossible." I stopped and examined the brownstone, focusing on the fire escape on the side of the building. "I think I took on the role of the kidnapper here because I was trying to keep myself from remembering what happened. Cro kept talking about painting the truth, and Leda brought up those pictures within a picture. The ones where if you stare at them long enough, the image eventually reveals it…"

I was interrupted by a vision of the mime mask blowing by me as I lay on the pavement, bleeding from a wound on my abdomen.

"Did you remember something?" Stella asked.

"The mime mask. Thought I made it up to keep myself from finding out I was the kidnapper, but I'm not sure about that anymore."

"When did you see it?"

"In a vision and later when the kidnapper was wearing it while performing a sidewalk mime routine. I then found him outside Jake's and chased him all the way to Steve's house that was on fire. I thought Gus was behind it, along with the kidnapping until I met him at Jake's and…" I faced Stella. "When did you turn in before all of this began?"

"I went to my room to meditate around eight."

"You fell asleep after that, which means I never overheard the phone conversation between you and Teddy where he told you he couldn't rule me out as a suspect in Jessie's kidnapping." I waved my index finger in the air. "And that must mean I never pulled a gun on Gus at—"

"You pulled a gun on Gus?"

"I didn't tell you?"

Stella frowned and slowly shook her head.

"Well, none of that matters anyway. Dot was serving us, and she died over five years ago, It couldn't have happened for real. And if I didn't meet up with Gus, he wouldn't have been around when the kidnapper called." I slapped my hands together. "Gus is the kidnapper! I was right all along!"

"Not necessarily. Discerning between fact and fiction here isn't a logical process. You could've replaced a familiar face with one you couldn't recognize."

"You really know how to rain all over my concert." I thought back to my last meeting with Gus when he shot me and what Stella said about how she knew I was dead. "I couldn't control his actions."

"You think he's here with us?"

"Let's go find out."

Death is convenient. When you know who you're looking for, it's easy to find them when you're dead. All you need to do is think about the person in your quest, and you instinctively know where to go. We walked for a block and found the grocery store Gus worked at. We went inside, and it was filled with customers in various stages of shopping.

"So this is where everyone's been hiding out," Stella said.

I picked up a pack of gum, opened it, and threw a piece into my mouth. Stella glared at me as though I had committed a major felony.

"None of this is real…remember?"

Stella's eyes popped open. "I should've had you make some baklava. I missed it almost as much as you." She rushed to the candy display case and grabbed a Snickers bar and a Kit Kat. "These will have to do." She snatched a few more chocolates.

We headed to the produce department. With no fear of dying from a heart attack that would've been my last stop, but I wasn't there for the dollar-forty-nine special on zucchini.

Gus was placing some apples in a bin. He pretended not to notice us when we walked up to him.

"What's up Gus?" I grabbed an apple from the bin and took a bite.

"They weren't washed."

I took another bite and talked with my mouth full. I savored the repulsed expression on Gus's face. "What's the worst that could happen to a man who takes a bite out of a dirty fruit when he's already dead?" I chomped off some more flesh from the apple.

Gus winced. "He'd probably get sent to hell for being a slob."

"Knew you were gonna say that." I kicked over the bin.

Apples rolled all over the floor, and Gus dropped to the ground on all fours.

"Why are you here?" Gus said as he crawled around gathering the apples.

"To continue our discussion."

"I told you we'd talk after I got off." Gus lifted the bin and placed it back on the cart.

"Are you really dead?" I asked.

"I was only kidding, Markos. You need to learn how to take a joke. I swear you haven't changed at all."

I capsized a neighboring banana bin. A few patrons gathered to watch, and I took a bow. Stella hit the side of my arm.

"Sorry, force of habit," I said.

Gus picked up a few bunches of bananas and returned them to the bin.

"Why are you doing this, Gus?" I said.

"Got bills to pay."

"You're dead. Who do you owe money to? God?"

Stella hit my arm again, harder. "Antagonizing him won't get him to talk."

"You should listen to your wife," Gus said. "She's obviously the one with the brains."

I was about to take a swing at him when Stella grabbed a cart from a shopper and pushed it at me. I jumped out of the way.

"We'll do this my way now," she said.

Stella approached Gus, and when she paused to place her hands on her hips, I knew the situation was about to get intense.

"You're in *big* trouble now, Gus." I crossed my arms and smiled.

"Did you take our daughter?" Stella asked politely.

"You too?" Gus lifted the banana bin. "Your husband is not the most rational person tonight. If I were you, I'd stay away from him."

Stella overturned a tomato crate, and I pressed my hand over my mouth to stop from laughing. The shoppers that gathered around us didn't exercise similar restraint, which made Gus appear as he used to moments before the guys in the football team shoved him into his locker. He got down on all fours to pick up the fallen produce.

"Unfortunately for you, I'm not any more *rational* than Markos," Stella said. "My daughter is missing, and if you don't tell me where she is"—she crouched in front of Gus, picked up a tomato and squeezed it—"your head will meet a similar fate."

Tomato guts dripped onto the floor. Stella threw the remains at Gus, wiped her hands on his shirt and stood.

Everyone applauded, and I joined in. Stella's grocery store rampage drew in the rest of the phantom shoppers. I pushed my way through to get a better view, and I wished I had some popcorn. This bardo production was getting interesting, and it was great therapy for Stella. I'd been trying to get her to loosen up for years. Between her outburst at the Jazz Room and here, she probably released twenty years worth of stress.

"Leave now, or I'll sue you both for defamation of character." Gus threw a few tomatoes in the bin.

"Your *character* should be the least of your worries now!" Stella glanced around, and I pointed to a cart filled with potatoes. She grabbed the cart and flipped it over.

Gus ran over to her. "Have you lost your mind?"

"I've lost more than that! I lost my life!" She darted to another cart filled with a variety of onions and knocked them over and did the same with the apples, pears, strawberries, oranges, and grapes. "And if I lose my daughter, I won't let you rest in peace until God damns you for an eternity!"

Gus crawled on the floor in a futile attempt to clean the mess. Customers huddled around him and laughed.

He sat up and waved his hands at them. "Get away from me!"

They all leaned down over him and laughed harder.

"Don't you have any shopping to do?" Gus put his hands over his ears. "Leave me alone." He rocked forward and back, crying.

The manager ran over. "What in blasted heavens is going on here?" He examined the mess and thrust his finger inches from Gus's face. "I moved you from the deli because you couldn't figure out the metric system. Thought this would be easier for you, but you can't seem to keep the produce inside their bins where they belong. Can't you do anything right?"

Gus stood up and clasped his hands together. "I'm sorry, Mr. Phipps. I'll clean everything up."

"Don't bother. I want you outta here. You're nothing but a failure, and failures got no business in the produce department."

"I'll pay for everything, Mr. Phipps. Please don't fire me," Gus sniveled.

"You better believe you're paying for this. It's coming out of your last check." Mr. Phipps stormed off, and everyone continued to laugh at Gus, including myself.

Stella looked as though she was about to work me over next. Admittedly, I enjoyed her threatening stare, and not in a masochistic way. Death surprised me in that way. One moment you're about to damn yourself to wherever the fiery vortex leads you to. In the next, you're laughing at your ex-wife who just trashed the grocery shortly after working over a jazz club where you had a weekly gig. Stuff like that doesn't happen when you're alive. When you're dead, anything goes!

Gus pushed himself out of the crowd, and we followed him.

"Leave me alone!" he said.

I forced him against the glass door. "I'll haunt you for an eternity if I have to."

"What do you want from me?"

"Your cooperation."

"To do what?"

"Find a way out of this phantom freak-show."

"I don't want to leave."

I let go of him. "Why would you want to stay? It's not as though your life is better here than when you were alive."

We turned to face a crowd of people who followed us over.

"This is all your fault, Markos!" He opened the door and left. Stella and I followed behind him.

"Everything was getting back to normal until you arrived," he said.

"Yeah, yeah, I know. You blame me for everything that's wrong with your life, but I still don't know why. Can you enlighten me? And please don't tell me all of this is over the scholarship."

"We're supposed to get rewarded for hard work."

"Oh jeez, are you kidding me? Man, can you hold a grudge."

He stopped and pointed his finger at me. "You never work hard. You waste, waste, waste. Meanwhile, those of us who appreciate hard work are passed over for the lazies like you. The lazies don't put any effort into what they do because to them everything comes easy. They're the ones who have all the friends, get invited to all the parties, and take on positions of leadership."

I flipped up my hands. "What's wrong with that?"

"Nothing, if you didn't get rewarded for being lazy. But you do, and it makes no sense to me. I worked hard. I practiced all my scales, learned all the repertoire, and it got me nowhere."

"It's because you listened to your father," I said.

"You're right. I should've rebelled and turned into a delinquent like you. Crime pays well." Gus waved his hand in the glistening haze. "How atmospheric. I suppose this jazzy wonderland is your creation? Even in the afterlife, Markos Adamidis is the star of the show." He put down his arm. "Well, now it's me who's calling the shots. Since you can't book your new gig without my help, I suggest you play my set list if you don't want to remain here for an eternity." Gus walked away.

I pulled him by his sleeve. "Your threats amused me when we were kids. Now they're just pissing me off."

"I haven't even begun yet. I'm going to make you wish you were in hell."

I pushed him. "If you're here with me, I'm already there."

"Get used to it. You'll be staying a while."

"What do you have to gain by continuing this?"

"Retribution. That's all I have left." He walked away.

I tried to follow him, but Stella called me back.

"You could try being nice to him," she said.

"*Nice* to him? He's more than likely the reason we're here."

She crossed her arms. "What you're doing now isn't going to help us find Jessie."

"What I'm doing? Who got him fired and made him the laughingstock of the produce department?"

"I lost control. That doesn't mean you have to follow my lead."

"But it was so funny to watch you go bananas all over Gus." I laughed.

"Shut up, Markos! This isn't funny! Stop treating this as if it's one big joke!"

"This is how I deal, Stella!" My anxiety levels returned to maximum. "You know that. It's always been like that for me. If I took everything seriously all the time, I probably would've entered that vortex, and you would've been left here all alone to deal with the neurotic produce boy." I walked to calm my nerves. "I don't get the purpose of this test. Am I supposed to suck up to a guy who more than likely killed me…and you?"

"You need to let go of him to free yourself from him."

"What if he harmed Jessie? Would you be able to let that go?"

Stella didn't answer me.

"Remember what you did to that tomato?"

She turned away from me.

"Letting go sounds practical in theory," I said, "but in practice it seems we're both having a hard time with it."

"What now?" Stella asked.

I watched Gus disappear into the golden mist. "He wants to start a war, I'm gonna give him one."

The Scholarship Blues

Steve had been a major influence in my life. His appearance reminded me of my Sunday school teacher, but when he played the guitar, he lit up like a pack of fireflies that stretched out as far as your eyes could perceive. That's how I always used to describe him to my mother and probably why I'd been seeing fireflies throughout this whole experience.

I studied with Steve throughout tenth grade and into the summer when my practicing intensified as I no longer had schoolwork to worry about. During one of my lessons, Steve tried to persuade me to try out for the high school jazz band when school started up again in the fall.

"They're going to offer a scholarship to the one that gets in. You want to give it a shot?"

"Let me think about it." I didn't think I could beat Gus. He'd been playing since he was five.

"I need an answer now. I'm setting up the audition schedule."

"Maybe next year then."

Steve picked up his guitar and played a scale. "What am I playing?"

"D-flat minor."

"How do you know this?"

"I know what it sounds like."

He then strummed a few bars of the blues with his fingers. "What am I playing now?"

"The blues...in F"

Steve pointed to my guitar. I picked up Ezza and played along.

"Where does your talent come from?" He asked. "Does it come from a book or from you?" Steve stopped playing. "Anyone can learn technique, but not style and expression. That comes from within, and you got it within, man...traveling outside to your fingers and to the strings that are the output of your within." He put his guitar on the stand. "Don't worry about the technique, it'll come with time."

I didn't believe Steve, but my mother did. She bragged about my *talent* every Sunday during coffee hour.

"You'll be the first one in our family who will do something important," she told me.

With both my mother and Steve pushing me to audition, I gave in. My mother was more excited than I was. "I know you're gonna go far, Markos."

I didn't believe her either, but I appreciated the plate of lamb stuffed peppers she made in my honor.

I enjoyed arranging music almost as much as playing. Taking a song no one would ever expect to hear in a jazz style and making it my own began during this time. For my audition, I played "What Is and What Should Never Be," as a mid-tempo swing. Steve bobbed his head up and down to my comping and singing. After I finished, he told me Jimmy Page would've loved my rendition. I left feeling confident but as the rest of the week progressed, my anticipation over how I played in comparison to everyone else took over. Everything Steve told me about my natural ability was forgotten. My technical shortcomings lingered in my thoughts every day and only disappeared when I slept.

On Judgment Day, Gus and I sat outside the music room waiting for the results of our audition to be posted. He attempted to act like my mentor, but his advice sounded more like his usual showing off. "I've been playing for years. Don't feel bad if you don't get in."

"Yeah, it's cool," I said while strumming a new tune I'd written.

"I'm sure there'll be more scholarships."

"I don't care. When I'm through with school, I wanna see as much of the world as I can."

"You should care. These days, most session musicians can't get a gig without reading music."

"Not in Europe," I said. "Steve said it's easier to find work there as a musician. I'm gonna live in a different country every six months."

Gus shook his head. "I can't wait to start college. I'll get to jam with the best musicians in the country."

One of Steve's students came over and posted the results on the bulletin board. Gus ran to see them, and I continued playing my guitar.

Gus scanned the list and then turned towards me. "I can't believe it. They picked you over me."

I froze and stared at the board.

"You couldn't even play a major scale last year."

I got up to check because I thought Gus was jiving me. When I saw my name, I was ambivalent over the news. Steve called it right with me, but I still wasn't sure about the scholarship.

Gus fixated on the board as though he thought his name would appear by some unseen magical force.

"Don't feel bad," I said, "you're a better player than all of us." I laughed. "You'll get to jam with all the best musicians in the country when you get to college."

If Gus's stare launched missiles, I would've been annihilated in that instant.

"Don't take it so seriously, man," I said. "Your playing is good enough to get you into a decent college."

He ran off without his guitar, and I caught up with him about a block away from his house.

"You forgot something." I handed him the case.

"I don't want it."

"You're quitting just because you didn't get the scholarship?"

"When I get home, my father expects me to tell him I won. When I tell him you beat me, he's gonna call me the loser he always knew I was and stop paying for my guitar lessons."

I extended the case towards him.

"Didn't you hear what I said? It's yours now."

"I don't play a Gibson."

"Learn."

"You'll change your mind tomorrow."

"Take good care of it."

As I watched Gus walk away I pitied him, which was strange as most of the time I couldn't stand the kid. When he mentioned his father, I knew what he was going home to. You can always relate to people whose family life is as miserable as yours.

In the middle of dinner, my mother got a desperate call from Gus's mother. Gus's father pushed him over the edge, and he left home with his suitcase packed.

"I'm going over there." My mother put on her jacket and grabbed her keys.

"Stay out of it, Maria. Don't go sticking your nose in everyone's business. George can handle his own kid."

"He's the one who made Gus leave. All that pressure he put on the poor boy, it was too much. I warned Mildred something like this would happen if George didn't ease up on him."

"If you ask me, George wasn't hard enough on Gus. Spending so much time on music is a waste of time. There's no money in it unless you become a rock star. And let's face reality here. Gus doesn't have a drop of charisma." My father pointed his finger at me. "What are you staring at, Eddie Fisher?" He laughed. "Yeah, you got the style, the attitude and the talent. You surprised me with that last one. Didn't think you had it in you. But the chance you'll be able to make a decent living plucking your fingers on six strings is almost nonexistent. Better use that tenacious brain of yours to get you into med school or law school."

"There's more to life than money," I said.

"Like what?"

"Like love." My mother smiled and kissed my father on the cheek. "I'll see you in the morning."

My mother left to counsel Mrs. Barras, and I went up to my room and inspected Gus's Gibson SG. Apart from the fact that I didn't like playing a Gibson because it was Gus's favorite guitar, it felt as though it was transmitting dark energy. I put the Gibson back in its case and shoved it under my bed. I was going to give it back to Gus when he returned home, but I never saw him again until my gig at the Jazz Room when he stared at me exactly as he did in our last meeting. He tried to conceal it with a smile, but I recognized the contempt. In all the years since, I couldn't erase his expression from my mind. Something about it gave me a sense of foreboding.

Chrysalis

jun - gle　　　that　　　still　　　is　　　　true.

　　I showed up at Gus's place armed with the blues in my soul and two guitar cases in my hands.

　　Gus opened the door and crossed his arms in defiance. "What do you want?"

　　"Do you still play a Gibson?" I set down one of the cases. "I nabbed this one especially for you. It gave me luck, maybe it will for you."

　　"Didn't Father Nicholas teach you that stealing is a sin?"

　　"Can't move further south than I already have."

　　Gus picked up the case. "Did you even try it?"

　　"No reason." I glanced down at my case. "Got my Ezza to keep me warm."

　　"Excluding Stella, you always went for the cheap-looking women."

　　"Either say it through your amp or lower your volume." I pushed myself inside. "As for me, I want it loud and smooth. Think you can still handle that?"

　　"Haven't played in years, but my fingers haven't lost their memory."

We both plugged into his stereo and played the blues in G. I soloed through the first twelve bars while Gus comped the chords. It was a surreal experience, jamming with someone who probably killed me and kidnapped my daughter. I hated to admit it, but I was having fun. Death is weird that way. Perhaps in some alternate reality Gus and I actually got along.

Gus took the next twelve bars and soloed. We did this a few times through, each of us trying to out-dazzle the other in our little guitar war. When my turn came to solo again, I readied to finish Gus off. I stopped playing and got out my Robert J. bronze slide from my pocket. I could tell Gus was impressed, and he did his best to hide it.

I played a solo and four measures before the turnaround, he paused to plug in his wah-wah pedal. After he wah-wahed through his solo, he wouldn't let me back in. He wanted the bigger kaboom. He started to *sing*. Gus did have that one on me, and he knew it. I had a good voice, but Gus had a smoother falsetto. He made up some cute little lyrics.

I played my guitar early.
Before I went to school.
Yeah, I played the guitar early.
I practiced like a fool.
Till Markos made the jazz band.
Guess my playing wasn't cool.

"Mind if I take the next pass?" I asked.
"If you promise not to sing out of tune."
I played a few more bars, cleared my throat and started to sing.

Where's my daughter Jessie?
Haven't seen her since I died.
Oh, where's my daughter Jessie?
Want her right here by my side.

Won't you tell me where you took her.

Let's get off this crazy ride.

Gus stopped playing. "This gig is over." He put down his guitar.

"This won't be over until we finish." I put Ezza in her case. "How long do you think we can stay here?"

"As long as we want. Time is nonexistent here."

"What are you afraid of?" I asked.

"Nothing. I like it here." Gus went to his desk and threw the newspaper articles of me into the trash bin.

"Why do you have those?"

"The time we went to see Kyria Thassoula, she put her hands over mine and after a few seconds, she pushed them away. Her eye looked terrified, and I asked her what was wrong. She pointed to the door and told me to leave and never come back because she couldn't read an empty. What did she mean by that? That I'm nothing? A nobody?"

"Could've meant she wasn't receiving your signal."

"You thought she was a fraud, but she wasn't. She saw right through me. I am empty." Gus tapped his chest. "Nothing inside here. No soul, no feeling, nothing…nothing but emptiness."

I could tell Gus believed what he was saying, but I didn't have time to be his shrink. My instincts told me to look out the window. Luckily, I listened. All the surrounding buildings were gone. "Think you should check this out."

Gus came over and looked outside. "My emptiness is spreading."

"It seems we have to move on," I said.

"I can't." He shoved me aside and ran off. I chased after him. There was no way I was going to disappear into oblivion all because Gus refused to face his demons.

Gus ran down the middle of the road, and I was close behind him. It took only a light jog to catch up. He wasn't an athlete when he was alive, and he wasn't much of one dead either. I pushed him to the ground and pinned him, face down, on the ground.

"You can't make me do this!" Gus yelled.

"I'm not making you do anything. Whoever booked us this gig wants us to finish the set and break down."

He started up with the crying again. "I can't, Markos. I can't live through my life again."

Gus struggled to free himself, and I jabbed one of my knees into his back. I wasn't angry anymore. I moved beyond anger back in his apartment. My motivation was to finish the night with my best performance. "You can't escape whatever you did. It'll keep chasing you until you face it. The truth can't be undone. We all eventually gotta pay." I stood and pulled Gus up with me. "And after you face it, no matter what you see, no matter what you hear, don't look back."

"Sodom and Gomorra," Gus said more to himself. "Lot's wife looked back and turned to a pillar of salt."

"Do you believe that happened?"

"I think it's a metaphor about how getting stuck in the past can hold you back."

"Whatever works. Let's get out of here."

During our walk back, Gus and I reminisced about our visits to Greece during the summers, our mothers' obsession with J.R. from *Dallas,* and all the gossip at coffee hour where I was often the main topic of discussion. The more we talked, the more it sounded like a conversation that could've taken place when we were teens. I hated the naturalness of it all, that I could picture him as a friend if all this hadn't happened. It was easier to view Gus as the man who more than likely killed me.

"Do you remember how we got here?" I asked.

"Do I remember? That's a tough one. There are so many things I forgot since I arrived here. I'm thinking there's a reason for that." He raised his index finger. "Like we're not meant to remember."

"Did you take Jessie?"

Gus's pace quickened, and I grabbed him by his arm.

He pulled away. "I don't remember a damned thing apart from coming to one of your gigs."

"What about those articles about me on your desk? What made you take the time to cut them out and save them?"

"I don't know how they got there."

"You expect me to believe that."

"Yes, for exactly the same reason you can't remember how you got here."

We continued our walk toward the brownstone, but there was nothing to show me if we were headed in the right direction. It was as though some instinctual guidance system was leading us.

"When I spent time with a religious cult in California, I believed a place like this existed," Gus said. "We were taught that when we died, we had to judge ourselves."

"Stella says we're in a bardo, a place that exists between life and death."

"My group believed enlightened souls pass through here without effort, but ones that suffered a trauma have a harder time. After I left the cult, I thought it was a lie told to us to keep us from leaving. I'm not sure if it was a lucky guess or if they truly understood some profound truth. The only thing I can say for certain is that Kyria Thassoula was right. I'm empty. Primed and ready to disappear into the nothingness like everything else here."

The gold haze extended in front of us and veered off to the right.

"It's like GPS," I said.

"Except it leads to nowhere."

We continued the remainder of our trek in silence. Without the buildings and street signs to show us the way, we had no idea where we were going. Everything recognizable disappeared. All I could do was hope the road would lead back to Stella and that she'd still be where I last left her.

The mist soon led us around another turn and up ahead where a light appeared. As we neared, I could see it was the porch light of the brownstone. Gus became more anxious. Like a convict being led to his execution, he walked with his head down and his shoulders hunched forward. He demonstrated his trepidation with an improvised blues song. It was as if we were part of some incorporeal chain gang, only we couldn't see who was leading us.

Gus sang his sombre death song, and I imagined the *plickity-plack, plickity-plack plack plack* of chains while marching in sync. Gus's voice still haunts me to this day. It was the most authentic I'd ever heard him. Too bad it took him dying to connect to it.

I'm leaving for my new home.

Can't look back, or I'll be doomed.

I'm heading for my new home.

Left the past inside my room.

Don't know where I am going.

Thank God I'm ending soon.

I'm heading to my new home.

Don't know where it might be.

Yeah, I'm heading to my new home,

Since the blues defeated me.

Will my new life be a new song,

Or my own ghost chasing me?

I agreed with Gus's sentiment, except that I had no idea what home meant anymore. The lyrics made it into my sixth studio recording. I credited Gus with the song, even though I could've gotten away with claiming it as my own. I respect the musician's code of honor. I never take credit for someone else's work.

I embraced Stella as soon as I saw her. "Just in case we all vanish into oblivion, I wanna tell you that I love you."

"I love you too."

We both faced the brownstone. Stella held my hand and leaned her head on my shoulder. I never knew how much I appreciated this small gesture.

"A lifetime of memories exist in each of those rooms," I said as I stared at what used to be our bedroom window. "If we walked inside now, would we see another day in our lives play back as the other parts of our lives did before on those giant screens? Each minute marked by an infinite time stamp, eternally captured as proof of all the decisions we made." I slapped my head. "Damn, I don't have my digital recorder. I sense a poem coming on."

I expected a sarcastic response from Stella about how my mind always focused on my work, but she kept her head rested on my shoulder. It was another sign that things were almost over. "I'm gonna miss this place. That's gotta mean something. Right?" I asked.

"I miss nothing," Gus said. "Nothing at all."

Stella had no response either, and that made me nervous. No more threatening Gus with bodily harm or even the mention of Jessie. Her silence was another reality punch to my head. We were in an unexplored domain, and I still couldn't discount the possibility that we were part of some vast computer simulation.

The fireflies returned in time to stop me from having a transcendental panic attack. Three of them hovered above us, humming as they faded and brightened to a rhythmic beat.

"Quarter time is truly universal," I said.

"Name that note," Gus said.

"Got no clue."

"Hah! Never heard of that one."

"I'm starting to hate these," I said as I swatted at the one in front of me. My hand went right through it.

"I never liked them," Gus said.

"I think they're lovely," Stella said in an enchanted princess-voice. She even looked like one when she extended her hand and one landed on her palm.

The whimsical fireflies of Nirvana next flew upward and hovered over each of us. They expanded into domes, enclosing us individually.

I tried to leave my dome, but each time I struck the wall of light, I was met with resistance, even though I felt none. It was the oddest sensation.

Stella seemed spellbound inside her dome. Her body glowed bright, and her face appeared relaxed and calm. On my other side, Gus lay in a fetal position. He pounded the floor with one of his hands, and from the way his mouth moved, it looked as though he kept repeating the word *no*.

Whatever mind-altering ether was in my contained environment, it started to affect me. I broke out in uncontrollable laughter, although I didn't find anything particularly funny. Every positive emotion hit me at once, and I couldn't stop myself from reacting. I wept, dropped to my knees and kept saying, "Thank you, thank you, thank you." I had no idea who I was speaking to, or if I was speaking with anyone at all.

The constant tension that lingered in my chest released, and I took in a deep breath. *Leave everything behind you,* I said, only I didn't really say it. The voice was mine, but there existed no thought behind the delivery. It was as though it was beamed into my mind. All my sadness, hatred, and regret poured into a dark, fizzy puddle of black smoke beneath my feet and seeped through the ground. This reminded me of my first heroin high, without all the weirdness and confusion. Within my chrysalis, I was filled with a bright, fluidic light and dissociated from all things of matter. I existed beyond words and conscious thought. My knowledge was more instinctual, and I unveiled my identity, beyond time, beyond space, beyond all my senses…and then I remembered.

On a Clear Night

Close your eyes, and dream a dream. A hap-py lit -

I stood on the ledge of the WXQX Building when "Crazy People" played, signaling it was time to take my meds. The wind blew hard, and my hair slapped my eyes making them tear. I spilled two pills onto my shaky hands and contemplated whether I should take them. It didn't take long to render my decision. I tossed the pills over the side, along with the bottle. I wanted to die lucid. One truth I unveiled during this experience is that we're limited in what we can control in our lives. It's amusing how you can know this and ignore it until it's nearing your time to check out. Then, as you stare over the precipice of denial, it suddenly dawns on you as though it were some major new revelation. *Oh yeah, I'm not immortal. I'm gonna die. And it would've helped if I figured this out sooner. I would've spent my efforts only on things that mattered to me.*

I was about to die, and I wouldn't see Jessie ever again. I was sure everyone would tell her how I'd been sent to Heaven and how we'd be reunited there one day. Believing in such a fantasy seemed silly to me, but now that I was about to die, I wanted Jessie to have enough of that in her life so that she could be happy. If I had the chance to speak to her again, I'd tell her fantasies weren't necessarily fiction. If she believed strongly enough in her dreams, she could make her own paradise on Earth.

My cellphone rang, and I knew my time was up. I did and didn't want to answer. This night was filled with such polarities. I answered and labored to keep my voice calm. "Since this is about to end, at least have the guts to use your real voice."

"Did you know from where you stand, you can see your old residence?" the kidnapper asked.

I searched every direction and stopped when I caught sight of a building fire a few blocks away.

"You have a big decision to make," the kidnapper said, "and you must decide quickly because time won't stop to wait for you. You can save your ex-wife, or you can fulfill your end of the bargain and save your daughter. Meet me here with your decision. I want to see your face when you tell me. I want to see your suffering and turmoil. Once I see it, you will have fulfilled your end of the bargain."

"That wasn't part of our deal."

"It was always part of mine." He hung up.

I ran all the way to the brownstone and found Teddy unconscious on the sidewalk. I checked his pulse and was relieved when I found it.

Leda opened the door. "I called the fire department." She ran over to us and gasped with her hands over her mouth when she saw Teddy.

"He'll be all right. Call for an ambulance, I'm going to get Stella."

I sprinted to the side of the building where the kidnapper was waiting for me, wearing a mime mask. He had a gun aimed at me and stood next to the fire escape. A gasoline can was on the ground next to him, and the whole area wreaked of gas. The major difference between the real kidnapping and the one in my bardo experience was that the kidnapper never asked me to identify him.

He removed his mask. It was Gus, which didn't surprise me. He made my suspect list.

"You were my first guess," I said.

Gus pulled down the fire escape ladder. "Have you made your choice? You only get one."

I glanced up at Stella's bedroom. The flames shot outside from the window.

"When this is all over, you'll know what it's like to be me," Gus said. "I want you to feel what it's like to have your life stolen from you."

"I didn't steal anything from you, Gus."

"After I left California, I spent a lot of time thinking about things."

I slowly approached him and stopped when he pulled back the hammer of his gun.

"My life's been one mess after the other," Gus said. "I thought it was just random bad luck until I traced everything that went wrong back to the point of origin. The scholarship should've been mine. What makes it worse is you didn't even use it. You're so ungrateful. You had a beautiful wife, and you took her as seriously as you did college. I would've appreciated everything you threw away so easily."

"It's not too late to stop this, Gus. Let me go up and get my wife."

"Unfulfilled desire leads to suffering." Gus kept his aim as he removed a lighter from his pocket. "Suffering can't be contained. It must be shared, and I'm sharing mine with you, Markos." He stared up at the window. "And you're sharing yours with Stella. Which is why her death will also be on you." Gus waved his gun. "You and me...we did this all together. I want you to understand that when you attend your wife's funeral."

Thick, black smoke now bellowed out the bedroom window.

"She should be dead right about now," Gus said. "That was my true intention the whole time."

A car door slammed, and I glanced at the road where Jessie stood, wearing her pink pajamas. I lunged towards Gus, and he shot me in the gut. I put my hand over my wound, and blood spilled from out of the sides.

Gus appeared vacant as he glanced up at the window and then back at me. He lit the lighter. "I'm going where I belong." He knelt down and touched the flame to the ground where he had spilled gasoline. He slowly stood as a ring of flames shot up and encircled him. He dropped his gun, put his hands together and began to pray. "Forgive me, Father. I know I'm a disappointment."

I pushed myself as far away from the flames as I could get and stared up at the bedroom window. The fire now came out of the next window over.

Gus surrendered to the inferno and fell to the ground. The smell of his burning flesh filled the air. I had to fight nausea along with the pain from my gunshot wound. I collapsed onto my back and looked up at the window. I couldn't do a damned thing to save Stella.

Teddy showed up and knelt beside me. "An ambulance is on its way. Sorry I didn't believe you."

"Save the sweet talk for Leda. Stella's up there."

Teddy eyed Stella's window, and he took off.

Jessie and Leda appeared next.

"Hang on little brother," Leda said as she knelt beside me. "An ambulance is on its way."

Jessie looked at Gus's burning body. Leda took her hand and directed her to kneel beside me.

"Why are you bleeding?" Jessie asked.

"I'll be okay," I said.

"That's a lot of blood."

"They'll fix me up at the hospital, and I'll be as good as new."

"Where's Mommy?"

I held Jessie's hand. "She'll be here soon. How about you sing me a song while we wait for her?"

The smoke from the bedroom window intensified, and I thought this was it for Stella and me. The thought of Jessie losing the two of us in one night distressed me more than my own death. I didn't want to leave her with the frightening last image of her murdered father and dead mother. That's the kind of event that causes nightmares and never escapes you no matter how hard you try.

Jessie looked back at the flames. "I can't sing when I'm scared."

"As long as you sing, everything will be all right. I promise."

She wept, and I squeezed her hand tighter. "What did Mowgli know about the red flower?"

"That's what the animals called fire," she said, "and it scared them. But not Mowgli. He wasn't afraid."

"I want you to be brave, like Mowgli. Can you do that for me?"

Jessie nodded.

"Good. Now sing to me, brave one."

"What song should I sing?" Jessie asked.

"How about your song?"

Leda put her arm around Jessie. "It would make me feel better as well."

Jessie began to sing, and I listened.

Confirmation

sum-mer in my jun-gle dream._____ Where no one ev - er_____ has to sle

I stared down at my body lying on the sidewalk.   "The truth can't be undone, and you paid up with interest."

Gus looked at his body that was still ablaze and then peered at me. "I wasted my whole life chasing after yours."

"I let go of everything."

"I can't," he said.

"Sentence wisely. Your judgment won't affect only you." I glanced up at Stella's window. "It didn't here."

"I'd like to say I'm sorry, but they're just words. They sound as empty as me."

"This isn't only about you. Don't share any more suffering. There's enough of that to go around."

Gus peered directly at me. His weird stare was gone, and his body started to fade. "Gibson is still the better guitar."

"In your dreams," I said, "but I wouldn't refuse to play one anymore."

Gus disappeared. I didn't know what verdict he gave himself, but I hoped he moved on. It's hard to explain how I could forgive someone who'd taken so much from me. I couldn't help but view Gus as a tragic soul. I'd seen him not only as a murderer and kidnapper; I'd seen him struggle to move beyond that. Had I not experienced our joint bardo, I might have been justified to judge him, which I hate doing even more than playing in a wedding band. I don't want Gus to hurt anyone else again. If reincarnation is real, as Stella believes, I'd prefer him to come back as a decent human being and not pass along any more of his pain.

I also decided to stop passing my pain along. To let go is to be free of all the hatred and vengeance that fueled me through most of my life. I may have been justified in my anger, but all I got in return was nightmares that haunted me each night and eventually cost me my marriage. I'm no saint. My letting go was fueled by selfishness. My need to be happy was more important than hating Gus and my father. I was ready to move on, take on a new identity, and disappear into oblivion or whatever else this bardo decided to throw my way. Whatever the outcome, I wasn't scared anymore. I wouldn't be around to remember anyway.

I continued to watch Jessie sing to me as Teddy carried Stella over and lay her gently beside me. After he performed CPR, she coughed, opened her eyes and smiled at me.

"I love you," she said. "Never forget that."

I remember being surprised by her proclamation. "I love you too." I held her hand, and that was the last thing I remember saying before dying.

An ambulance pulled in front of the brownstone, and medics hurried over with two stretchers.

Stella's ghost knelt in front of Jessie. "I'm so glad I got a chance to be with you one last time."

"I think I can let go now," I said, staring down at my body.

"So can I." Stella watched the medics set down their equipment. "We're out of the bardo."

"We better say what we gotta say. I don't want this to end until I tell you how I feel about you."

I reached down for Stella's hand and pulled her up to me. "I hope I find you again."

Stella hugged me. "I hope so too. I'm going to miss you."

The medics began to work on our bodies with defibrillator paddles. We were both flat-lining.

"What if we don't find each other again?" Stella asked.

"I know I'll find you. You've got an adventurous spirit. Wherever you end up, you'll be hard not to notice."

I started dancing with her while singing "Stardust." After one verse, I twirled her around and dipped her. "Next time around, I'll be a full-time player." I lifted her up. "I wanna be in all the pictures on our wall. Not just on one small family portrait."

The medic gave me another jolt with the paddles, and I spoke faster than my usual pace. "I'll miss hearing you play your piano, I'll miss hearing you sing, I'll miss your smile when you watch Jessie sleep at night, and I'll miss your homemade Bengali spice tea. And even though I may not remember any of this, I'm gonna sense something's missing until I find you, and we're a duo again."

We kissed as I was given a final jolt by the paddles.

A bright light flashed, and I felt a chill surge through my whole body. I regained consciousness, and Jessie was singing to me.

Leda hugged her and cried in relief .

At first, I despaired over my return, especially since I finally reconnected with the woman I love. Now she was gone forever. *Forever.* The word took on a whole new meaning for me that night. Why couldn't I appreciate Stella while she was alive? That question would have tortured me for the rest of my life had we not had our closure. Her last words to me meant everything. I still find it hard to grasp that time was nonexistent where we were, and for a brief moment, Stella returned to me to tell me she loved me and to never forget. I needed that confirmation as much as I needed to hear "Jessie's Song" to pull me back into my life.

"Daddy! I knew you'd be okay. I knew you'd hear me!"

When Jessie smiled, I understood I was where I had to be.

"Thanks for coming home, Daddy."

"I heard you singing to me." I hugged her.

"I was brave, just like Mowgli."

"You *are* brave."

The medics lifted me onto the stretcher, and I watched other medics roll away two stretchers with filled body bags. I looked back at Jessie and couldn't help but smile when I saw her face. I never knew it was possible to experience joy and sadness all at once, but I can say it's possible because I felt it that night.

Sometimes, when I see a baby, I'll wonder if it's Stella. I have no way to know for certain, but it's fun to imagine finding her again before I die. We may not meet again until many lifetimes from now, but I'm comforted to know we'll always be connected to each other. From unrecognizable worlds to ancient Egypt and modern-day New York, our paths had crossed many times. A part of me will always belong with a part of her.

I still don't believe in God, which may seem strange considering all I've been through. However, I'm not an atheist anymore. I've accepted there are some things we can never fully comprehend, even as we experience them. I'm okay with leaving everything at that. It's enough for me to know we continue. Somewhere in another life, in another place, Stella and I will be a duo again.

Poems By
Markos Adams

White Orchid

The white orchid in her hair.
Ornament of pleasure or a symbol of longing?
In front of the stage where I'm performing,
She sits attentive upon a chair.

Candlelight shines on her probing stare.
I remember her eyes, her skin, her face,
The white orchid in her hair.
A vision I'll never forget or replace.

Her ears on me, I fear she'll share,
My thoughts behind the strings.
Their plucking always swings.
Shining bright beyond the glare.
The white orchid in her hair.

Red Flowers

Red flowers awaken my mind.
I smell the life I left behind.
An astral world or loony bin?
I party with the Seraphim,
Until I have to self-rewind.

What is the I, as I was defined?
Am I now of a different kind?
A florist who now lives to trim,
Red flowers?

Past and present, all combined.
As the calling so divined.
Hidden in an ancient hymn,
Within this dream I have designed,
Red Flowers.

Bopping in the Slipstream

I took a high dive.
Defunct or alive?
I'm free.
Away from that jive,
My mental hard drive.
Empty.

A mellow death song.
I'm playing along,
Comping.
But what if I'm wrong?
Nowhere to belong.
Nothing?

Asleep or awake?
My mind takes a break.
Closed shop.
I might be a flake,
But my heart can't fake,
Bebop.

From here I can't flee.
A fait accompli.
I'm here.
A ghost enlistee,
I haunt what was me.
No fear.

The dead and I meet,
And talk near the street.
No con.

I'm tapping my feet,
And swing to the beat.
Jam on!

The stars will portend,
The moon's newest trend.
Slipstream.
Each step toward my end.
My soul will ascend,
This dream.

Neuron Symphony

Each night I play inside my dream.
I wake up somewhere in midstream.
I hear the music calling me.
Performed by a neuron symphony.

The ground is pulled from under my feet.
I land on a familiar city street.
A mystic realm where spirits roam free.
Performed by a neuron symphony.

Familiar faces shadow each day.
The remnants of a past today.
No hiding from this ghostly spree.
Performed by a neuron symphony.

Existing somewhere between two scenes.
My past projected on multiple screens.
Moving toward a reborn version of me.
Performed by a neuron symphony.

Death is Funny

Death is funny once you realize you're dead.
I strut along freely without worry or fright.
Sit at a cafe and have a sweet bite.

Heaven's not like anything I've ever read.
I can play my guitar at a club late at night.
Death is funny once you realize you're dead.

Since my arrival, my past has all shed.
Distant eternal, I sit and I write,
Of past loves and old rivals back in the spotlight.
Death is funny once you realize you're dead.

Walking Dead Street

We're joined in a timeless promenade.
No roadblock left to halt our parade.
No angels or demons to lead us along.
We no longer know where our spirits belong.

We amble along on Walking Dead Street.
A temporary mind retreat.
Staircase down to an eerie station.
Where a train departs to Reincarnation.

A nonstop trip to the other side.
Relax onboard and enjoy the ride.
Throw away all our superstitions.
Embrace our fears as we reposition.

A new life awaits as our old ones end.
An infinite loop, where our thoughts transcend.
I capture your image within the illusion.
I'll carry it along my soul transfusion.

Supernal Internal

Stuck in between my phantom's plight.
Trapped in a barrier of subjective creation.
Color emotions splattered in a tapestry of illusion.
All streets lead to my eternal might.
The truth exposed under the city light.
A spectacle of thoughts ignite a whirlwind delusion.

Death's calling whispers an unwelcome intrusion.
The reveal is clear as air from this height.
I can't change the outcome of this tragic diversion.
Not a shout, nor a whisper, my closing nears,
In constant motion to the outer margin of night.
A voice sings to me during my lonely excursion.
Lifetimes and dreams intertwine,
Connected and deciphered by my internal sight.

Ezza's Song

Your eyes called me into your guarded truth.
Beneath the false smile painted on your face.
Hiding the pain of your long lost youth.
A time you've worked hard to erase.

The sparkle of your heavenly voice
Now enters my ears as a celestial song.
In reverence to you I now rejoice.
Your support helped make me strong.

Because of you I outgrew my friends.
You helped repair my groggy mind.
For that my love for you transcends,
The lonely life I left behind.

On the rooftop, under the moonlight,
We spoke, and we were less lonely.
I'll never forget our last starry night.
My beloved one and only.

Jessie's song

Eleni Papano

Close your eyes, and dream a dream. A hap py lit tle
eyes, they come to me. I sing my song un

sum mer in my jun gle dream. Where no one ev er has to sleep.
der a sha dy ban yan tree. A qui et place where I can stay.

Where wolves and ti gers and pan thers creep. I close my
Sit with my friends and play all day.

play all day. Trust in me and fol low a long. When ev er you hear me

sing my song. Hear my call you'll ne ver go wrong as long as you hear my song I go

home when the moon is high. I can not stay be cause my mom and

dad will cry. chil dren have par ents to go home to. Out in the

jun gle that still is true.

Acknowledgements

Jessie's Song had taken the longest time to come together, and I had gone through three major revisions when it was in screenplay format. Nevertheless, I stuck to it because something told me there was something special about this story. This is why I begin with my deepest heartfelt thanks to you, Mom, for raising me to be critical-minded and teaching me that I could do anything I wanted in life as long as I believed in myself. It took me many years to understand the wisdom behind your words, but I do now. It also took me many years to agree with you when you told me I should be an author. You were right!

Thank you to my husband, Russ, for reading all my stories and giving me the critical advice that I needed to take this book to the next level.

Thank you to my daughters, Daphne and Tiggy. Your support encouraged me from the start to finish of this book. And thank you, Daphne, for being the perfect little model. You helped bring Jessie to life.

Thank you Hal Croasmun. Your screenwriting course is where I had come up with the concept for Jessie's Song. It's nothing like what we had discussed, but your class is where I planted the seed, and for that I'm indebted to you.

Thank you to Erica Orloff for editing my book. Your insights made me ask some questions which lead to further breakthroughs and helped deepen the characterization of Markos Adams.

Thank you to Dr. George and Amy Jirsa-Smith, who proofread my manuscript and helped make it ready for publication.

I would also like to extend my thanks to Margaret Duarte who beta read for me. I deeply appreciate your support.

A big thanks to Readers' Favorite for being a valuable support system for indie authors.

Thank you Maria Beltran for being the first to review and give Jessie's Song five stars.

I'm forever indebted to Jamo Lorswal for getting me started with screenwriting, which led me to discover my talent for storytelling.

And finally, thank you, Anthony Randazzo, for turning me on to Billie Holiday at Wayne on Wheels skating rink in New Jersey. Who would've thought this Jersey gal would end up majoring in jazz and then follow it up with a book about a jazz guitarist? Life is funny that way

Additional thanks to the places where I composed *Jessie's Song:*

At home in Waianae and Pukalani
Starbucks
Dr. Kim Orthodontics - Aeia
Kapolei Public Library
Hickam Air Force Base Library
Spark M. Matsunaga VA Medical Center (Sparky's Place)

Music that inspired me the most during the writing of this book:

Robert Johnson
Wes Montgomery
Assemblage 23
Lustmord
Robert Rich

About the Author

Eleni Papanou wrote her first poem when she was an outcast at school. Honored with the name, "Greek Freak," she started to feel like one and believed life was plagued with torment and endless suffering. A spontaneous kundalini awakening thrust Eleni on a spiritual path and constantly tested her to the breaking point by challenging her world-view and everything else she held sacred. Through visions and personal insights, Eleni eventually discovered the Universe has a sense of humor. She started laughing more—mostly at herself—whenever she caught herself taking things too seriously. After many years on the path of self-rediscovery, along with the addition of a husband, two daughters and a bout with cancer; Eleni had a lot to say. Having already written several screenplays, she decided the most fulfilling method to articulate what she learned was in novel form. The book you now hold in your hands is a product of that desire.

Visit Eleni's personal blog at http://elenipapanou.com for news and updates

Other Books by
Eleni Papanou

Unison - Book One of the Spheral Series - A man is condemned to relive his life until he uncovers a suppressed memory. Available at Amazon and other online retailers.

Beyond Omega's Sunrise follows a group of people on the eve before Earth's destruction. Linking them together is a shuttle crash that happened ten years prior and ties to their fate that will become apparent by the next Sunrise.